## "Come to Home Away From Home, Abby. Spend Christmas there."

The solution was perfect. For her. And for him. "The position of housemother is still open," Nick said quietly.

He'd be helping her—giving her a houseful of needy girls to love. Giving her purpose.

He'd be helping the girls, too. Brit, who was holding something back. Kaylee, who was hurting far more than she let on. Even Becca, who needed mothering...

"I can't, Nick." The words were a crushing disappointment.

"I've got seven girls who need a woman's care, Abby, especially now with the holidays approaching."

"Aren't they going home for Christmas?" Abby sounded surprised.

"If they were wanted at home, they wouldn't be here to begin with."

"Oh." He'd never have believed a single word could say so much.

But it was all the incentive Nick needed to push her a little more. "You owe me one, Abby," he said, collecting on a debt he'd never considered a debt to begin with. "Just until after Christmas?"

Dear Reader,

This is a special time of year for me—and a special story. I believe in Christmas. In the magic that weaves itself around the season. And in Santa Claus. To my way of thinking, elves and Santas come in all sizes, shapes and colors. Elves are the boys and girls whose eyes glow with wonder, who bring the excitement of Christmas back to those who've lost it. They're the parents who find a way to have that special something under the tree for the son or daughter who will truly appreciate it. They're the friends who call someone who's alone and offer an invitation to Christmas dinner.

Santa Claus is a doer. He exists in those who know about the magic of love, who see a need and address it. Who enrich the life of someone else just because they can. Santa Claus is a spirit, a power that comes over normal mortals and gives them the ability to do something extraordinary for someone else. To buy something they wouldn't ordinarily buy, to do something they wouldn't ordinarily do—simply to make someone else smile.

A Santa Claus wants only to make his or her small portion of the world a better place. Santa Claus is anyone who believes in the power of love.

To each and every one of you, I wish a very merry Christmas—and a visit from Santa Claus!

(And to anyone who wants to enjoy some of the delicious Christmas cookies Abby discovers, I'll share a couple of my mom's secret recipes with you. You'll find them at the end of the story.)

I love to hear from readers, at Christmas or any other time. You can reach me at: P.O. Box 15065, Scottsdale, Arizona 85267-5065 or on-line at http://www.inficad.com/~ttquinn.

*Tara Taylor Quinn*

# THE HEART OF CHRISTMAS
## Tara Taylor Quinn

TORONTO • NEW YORK • LONDON
AMSTERDAM • PARIS • SYDNEY • HAMBURG
STOCKHOLM • ATHENS • TOKYO • MILAN • MADRID
PRAGUE • WARSAW • BUDAPEST • AUCKLAND

ISBN 0-373-70817-3

THE HEART OF CHRISTMAS

This edition published by arrangement with Harlequin Books S.A.

® and TM are trademarks of the publisher. Trademarks indicated with ® are registered in the United States Patent and Trademark Office, the Canadian Trade Marks Office and in other countries.

**Printed in U.S.A.**

For Patty Bodell Meredith, who showed me
that caring is a strength,
not a weakness.
I cherish her friendship.

# CHAPTER ONE

THE FIRST THING she noticed that morning was the Christmas decorations.

Walking the picturesque, sleepy block from the bagel place to her shop, Abby wondered how many little Oxnard elves it had taken to bring about the festive transformation since she'd left work the evening before. Someone in this small coastal town just north and a little west of Los Angeles had been way too busy. She could hardly believe what she was seeing. It wasn't even Thanksgiving yet, and smiling plastic Santas were flapping in the breeze.

Perhaps they were fitting, those reminders of the upcoming holidays. They'd appeared like magic— but, then, people who believed in Santa Claus believed in magic, and usually in dreams, too.

Abby's dream was about to come true.

It just wasn't her dream anymore. It never had been *hers*. It had always been *their* dream. She and her sisters. All three of them. Together. From the moment of their conception they'd been together. Shared everything. The dream had been no different.

But the other two were gone now. One dead. And one so unreachable she almost felt dead to Abby. Two-thirds of the dream was dead. Two-thirds of Abby was dead.

She walked. She looked. She thought. She just didn't feel.

She'd lost her faith.

So far removed was she from the world around her that she didn't even hear anyone approach. Didn't know she was in danger. Had no warning until suddenly the shoulder strap of her briefcase was pressing into her back, her bagels were rolling on the ground at her feet and a steely arm was around her neck, forcing her off the sidewalk and into the vacant alley used for deliveries by the surrounding businesses. Stumbling from the force of the body hurled against her, she tried to scream, but no sound came out. She tried again, panicked, clutching desperately at the arm choking the air from her throat.

Hot breath panted against the back of her neck as Abby dug her fingers into the arm, knowing instinctively that she wasn't going to be able to save herself. The arm was too strong, the hold too determined. With a sense of horror, she felt her assailant's other hand grope for her face. She was choking on terror and trying frantically to breathe. To keep her nose and mouth free. To stay conscious.

She was going to die.

"Hey!" a man called from the sidewalk.

And then, just as suddenly as she'd been accosted, she was free. Her assailant's arm was wrenched away, bruising her throat with the force of its release. Stunned, Abby fell to the ground, gravel digging into her thigh through the dress slacks she wore. She was free. Miraculously, unbelievably, free. She tried to draw breath into her tortured lungs—and couldn't.

She was vaguely aware of the short scuffle behind her, the grunts. But it was only when she heard two

sets of footsteps running down the alley that she
started to shake. And to breathe again. Harsh, gasp-
ing, painful breaths that burned her throat, her chest.
Lying there, dazed, she dragged air in greedily.

Until footsteps returned.

*Oh, God. No!*

Scrambling desperately to her feet, Abby prayed
she could make it out to the street in time. Surely
once there she could attract attention, in spite of the
early-morning hour. If only she could make it out to
the street...

"Hey!"

That male voice came a second time, but it sounded
different—more concerned than threatening. And
slightly winded.

Abby faltered, her whole body shivering with
fright, just as an arm reached for her again, a different
arm, one that caught her around the waist—gently.

"Steady, there," the man said. "Are you all right?
Do you need a doctor?"

Abby shook her head, but which of his questions
she was answering she didn't know. She knew only
that she was afraid to move. She wanted to be left
alone, to hide, to run.

Her body continued to tremble. She stood frozen
in the stranger's grasp.

"It's all right. You're okay now. It's over...."

His words penetrated slowly, although the deep,
even timbre of his voice was soothing. Abby turned
into him instinctively, burying her face in the warm,
solid haven of his chest, listening to his heart beating
a hurried tattoo. It was over. She was safe.

"It's all right," he said again, softly, smoothing an

easy hand over her hair as he held her securely within his arms.

Her chest shuddered with sobs, shocking her, drawing her attention to the front of her savior's crisp white shirt—wet with her tears. Abby never cried. She was the strong one.

Embarrassed, she pulled out of his hold.

"I'm sorry." Tucking her straight blond hair self-consciously behind her ears, she took another step back from him, trying to calm herself. To wipe her eyes without making him more aware of her tears. "I don't usually fall apart like that."

"I don't guess you get attacked on a regular basis, either."

Abby looked up at him then, this stranger who'd saved her. His face was lined, not so much with age as with having lived. His dark hair, thick and a little long, as though he didn't bother with it much, didn't have even a hint of gray. But it was the depth of concern she saw in his gorgeous brown eyes that took her breath away again.

"No. No, I don't," she finally answered, still staring up at him. He was easily a good six inches taller than her own five and a half feet.

"I tried to catch him, but he had the advantage of knowing the neighborhood."

"If you hadn't come along..." Abby's voice trailed off as she was suddenly beset by a fresh surge of panic. She'd have been badly hurt by now. Maybe even dead.

"But I did come along," he said softly. "I was in the right place at the right time. It was obviously meant to be."

The words were so strong. So sure. So full of baloney. Maybe once she'd believed in things she couldn't see, things beyond human understanding. In "powers that be" looking out for them. Maybe once she'd secretly believed Audrey's tales of Prince Charmings and happily ever afters, too. She knew better now.

"I suppose I should call the police," she said.

Reaching into the inner pocket of his suit, the man pulled out a small cellular phone and unfolded it. "Use this," he said, dialing 911 before he handed the little phone to her.

Abby was strangely glad of his presence beside her as she reported the attack. She listened to the unemotional female voice on the other end of the line, answering questions about her whereabouts and condition, declining an ambulance. She felt like some kind of freak.

"They're sending someone," she said, still holding his phone, as though there were someone else she needed to call.

He led her to a pretty white bench out by the street. "We can wait here."

"You don't have to stay." She no longer needed a savior, wasn't looking for a prince. She was perfectly capable of taking care of herself.

"Of course I do." He sat down. "I can give a much better description of the guy."

Abby sat down, too. He had a point. A valid point that had nothing to do with her not wanting to be there alone. He was staying because the police would need to talk to him, not because Abby was scared out of her wits.

"You're sure?" she asked, looking over at him. "You don't have someplace else to be?"

"I finished a breakfast meeting earlier than I expected and I have another appointment just down the street at eight." He glanced at his watch. "I've got a few minutes."

There were those eyes again. So compassionate. So warm. And she'd been cold for so long....

"Thanks," she said, finally handing back the telephone. She'd been thinking about getting a cellular phone herself—except that there was no one who needed her to be that accessible.

"I'm Nick McIntyre, by the way," her rescuer said. He slid the phone back into his pocket.

"Why do I know that name?"

He shrugged. If he knew why, he wasn't saying. And Abby was too rattled to figure out where she might have heard—

*"Love's Way!"* She suddenly remembered. She had the book at home someplace. Maria had given it to her, said it was a national bestseller that had helped millions of people. Said it would help Abby. Something about how acts of love, support and compassion were more valuable than words or feelings.

The book had been written by a Nick McIntyre; was it the same man?

"You've read it?" he asked.

Abby shook her head. She could hardly tell him that when she'd found out the self-improvement book had been written by a psychiatrist, she'd been afraid to open it. Afraid she'd find out she was crazy after all.

"It's not for everyone—too academic." He grinned at her. "I like my second book much better. It brings the actions-versus-feelings theory down to an everyday workable level."

"You're *that* Nick McIntyre!"

"I hope that's not a problem."

He grinned at her again, and Abby blushed, realizing how taken aback she'd sounded. "Of course not." Leave it to her to be rescued by a man with a medical degree who made his living teaching people how to love. "I'm Abby Hayden," she said to cover her awkwardness.

He smiled, his warm brown eyes still gleaming with compassion. "Nice to meet you, Abby." He actually tipped his head to her like the Prince Charming of Audrey's dreams. "In spite of the circumstances."

As her gaze met his, connected, a split-second spark of excitement shot through Abby. Shocking her. Not so much because he'd inspired it—the man was to die for—but because she'd felt it at all. Felt something good.

Or maybe she'd just *imagined* she had.

"In spite of the circumstances." Abby couldn't help wondering, as she sat there waiting with him, cloaked once again in numbness, what might have happened if she'd met him under other circumstances. Say, two years earlier, before everything had fallen apart. Before she'd begun to doubt herself. Before she'd discovered that her love for others was a curse to them, not a joy.

"SLIGHT BUILD, strong and wearing a Dodgers baseball cap?" The Oxnard policeman—"Officer James," his tag read—recited from the small tablet he held.

"Yes," Nick concurred.

"What about eye color? You didn't see his face at all?"

"Unfortunately, no," Nick muttered, feeling Abby's discomfort beside him as she shifted her weight from one foot to the other. "I got only that one glimpse when I hollered and he glanced around, but the alley was darker than the street where I was standing and his face was shaded by the cap."

He wished he could tell the cop more.

"What about you, ma'am? Did you get a look at his face?"

Abby shook her head. "Just the work boots and the pant leg of his jeans," she said, in complete control as she repeated what she'd already told the man. Other than those first few minutes after the attack, she hadn't missed a beat—or shed another tear. "They were designer jeans," she added.

Nick stared at her. *Designer* jeans?

"I'm a fashion designer," she told the policeman, who nodded and wrote it down. Abby spelled the name of the jeans' French maker.

A fashion designer. But even so, in the midst of an attack, she'd noticed the style of the guy's jeans? She had to be the most levelheaded woman he'd ever met.

"Were you carrying a purse?" the policeman asked.

Abby shook her head a second time. "Just my briefcase." She indicated the leather satchel that rested against her hip; its long strap crossed her body, leaving an enticing view of the breasts it rested between on the way down to her waist.

"Were you wearing it like that?" Officer James asked.

"Yes." Abby clutched the strap. "That's what I felt first," she explained, "the strap pressing into my back as he slammed against me."

"Chances are that's what the guy was after," Officer James said.

Nick tapped his knuckles on the white bench beside him. "You think the briefcase was the target, rather than Abby?"

"Yeah," Officer James said, "I do."

The expression of relief on Abby's beautiful features was unmistakable, but was too quickly gone, replaced by the same vacant-faced fear she'd been wearing since her attack.

"He was strangling me," Abby said, the words soft but in no way weak.

The policeman nodded thoughtfully. "He tried to get your bag, and when he realized you were wearing it over your head instead of just over one shoulder, he panicked."

Abby didn't seem completely convinced, but Nick agreed with the officer's assessment. And he ought to know. He made his living understanding what motivated people, helping them to understand themselves and one another. Someone desperate enough to attempt a mugging in the first place would certainly panic when the plan backfired.

After a couple of other questions, they made a quick trip to the alley, where the only evidence of Abby's attack was the strewn gravel and the scattered bagels—which they gathered up and threw in a nearby garbage can. Officer James closed his book. "I'll have some men search the area," he said, looking in the direction Abby's attacker had fled. "But if, as I think, this was simply a botched mugging attempt, the guy's long gone."

The doubt on Abby's face told another story, but she didn't say anything more.

"I'm guessing the guy was young, based on his strength and speed and the fact that he panicked so completely," the officer continued. "Probably just a kid."

*Just a kid.* A kid who'd almost killed one of the most beautiful women Nick had ever met. Just a kid. A reminder that no matter how many hours he squeezed into a day there was still so much work to be done. So many messed-up lives that needed to be straightened out, so many despairing people looking for a little hope.

Abby looked like she could use an injection of hope herself as she shook hands with Officer James, promising to call if she thought of anything else. The minute he'd climbed into his patrol car, she began to brush at her sleek black slacks and matching vest, as though she could rid herself of the entire episode if only she brushed hard enough. Her business attire was none the worse for wear, other than a little gravel dust on one leg—which she quickly took care of.

"Thanks again. I owe you one," she said when Nick didn't leave. She was still fidgeting with her clothes.

A fashion designer, she'd said she was. She looked more like a model. And yet, there was something so no-nonsense about her. Something that attracted Nick almost as much as her shining blond hair and striking, unforgettable face. Her control intrigued him.

"Have dinner with me." The words were out of his mouth before he'd even considered them. Considered the fact that he didn't have time to pursue an attraction.

She hesitated, and Nick was afraid she was going

to turn him down. Really afraid. Like her answer was important.

He tensed, uncomfortable. The internal voice of self-discipline that governed his life reminded him of the risk he'd be taking if he put too much stock in a dinner invitation, in the dinner itself...in the woman.

Of course, he couldn't remember the last time a woman had refused to have dinner with him. His reaction was probably no more than latent male ego sneaking up on him.

Or perhaps it was the doctor in him, the counselor, wanting to take that empty look from her eyes.

"I understand your being leery, especially considering what just happened," he said, more comfortable now that he understood his own motives. "I am, after all, a total stranger."

Meeting his eyes for the first time since the policeman had left, she said, "It's not that...." And then, "Yes, I'd like to have dinner with you. Thank you."

"Would seven o'clock tomorrow be all right?" he asked, having run through his mental calendar, searching for a couple of free hours to spend on dinner with a beautiful woman. Tonight was out for sure. He had that session with the family out in Mission Viejo.

"Sure." Abby lifted her briefcase over her head, then removed the strap from around her body. "Any night's fine."

Nick smiled. "Great."

It sounded as if she was completely unattached. Which shouldn't matter to him at all.

But it did.

ABBY KEPT her appointment later that morning with the clothing manufacturer she'd been courting for more than a year. Considering the start to her day, she could have called to reschedule, but saw no real reason not to go. It wasn't as though she had anything better to do that would help her forget the horrifying attack. Or anyone to run to for comfort. And even if she'd had somebody who'd lend her a shoulder to cry on, she'd still have kept the appointment.

She wasn't going to let fear, or the irrational notion that the attack had been anything more premeditated than a simple mugging, keep her from carrying on. That was what Abby did. She carried on. When they were growing up, she'd known with complete certainty that her sisters looked to her for their cues, their example. If Abby could cope, so could they.

Anna and Audrey had needed her—or so she'd thought—and she'd somehow taken over all the responsibility, all the decisions, for the three of them. She hadn't been much more than seven that time she'd baked cookies for Audrey to take to school because their mother had forgotten to bring some home. If Abby remembered correctly, her mother hadn't even brought herself home that night.

And then there'd been the time no one remembered to pick up valentines for the three of them to trade at the party at school—in spite of the fact that Abby had called both her parents to remind them. That was when Abby had first started drawing. She'd stayed up way past her bedtime, making valentines for Anna and Audrey to give away. She'd meant to make her own, too. She'd just fallen asleep before she got to them.

And there were the nights when one of her sisters was sick either physically or at heart and their mother was pulling another all-nighter at the office, or her parents were out of town. If Abby hadn't stepped in to fill their shoes...who would have? Who'd have held Anna's hair while she threw up, or dried Audrey's tears as she swept from one true love to another? Who would have made sure Audrey did her homework assignments? Or helped her get ready for her first big date—the homecoming dance at school their freshman year? Who would have been there to quiet Anna's fears when she'd been the first to get her period—and hated it and herself?

Certainly not the line of strangers her parents' baby-sitting service sent over. Sure, until the girls were twelve or thirteen, there'd always been someone in the house with them when the Haydens weren't, but never the same someone—at least not on a regular basis. Because the Haydens kept such strange hours, both freelance corporate attorneys, they had one of their secretaries call the service each day with a fresh work order. The girls never knew, when they got off the school bus each afternoon, which of the many women the service employed would be waiting for them—or if one or the other of their parents would be home, instead, holed up in his or her office. Only once in all those years had they had the same woman enough times in a row that she'd actually learned to tell the girls apart.

It meant that always the responsibility for her sisters' lives had rested on Abby's shoulders. Always she'd borne the weight of their needs. For as long as she could remember.

Abby's stomach fluttered uneasily as she waited on a couch in the reception room of Doug Blair's office. It was more than a year since Abby had first approached him with the designs for her line of durable but fashionable girls' wear—a line that Abby, Anna and Audrey had been producing on a small scale ever since their senior year in college. Doug had finally said he was ready to make an offer.

Until now, sitting in the plush, sound-buffered office with fashion magazines on the table in front of her, she'd felt nothing in regard to Doug's call. But now that the moment was upon her, she wanted Doug's offer to be good. For herself, but for her sisters even more. It comforted Abby to think of them smiling, gloating with pride at their success. If only Audrey hadn't died. If only Anna hadn't run off to New York demanding that Abby not contact her, if she hadn't been in the subway crash that had wrenched away all her memories.

Glancing at her watch, noting that Doug had kept her waiting more than fifteen minutes, she considered taking her portfolio and heading straight back into the Southern California sunshine. The flutters in her stomach had multiplied, until her entire midsection was churning with nerves.

She was afraid Doug Blair was going to try to take advantage of her. That his offer was going to be insulting. Had she encouraged her sisters to sacrifice, to work long, hard hours for nothing? Had she led them wrong here, too? Let them down one more time?

For a second there, she almost wished for a return of the void that had left her so emotionless these past months. Surely numbness, a sort of living death, was preferable to this torment.

"Ms. Hayden? Mr. Blair's ready to see you now."

Armed with her portfolio, and with the faith her sisters had so blindly placed in her, Abby entered

Doug's office, completely in control again. Her designs were good. Selling them would be a final good-bye to her triplet sisters, to the life they'd shared.

"WE WOULD ALSO expect you to design exclusively for us for a minimum of three years. We'd like you to continue with entire lines, as you do now," Doug Blair was saying, his bushy eyebrows meeting above the bridge of his nose.

Exclusive rights. Entire lines. Abby sat silently in the modern-framed upholstered seat in front of his massive metal desk. She'd heard his words, but her brain couldn't seem to function beyond the unsurpassable sum of money the manufacturer had just offered her.

He was leaving her no choice but to sell to him. To say that goodbye.

"I'm sure you'll want to have your attorney go over this," Doug said, handing her the official-looking paperwork.

Abby nodded. Yes. An attorney. That would buy her some time. Because she hadn't realized, until just that moment, how badly a part of her didn't want to sell the business at all. It was the only thing she had left of her life with Audrey and Anna—except a lonely beach cottage filled with remnants of the lives her identical sisters had left behind.

She flipped through the papers, more because she knew Doug expected her to do so than because she could make sense of any of them.

And then, turning back a page, she saw that astronomical sum again.

"How soon do you need an answer?" she asked.

"Yesterday." Doug smiled for the first time that

morning. "We'd like to begin production in time to get something on the racks by spring."

"That soon?" She wasn't ready to change her life so drastically. Not yet. Not so quickly. So irrevocably. "I have my shop, my staff. Inventory. Orders I've already committed to fill."

"When you read those—" he nodded toward the pages she held "—you'll see we've attended to all that."

Abby continued riffling through the thick packet of paper. These things were supposed to take time. Lots of time. Doug had waited a whole year to even make an offer. She'd expected at least another year to adjust to the coming changes. Time for Anna to recover, to remember who she was, remember Abby, remember that they had a shop to sell...

"Your shop is to be closed by January 1, which gives you through the holidays to sell whatever inventory you have in stock. The two women who currently work for you are being offered the opportunity to interview with us. We can always use seamstresses of their caliber. Any additional orders you receive will be filled by us."

Abby nodded, sliding back into the familiar void she'd been occupying for most of the past year. She'd be a fool to turn down Doug Blair's offer. All the details had been dealt with. She'd be set for life.

But what life? She wouldn't even have a business to run. The more than forty hours she spent in the shop each week—arranging, ordering, accounting, selling, working with the customers who'd become almost friends to her—would, instead, be endless hours mocking her with their emptiness.

"I think you'll also find the deadlines for the designs for your fall line, and all future lines, to be quite manageable,'' Doug said, sitting back in his leather office chair, hands folded over his rock-hard belly. ''If not, they're negotiable.''

She'd still have the designs to do. But that wasn't a job. Or even a full-time endeavor. She drew in the evenings. To relax. Because drawing was the one thing she did for herself.

Doug Blair waited, the picture of a patient man, although they both knew he was anything but. He was too trendy for her taste, in his pristine, pleated pants, colorful tie and suspenders to match. And too sure of himself.

But he was fair. The best in the business. And with the money he was offering, plus the guaranteed purchase of future designs, he was giving her the chance of a lifetime. A lifetime that had come frighteningly close to ending just that morning.

''Can I have until tomorrow?''

# CHAPTER TWO

ABBY WASN'T SURE how she made it home, couldn't remember the whole stretch on the 101. But she was strangely glad to be parking her Mustang convertible next to the beach cottage that had become more of a tomb than a home over the past months. She just wanted to be there. Where she was boss. Even if only the boss of empty rooms and painful memories.

She ought to get a cat. A living creature to breathe the air, shake up the dust so the cottage didn't resemble a morgue every time she walked in the door.

Or a dog. She'd really prefer a dog. A companion. He'd bound out to greet her, maybe even bark an enthusiastic welcome when she came home. A dog would *need* her affection. She wouldn't be able to hurt him with her love.

It wasn't like she wouldn't be home to take care of a puppy. Not if she accepted Doug Blair's offer. She'd be home so much, bugging the poor thing, he'd probably file a complaint with the animal rights activists.

Stripping off her clothes as she headed back to her bedroom, Abby tried to ignore the closed doors she passed along the way. She didn't want to think. Didn't want voices from the past to hurt her with memories of happier times. Times like the day the three of them had first seen the cottage, a bit run-down but exactly what they'd been looking for. She didn't want to remember how excited they'd been as they'd written an offer on the place that same evening.

What she wanted was to shower off the morning's grime. Wash away the disgusting sensation of her attacker's touch. Though, now that she thought about it, she hadn't felt any arousal in that body pressed so intimately against hers.

Abby was undeniably relieved that she probably hadn't been a potential rape statistic. But she had to wonder if that meant the guy really had been out to kill her. *Why her?* Try as she might, she just couldn't convince herself the attack had been nothing more than a random mugging gone bad. She'd been so certain the guy wanted her dead. Was she losing her mind? Had the long solitary months finally gotten to her? Drained away her ability to handle any kind of crisis?

Abby stopped in front of her bathroom mirror, afraid to meet her eyes there, to confront the fear she was trying so desperately to ignore. She was overreacting. A part of her was still rational enough to know that. Her mind was just feeding on the ever-present memory of Audrey's murdered body lying on the beach behind their cottage.

The police investigation had been closed months ago. According to the report, Audrey might still be alive today if she hadn't resisted the attack. A random incident that had backfired, a panicked perpetrator. Just like this morning.

Except that Audrey had never resisted anything in her life. Particularly not a man.

As much as Abby had adored her baby sister,

younger than her by almost half an hour, she'd been aware of Audrey's weaknesses. Was only just beginning to see that she'd probably been the cause of them. Audrey wasn't a fighter. She wouldn't have said no. She'd have begged. She'd have cried. She might even have tried using her immeasurable sex appeal. But she hadn't known how to fight for anything.

She'd never had a reason to. Everyone loved Audrey. And Abby had fought all her battles for her.

Sweeping the cosmetics she'd left on the counter that morning into one of the vanity drawers—thinking how much Anna would hate her doing that—Abby finally forced herself to look in the mirror. To stare down the brown eyes gazing back at her with that mixture of apprehension and defiance. She was being ridiculous. She had nothing to fear. Audrey's death had been a senseless, random incident. Her own attack that morning had been, as well.

The Hayden triplets were beautiful women. California blondes with a touch of angel and a dab of come-hither. Male interest in them had been compounded by the fact that they were identical triplets. They'd been fighting off curious stares since birth, and more overt advances since puberty. And they lived in L.A., which was quickly becoming one of the most dangerous cities in the United States.

Random acts of violence were almost commonplace in Los Angeles. And that was all either attack had been. Maybe if she kept repeating that…

Abby's gaze left her eyes and traveled lower, over cheekbones that were too soft to fit her personality but had looked perfect on Audrey. Across a slender nose that Abby had always liked better on Anna than

on herself. Past the full lips that shouldn't be trembling—but were. And then she looked at her neck and
started to shake. There, just below where her collar
had been, was an ugly red welt that encompassed half
the circumference of her neck. Staring at the angry,
purpling swollen flesh, Abby felt sick to her stomach.
And afraid.

Someone had tried to kill her.

"OH, DADDY, please answer." She'd never have said
the words aloud if she hadn't been alone.

Abby's parents, retired corporate attorneys turned
entrepreneurs—perfume-entrepreneurs at the moment—had buried themselves even deeper in their
work since Audrey's death, making them more un-
attainable than ever to their eldest daughter.

Hearing her father's deep baritone on the voice
mail in his home office, she was tempted to ask him
to call, tempted to tell him about Doug Blair's offer.
Her parents would insist on looking over the contract
for her. She wasn't going to sign with Doug until they
did. But she wasn't calling them about Doug's offer.
She was calling because she needed her father's reassurance. Needed to know that he believed Audrey's
murder was just what it had seemed—a completely
random, unpremeditated act of violence against a
beautiful woman alone on the beach. In addition to
the police investigation, which he'd followed daily,
Lincoln Hayden had hired one of the top investigative
firms in the country. Other than determining that Audrey did, indeed, date a lot of men, too many to count,
they found no one who didn't think she was "fun,"
"great," "lovely." No one who appeared to have any
grudge against her. Abby needed her father to tell her

she was being ridiculous, that there was no connection between her sister's murder and her own attack earlier that day.

But as usual, he wasn't available. She'd thought her parents would be more accessible when they moved their business into their home office. But on the contrary. Neither of them was there later that night, when she tried a second and then a third time to reach them. She left a message about Doug's offer after the third call, desperate enough to hear from them that she pulled out the artillery she knew would work. But after the fourth unanswered attempt, she gave up. And reassured herself. Again and again throughout that long, lonely night. She reassured herself. Just as she'd been doing all her life.

By morning, she was once again firmly ensconced in her eerie gloom, her emptiness. The fear couldn't follow her there. She had nothing to fear in the living death. Everything had already come to pass.

"PASS ME the Richter file, would you, Sal," Nick said, lowering the phone as he spoke to his secretary. He was on hold, waiting to hear from his government contact about funding approval for the new Richter family counseling program. He hoped to fit in another call to Abby Hayden after that.

Sally pulled a file out of the stack in her arms and set it before him. "You have a meeting with the mayor after lunch, Nick. He faxed over a proposal this morning for hospital affiliation with the clinic. And that Mrs. McDonald you saw in Mission Viejo last night returned your call." Sally placed the list of messages in front of Nick. "Your agent called," she continued by rote. "Wants to know if you can have the book in a couple of weeks early. Oh, and Charles called. Something about that new housemother...."

Nick nodded, his adrenaline pumping as he juggled four things at once, still on hold.

"Call my agent, will you, Sal." Nick opened the Richter file. "Tell him he'll have the book early." He was already glancing over the notes on the funding for the Richter program at the free clinic in South L.A. by the time she nodded.

He'd attack Sally's list next. Oh, yeah, and he wanted to get in that call to Abby, too. He'd tried a couple of times since her attack the morning before— just to make sure she wasn't suffering any aftereffects from the assault—but the first time he called, there'd been no answer. And then, when he'd tried again before going to bed last night, her line had been busy. He'd been disappointed not to reach her but had eased his regret with the knowledge that she'd had someone to talk to. She wasn't alone. And frightened. Needing—

Before Nick's thoughts could take him any further, a voice came on the other end of the line.

"Nick?"

"Yeah?"

"It's a go. You got the funding."

*Thank God.* All it took was a year of council meetings, hours of gathering statistics, testimonies from potential clients, an inconceivable amount of begging and Dr. Nick McIntyre's agreement to donate ten hours a week—free of charge.

"We got it, Sal!" Nick called a few moments later as he dropped the phone in its cradle. The program had been her idea.

He handed her back the Richter file as she appeared in the doorway that led from her office to his.

"They gave us the money for the program?" she asked, her face hopeful.

Nick nodded, gratified to see the smile spread over her beautiful though usually staid features. Her smile lit up her face like lights on a Christmas tree, and appeared about as often.

He'd found Sally in South L.A. four years before, shortly after her mother, Eleanor Richter, had been beaten to death by her own husband of thirty years. Nick could only guess how many of those years Sally had also suffered her father's abuse—before she'd moved on to a young husband who'd given her more of the same.

"You'll let me go there?" she asked now. "Work at the clinic with you?"

Not if he could help it. She didn't owe a damn thing either to those people or to him for her escape from a hellish life.

"We'll see, Sal." He toned down his refusal, knowing that saving her pride was almost as important to her recovery as never stepping foot on those streets again. "But don't count on it. I really need you here. I'd lose myself in an hour if I didn't have you keeping track of me."

Nick didn't miss the flash of relief that crossed Sally's face before her features settled back to their usual stoic expression.

"You don't need me, Nick. We both know I'm the beggar here."

"What we both know is that this office couldn't run without you." Truth be known, his *life* couldn't run without her. "Now, where's that proposal from the mayor?'' He looked through the piles on his desk. ''Did you bring it in?''

''Right here.'' Sally slid the faxed sheets from beneath the phone list she'd brought in earlier.

Which only proved his point. He'd never make it without her.

''AS WE SAID last night, Mrs. McDonald, the mistake has already been made and nobody regrets it more than Kaylee does.'' Several hours later Nick was finally able to return the first of that morning's calls. ''But for your own sake as much as for Kaylee's, you must get beyond the mistake to the solution. To Kaylee's future.'' He dropped his pen on the notepad in front of him. He could talk until he was blue in the face, talk sense, talk calm, rational, levelheaded facts. But he had yet to find a cure for the bone-deep pain that came with irrevocable mistakes, with betrayals and tragedies. He hadn't yet found the words to take that pain away.

Only time could do that, and Kaylee didn't have time to wait for her mother's disillusionment to taper off enough to allow rational thought.

''She's ruined her life, Dr. McIntyre,'' Mrs. McDonald cried, her agony so clear over the telephone wires between L.A. and Mission Viejo.

Kaylee was an honors student with a perfect grade-point average. The president of the French club and secretary of the debating team. She was also sixteen years old and pregnant.

''Her reputation will be ruined when people hear,'' the woman moaned. ''She won't be able to finish her junior year, and then what kind of future will she have? She was almost guaranteed a scholarship.''

"Let her come to Home Away From Home, Mrs. McDonald," Nick pleaded, as he had for more than three hours the night before when he'd helped Kaylee McDonald break the news of her pregnancy to her widowed mother. "At least bring her for a visit, look the place over—"

"How could that boy do this to my Kaylee?" Mrs. McDonald interrupted, still not able to hear what Nick had to say. "How can he tell her he loves her and then just walk out on her? Why is she the one who has to pay the price?"

Telling Mrs. McDonald that the boy was going to have to answer for his actions sometime wasn't going to do a bit of good. Nick knew that. He just didn't know what *would* make a difference.

But he'd promised Kaylee he'd help her. She was a distraught, plain little blonde whose head had been turned by the high-school quarterback's sudden and completely unexpected attention. The young woman's heart had been crushed when she'd found out that Joe Cunningham's interest had only been the result of the challenge she'd presented, that her virginity was the only thing he was after. Once he'd taken that, there hadn't been anything else of her he'd wanted. Not her love. And certainly not the child he'd left her with. The child she'd already decided to give up for adoption.

She needed her mother's moral support. Not her castigations or her anger. She needed Home Away From Home.

Nick had first heard of Kaylee through one of the many high-school guidance counselors he worked with throughout the city. After he'd met with her, listened to her story, seen the innocence still shining through the pain in her eyes, he'd known he had to assist her. Somehow.

"Do you still love your daughter, Mrs. McDonald?" Nick broke into the woman's mounting accusations against Joe Cunningham, his frustration no longer as controlled as it had been.

"Of course!" The woman stopped crying for a moment, shocked.

"Then she needs to know that," Nick said. "Now."

Other than a couple of sniffles, Mrs. McDonald's end of the line was silent.

"Kaylee can't bear to go back to school, to face everyone when the evidence of her mistake becomes obvious," he said, sensing that he finally had her mother's attention. He didn't add that Kaylee would rather die than have her younger brother see her grow big with an illegitimate baby.

"I know," Mrs. McDonald said softly. "Kaylee's really a shy girl. That's why she joined the debating team last year, to help her open up. This humiliation will kill her."

"And neither one of you will consider abortion."

"No."

Kaylee had sounded exactly like her mother when Nick had asked her the same question.

"You have a good job, Mrs. McDonald, one you enjoy. A nice home. Your son is just starting junior high. He has friends. A life in Mission Viejo."

"Yes."

"A life neither of you wants to leave."

"No, we don't."

"Let Kaylee come to us, Mrs. McDonald," Nick said, more telling than pleading now. Kaylee needed a place to escape for the duration of her pregnancy. But even more, to heal. To be around other girls who'd made mistakes, but who would all survive their mistakes together. Become stronger, better people because of them. Who would go on to have good lives in spite of them.

"I don't know...."

"At Home Away From Home, she could finish her junior year with tutors until she has the baby, living with other teenage girls who are also giving their babies up for adoption. She could be back in school by next fall and graduate with her class. She won't lose her future."

Nick couldn't promise that she wouldn't pay for her mistake in other ways. But he'd see that the price was as small as it was in his power to make it.

"I don't want her to leave home."

The woman started to cry again. But Nick knew that he'd won. That Kaylee would get the help she needed. As soon as possible he'd introduce her to Brittany, one of Home Away From Home's current residents. If anyone could reach Kaylee, Brit could.

Glancing at his watch when he finally hung up the phone, he uttered a soft curse. He was cutting things too close. Again. He had half an hour before he was due to pick Abby Hayden up for their dinner date. He never had gotten through to her. And he still hadn't spoken to Charles.

NICK CALLED CHARLES from his cellular phone on the way to Abby's shop. Half of the husband-and-wife team that kept the old mansion running, Charles never called unless it was important. Nick just hoped to God the electrical problem they'd discovered on the third floor wasn't something major. He needed one of those rooms for Kaylee.

"The new woman isn't working out, Nick."

Charles's gruff voice gave him the bad news right off. Sliding his four-wheel-drive utility vehicle behind a red Camaro in the lineup to get on the 101 to Oxnard, Nick asked, "How so?"

He had a full house at Home Away From Home, and Kaylee McDonald on her way. Without a housemother, a woman to watch over the girls, discipline them, guide them, listen to them, love them, chaperone them, enforce lights-out, ensure that they all stayed snug in their beds at night, Home Away From Home couldn't operate.

"She ain't good with the girls."

Nick frowned. Mrs. Leonard had seemed a little stern to him, but for most of the girls at Home Away From Home, a little firmness wouldn't come amiss— as long as it was administered lovingly. For many of them a firmer hand, a bit more supervision, could have prevented their stints at a home for unwed pregnant teens.

"She talks down to them, like they're some kind of trash," Charles said. "Marianne found Brit crying this morning, in that closet underneath the first-floor stairs. That damn woman told Brit if she wanted to do what's right for her baby, she'd give it away like the rest of them. Said Brit's baby was an innocent bystander that deserved a nice moral family to give it values." He snorted disdainfully. "Said some other stuff that was even worse."

Nick slammed on his brakes six inches from the bumper of the red Camaro. "I'll start looking for someone to replace her first thing tomorrow."

Sure—in between the sixteen other things already on his calendar. Making a mental note to leave a message on the office voice mail for Sally before he went to the clinic in the morning, Nick told Charles he'd squeeze in a few minutes to see Brit the next day. He asked the handyman about the new hot-water heater he'd purchased for Home Away From Home, glad to hear something was working out, before ringing off.

If he hadn't already committed himself to dinner plans, he could have used the evening to start making calls for a replacement housemother. And to fire the one he already had.

Right before the holidays, neither task would be easy.

But he *had* made a commitment to dinner—a commitment he wanted to keep. For purely professional reasons, he told himself. Nick was used to helping people; in fact, his entire life was devoted to it. But even he found yesterday's experience outside the norm. Rescuing a beautiful woman from a hoodlum—in broad daylight, no less. He wouldn't be who he was if he didn't do a follow-up visit. Just to make sure she was recovering from the incident.

And if he enjoyed dinner, was even looking forward to it? Well, he loved his work. There was no law against that.

NICK MCINTYRE was late. Abby paced her small shop, wishing she hadn't told Jeanine, one of her seamstresses, that she was fine there alone. Because she wasn't. She'd done a good job of convincing the two women who worked for her that yesterday's attack was over and forgotten; she was nowhere close to convincing herself.

Peeking through the blinds into the darkening street, Abby gnawed off the lipstick she'd applied only fifteen minutes earlier. The same blue car was rounding the corner for the third time. Slowly. Probably looking for an address. Dusk had fallen, making identification difficult. Of street numbers. Of faces.

Abby couldn't see who was driving. Annoyed with herself for trying, she let the blind slide back into place and, staying in the shadows so as not to be conspicuous to any untoward passerby, grabbed a tube of lipstick out of a drawer behind the counter. If she didn't watch herself she'd end up a paranoid old woman, just like the wrinkle-faced Old Maid in the card game Audrey used to make her play over and over when they were little. Abby had grown to hate that game.

Catching a look at herself in the mirror of the antique bureau that held extras of the flower-appliquéd overalls, Abby smiled. She'd sure loved to hear Audrey carry on when Abby or Anna were left with the Old Maid, though. Their younger sister had had a real flair for dramatics. She used to make Abby and Anna roll with laughter as she spoke in the imaginary old woman's squeaky voice and acted out her bony-necked antics.

What Abby would give to play a game of Old Maid again....

And that kind of thinking was going to ruin what might be the first good evening she'd had since Anna walked out on her last April.

Lipstick open and firmly in hand, Abby inspected the outcome of an hour of dithering that afternoon in preparation for her date with Nick McIntyre—a man who'd been teasing her thoughts at the oddest times over the past twenty-four hours.

She knew so little about him. Only that he was a shrink with a medical degree, turned celebrity author. And that he saved damsels in distress. Oh, and that, for a minute there, he'd made her feel something good.

Abby wasn't sure she wanted him to inspire that peculiar sense of excitement a second time. She did want to feel again, wanted it badly. But she wasn't ever going to love again. Of that she was certain.

And where else could the sweet attraction she'd felt the day before lead, except to entanglements she'd never allow?

So why, late last night, had she pulled one of Audrey's little black dresses out of the closet? Why was she walking around her shop in black hose and heels, with her blond hair brushed and shiny, flowing over her shoulders with that tiny hint of curl at the ends? Just as she'd seen Audrey do so often—for so many different dates.

And why was she reapplying the lipstick she knew she was only going to chew off?

It wasn't as if being without a date was new to her. She was probably the only twenty-eight-year-old virgin in the state of California. Not that she was particularly embarrassed by her inexperience. At least not anymore. Never having slept with a man was, by far, the least of her shortcomings. She'd been so busy trying to keep Audrey out of mishaps when they were younger she'd barely had a chance to get as far as necking a time or two herself, let alone developing a relationship that went any deeper than a few wet kisses. And later, when they were all adults, she'd never found a man who'd understood her commitment to her sisters. Men had a tendency to want to come first in their women's lives.

None of which explained why, when she was struggling so hard to find out if she had a purpose outside her sisters, trying desperately to be whole all by herself, she was pretending to be something she was not.

In more ways than one. She might be emulating her identical sister, but Nick wouldn't even know she was a triplet.

She didn't intend to tell him.

For once she wanted to be known simply as Abby Hayden. Not Abby, Anna and Audrey Hayden. Not one of the Hayden triplets. And that made her feel guilty as hell.

The deception, on the other hand, did not. She had a right to her secrets. But more, she had a right to be her own person—just Abby—whoever that turned out to be. She *needed* to be her own person. She'd been left no other choice.

Satisfied with her appearance if not her thoughts, Abby once again paced to the window. She used to love this hour or two after closing time, alone in her shop. Audrey always went home to make dinner as soon as the last customer left and Anna usually went with her while Abby stayed behind to work on the books. Abby hadn't always started the day's accounting right away. She'd often pulled a chair into the open doorway of the shop and simply watched the day end. Just sat there, doing nothing more than whiling away the minutes—communing with the coming night. Those hours were the only ones Abby had ever had to herself. She'd cherished them.

Tonight, rather than communing in an open doorway, she was locked in, avoiding the night, the falling dusk. And watching for her date through the slats of tightly shut blinds. The door to the record shop next door slammed, followed by the clicking of a dead bolt. Abby's heart hammered, her nerves clamoring beneath her skin. She was really alone now. Even Raymond had gone home.

She jumped as the antique clock on the wall behind her chimed the quarter hour. Nick had said he'd pick her up at seven. What if he didn't show? What if she'd looked forward to this night only to be disappointed? What if she had to walk out back in the dark, to her Mustang, all by herself?

A bronze-colored Ford Bronco she'd never seen before pulled up in front of the shop. Abby started to sweat as she saw the headlights go off. She dismissed the possibility that it could be Nick's car; she figured him for the Mercedes type. None of the surrounding businesses was open. And none of the proprietors drove a Bronco. She should never have told Nick she'd wait for him here.

But she hadn't wanted him to come to the beach house, either.

Peeking through the blinds, she held her breath as a rather imposing man got out of the Bronco—and then gasped with relief when she recognized Nick. So she'd been wrong about the expensive sedan. He was dressed just as he'd been yesterday morning, in a dark suit, white shirt and tie, his hair hanging over the collar of his unbuttoned coat.

Quickly, before he could get close enough to hear, she slid open the dead bolt on the shop's front door, then hurried to take a seat on the stool behind the counter. She'd just picked up her pen and barely had time to bend over the ledger before she heard the bell over the door signal his arrival. She couldn't have him thinking she'd been sitting there scared out of her wits in her own shop.

Or waiting for him like some excited schoolgirl with an adolescent crush.

"Hi," she said, getting to her feet, calm now that he was finally here. Now that she was no longer alone.

"Hi." He saw her and stopped. Just stood there in the open doorway, staring, while Abby came slowly toward him in her short black dress.

And Abby knew suddenly that she'd made a huge mistake. She'd walked straight into a danger that might very well turn out to be more threatening than any she'd had the good sense to fear. His eyes were penetrating and hungry. Finding an answering hunger in her.

A hunger she could never assuage.

Losing her own life was one thing, but ruining someone else's was something she was never going to risk doing again. Not ever.

# CHAPTER THREE

"You get enough to eat?" Nick asked, smiling as Abby scraped the last of her chocolate mousse off the china plate in front of her.

Not looking the least bit self-conscious, she shrugged, sliding the empty fork into her mouth for one last taste. "I'm not much of a cook," she said. "And no fool, either. I take it when it's offered."

She'd done it again. Tempted him to come back with a remark that would have sent the attraction simmering between them up in flames.

"So, are you going to accept Doug Blair's offer to buy you out?" he asked. She'd told him about the pending deal over the shrimp teriyaki they'd consumed almost an hour ago.

"I don't know. Probably."

"What's holding you back?"

"Pride, maybe. Not having a business to run."

Her eyes shadowed, as they'd done several times that evening, leaving Nick to wonder about the silent thoughts behind those bleak expressions. She'd assured him when he'd picked her up earlier that she'd recovered from the attack; she'd admitted that the incident was just one of those inexplicable things that sometimes happen in life. And then she'd immediately changed the subject. That alone made him suspicious. He would've felt better if she'd talked about the mugging, the aftermath.

"If you enjoy running the shop so much, why offer to sell in the first place?" he asked.

"It's not the shop so much," she said, frowning, weighing her words as though choosing which ones to share and which to keep to herself. "I'm just not the type of person to enjoy a life of leisure. I wouldn't even know how to begin."

He could relate to that. "So find something else to do."

"I don't know where to start," she admitted.

The lost look in Abby's eyes bothered him. A lot.

"I majored in fashion design in college," she continued. "It's all I know."

"What about your free time?" he asked. "You must have hobbies, things you did in high school or college that you enjoyed. Something you could pursue more fully."

"Hardly," Abby said, not a trace of humor in the little laugh that accompanied her words. "You're looking at the world's most boring person." She took a sip of iced water that had long since lost its ice. "I spent my whole life raising myself and my two sisters. If it wasn't practical or necessary, I didn't do it."

He felt another tug on the heartstrings that weren't available. "What happened to your parents?"

"Nothing happened to them. They're great people. They just weren't great parents."

"How so?"

Abby shrugged, though, strangely, the bleakness that had shadowed her eyes wasn't quite so noticeable.

"They just weren't around. We hardly ever saw them."

She didn't seem to suffer any bitterness over the fact; rather, she sounded as though she'd just accepted her parents for who they were. Nick wasn't sure he'd have been so generous.

"Most nights," she went on, "if they came home from the office at all, it was long after we were in bed." Abby's elbows rested on the table, her chin on her folded hands. "I learned very early on not to rely on them. No matter how many times I'd call and remind them of this or that, they were bound to forget. Eventually, I quit wasting the time on phone calls and just took care of things myself."

Nick recognized eldest-child characteristics. And more. He saw a child who'd been disappointed time and time again. A woman who'd lay down her own life for those she loved, who was strong and capable. Who intrigued him more every moment he spent with her.

Her parents were another story. "They had no right to do that to you."

"They did the best they could, Nick," she said, immediately defensive on their behalf. "They provided very well for us. We always had the best that money could buy—clothes, homes, housekeepers who kept everything immaculate." She stacked sugar packets, making a little house while she talked. "And in the evenings they'd always arrange for the baby-sitting service to send someone over."

"The same someone?" Someone they could bond with. Someone to care.

"Not usually."

"So what about love?"

"They loved us. We always knew that." She toppled her house of sugars. "I remember nights when they'd come home late and they'd sneak into our room, hand in hand, kiss us all good-night and whisper that they loved us," she said, a fond smile curving her lips. "They just didn't know what to do with us."

As hard as he tried, Nick couldn't remain completely unaffected by her compelling brown gaze. "They're lucky to have such a forgiving daughter."

Abby just shrugged. And the shadows were back.

"Do your sisters live nearby?"

"Nope." That was all. Nothing else.

But before Nick could comment, their waiter stopped by for the third time since he'd carried away their dinner plates to ask if there was anything more they wanted. Looking around, Nick was surprised to see that they were the only diners left. They had to let the guy close up and go home. *He* needed to get home. To slog through some of the paperwork he hadn't had time for that day. To check through his files for an interim housemother. To grab a couple of hours' sleep.

"You want to go somewhere for a drink?" he asked.

"Sure." Abby seemed almost as eager as he was to prolong the evening.

He ignored the voice of self-discipline warning him of imminent danger, as he paid the bill and escorted her out to his Bronco. Just one evening. He was only asking for one evening.

Searching for a place that would be quiet enough for conversation but busy enough for anonymity, Nick drove slowly through the streets of Oxnard. The car was still cool from the November air, the streets were quiet, yet filled with the promise of upcoming festivities. Santas smiled from shop windows, garland hung from streetlights. Cutouts of turkeys and corn on the cob adorned grocery store windows. And an intriguing, beautiful woman was sitting beside him.

"I love this time of year," he said, wanting to take Abby's hand, to hold it against his thigh while he drove.

If she'd been any other woman, any of the women he occasionally dated but had never grown attached to, he might have.

"Winter?" she asked, her brows coming together in contemplation.

"The holidays." He loved the excitement, the goodwill. Most of all, he loved the promise of hope, of better things to come. He wondered, for just a second, what it would be like to have Abby play a part in his own holiday celebrations.

"You can have 'em," she said, no longer contemplating anything more than the traffic in front of them. For the first time that evening her features bore the resigned expression she'd worn most of the time he'd been with her the morning before.

"You don't mean that."

"Yeah, Nick, I do."

The holidays were hard for some people; he knew that well. But usually those people were all alone in the world, often living lives that had somehow lost meaning. They weren't Abby.

"What have you got against the holidays?" he asked, feeling almost threatened by her attitude. Abby was a damn smart woman. A dependable woman. Her life of commitment to her loved ones was the embodiment of everything the coming holidays stood for. Why didn't she see that?

She made a noncommittal gesture. "They're depressing," she said. "Maybe we should just skip the drink. It's later than I thought."

"Fine." He turned toward her shop. "So what's depressing about the holidays?"

"They just are, okay?"

He should simply let it go. He knew he should. But... "Thanksgiving, Christmas—they're the essence of hope, Abby. Of promise. Of love."

"You really are straight from a fairy tale, aren't you?" Abby asked, her voice husky with laughter. "Yesterday you're a knight in shining armor—today you're St. Nick. Makes me wonder who you'll be tomorrow. Prince Charming?"

There was no derision in her tone, but no real humor, either. Just a dash of disbelief, and the very clear message that he wasn't going to change her mind.

Which was just as well, considering how personally he was taking this attitude of hers. As if her private feelings and beliefs were any concern of his. He wasn't looking for a romantic attachment—or any other kind of attachment, for that matter. He of all people knew how much time had to be invested to maintain a healthy relationship. And with his priorities, he didn't have that time.

Pulling into the driveway behind Abby's shop, he turned off the Bronco's headlights as he stopped beside her Mustang. Other than a few fairly dim security lights, they were in darkness.

"I'm just a man, Abby. Nothing more."

"What kind of man?" she asked softly.

Her voice filled the night with an intimacy he suspected she didn't want any more than he did. He turned, putting his arm along the back of the seat they shared, his fingers mere inches from her shoulders.

"Just a man married to his work," he said. "I'm no saint, no knight, no prince. I'm not even all that charming."

"So what do *you* do in your spare time, Mr. Uncharming?" she asked.

He could hear the sudden smile in her voice, and found himself smiling in return. "It's been so long since I had any spare hours I really couldn't say."

"Writing a few books takes up that much time?"

Nick shifted in his seat. "I, uh, do a bit more than write books." Usually on the listening end of conversations, he wasn't used to talking about himself.

"Like what?"

"I specialize in family counseling."

"Oh." He could just hear her replaying what she'd said about her parents. "You still see patients, too?"

"Mmm-hmm."

"Where? You have an office close by?"

Add tenacious to Abby's list of character traits. "I have an office in Beverly Hills and a part-time practice at the Hollywood Clinic. Aside from that, I see teens through a program I direct in the Los Angeles school district, I counsel patients twice a week at a family counseling center not far from here, I'm in the process of piloting a family counseling program at a free clinic in South L.A. and I'm the director of a home for pregnant teens."

"Oh."

Nick laughed. "That's it? Oh?" he asked.

She shifted toward the door. "Does this mean I have to call you 'Dr. McIntyre'?"

"Not unless you intend to be one of my patients."

"Nope."

"Good. Because I'm not sure I'd be able to examine you objectively," he said, which, considering his intentions—to remain unattached, to keep things impersonal—was entirely the wrong thing to say.

"Oh."

"Any more questions?" Nick asked, needing to diffuse the energy pulsing through the Bronco. To say good-night and never see this tempting woman again. What was it about Abby that was getting to him, that made her different from every other woman he'd ever known? He realized that if he didn't leave soon, he was going to do something he'd regret.

"You actually run a home for pregnant teens?" she asked, as though she just couldn't quite picture it.

"I don't actually run it, no," Nick explained, his fingers having somehow found her shoulder. "I've hired a couple who run the house itself. They live on the property in a renovated guest house. And there's a live-in housemother who sees to the girls."

"So where do you fit in?"

"I counsel the girls—and their families when necessary." He also owned the place, financed it with some of the money he made from his books.

"How many are there? Girls, I mean." Abby's voice took on a sad quality, almost as if she could feel the pain of the young women whose lives were so out of kilter.

That was when it hit Nick. He might have found a way to keep Abby in his life for a little longer. Strictly business, of course.

"There are six at the moment," he said, his mind reeling with possibilities. "Soon to be seven."

She was silent and Nick rubbed his fingers along her shoulder while he figured out how to present her with his plan.

"What happens to them, you know, afterward?"

"Most of them return home, try to resume normal lives." He thought of young Kaylee. "Finish school. Go to college."

"What about the babies?" Abby asked, shocked.

"With the exception of one young woman who's there now and who's keeping her baby, Home Away From Home is specifically for girls who have already decided to give up their babies for adoption. We work with a couple of first-class adoption clinics to place the babies, and the girls all have the opportunity to interview prospective families. They can choose the adoptive parents themselves, if they want."

"It's gotta be so hard..."

Abby's voice trailed off, and Nick had the feeling once again that he'd lost her to another time, another place. A place he was becoming more and more eager to visit with her. He wanted to find out what caused the sadness he saw in her eyes. To replace that sadness with smiles.

He wasn't sure anymore whether his reasons for wanting to help were professional...or personal.

ABBY KNEW IT WAS TIME to say good-night. To slide from the warmth of Nick's Bronco to the cold Mustang waiting to take her to an even colder home. Nick's talk of babies had brought it all back to her. Her life. Her loneliness. The fact that she had an identical triplet with whom she'd always shared every thought, every feeling. Anna, who was at that very moment pregnant—and unmarried. And shutting

Abby out. Anna was suffering from hysterical amnesia, living clear across the country and refusing to speak to Abby until she remembered why she'd left home in the first place.

Thank God Jason was with her....

"I've gotta go," she said, reaching for the door handle.

"Abby, wait." Nick grabbed her shoulder and gently turned her toward him.

She thought he was going to kiss her. Wanted him to kiss her more than anything, wanted to warm herself at the fire she somehow knew he'd ignite.

"I might have the perfect solution for the extra time you'll have on your hands if you accept Doug Blair's offer."

"What?" Okay, so he wasn't going to kiss her.

"I need a new housemother for Home Away From Home, at least to see me through the holidays, but permanently, too, if you'd be interested."

"Thanks, Nick, but no." She didn't even have to think about it.

"You'd be perfect for it, Abby," he said, still holding her shoulder. "I admit it's a lot of work, being guardian to half a dozen teenage girls, but it's rewarding, too."

Now she *had* to leave, to feel the cold air in her Mustang against her heated cheeks. To go home. To be alone.

"I'm sure it is," she said, "but I can't do it. I'm sorry."

"You haven't even thought about it."

"I don't need to." She sat forward, away from the touch of his fingers. "I've spent my whole life taking care of people, Nick. I'm done now."

His hand dropped to the seat. "It sounded to me like you'd enjoyed caring for your sisters, Abby. I'm sorry. I didn't understand."

He still didn't understand. And Abby wasn't sure she could—or should—explain it.

She was afraid to open up to him, to be vulnerable in any way. But she was even more frightened that she might never see this man again. He'd given her several hours of forgetfulness that evening. He'd made her feel good. And that was more valuable to Abby than he'd ever know.

"I did enjoy caring for them, Nick, but in the end, I gave everything I had and was left with nothing."

"How can you say that?"

"They're both gone," she said. "And I have nothing to show for all those years but emptiness. An empty beach house. An empty life."

"Parents have to let go of their kids, Abby. It's part of life."

"They weren't my kids—they were my sisters, my best friends. It never dawned on me that they wouldn't always be there."

"But doesn't it still make you feel good knowing you made their lives a little easier, a little happier?"

Abby yanked open the door, letting in a gust of night air before she suffocated. "Not me," she said. "In the end, I failed them both."

Nick didn't say anything. Just sat there, staring at her in the near darkness. She wished she knew him better, wished she knew what he was thinking. Most of all she wished she hadn't disappointed him.

"Can I ask you something?" Her voice stuck in her throat, a hoarse whisper.

"What?"

"Why did you ask me out tonight?"

She hadn't thought the question would be so difficult, had just wanted to hear him acknowledge the strange attraction that had sprung so immediately between them. But Nick didn't seem to have an answer. He continued to sit still, watching her.

And then she understood. Hell, he'd practically spelled it out for her when he'd listed his unbelievable number of pastimes. "It's because you're a counselor, isn't it? You felt obligated to make sure I wasn't suffering from yesterday's attack."

"Yes."

"I see." She stepped out of the car without another word, shut the door and walked calmly to her Mustang. The first *good* feeling she'd had in months, and it turned out he'd only been taking pity on her. For a couple of hours, she'd almost started to believe in fairy tales again. She'd thought the night actually held some mysterious magic. Would she never learn?

Hearing the Bronco door slam, Abby froze, her key in the lock of her car. What did he want now? To take her temperature? Give her an office hour?

"I don't need your help," she said through gritted teeth, facing her car. She was not going to humiliate herself further. She was not going to cry.

His arms slid around her from behind, gliding over her stomach, pulling her up against him. Completely against him.

"I was intrigued by the strongest, most compelling, most beautiful woman I'd ever met," Nick said, his breath warm on her neck.

There was no hiding the evidence of what he was trying to tell her. He held himself firmly against her and his body told her in no uncertain terms. But still... "Intrigued professionally?"

"Personally," he said, burying his lips in the tender flesh between her shoulder and neck. Kissing her there. Igniting the flame Abby had begun to think she'd only imagined.

She turned in his arms, but before she could raise her lips for his kiss, he was gone, striding back to the Bronco.

Abby watched him go, bereft, perplexed and intrigued herself. After unlocking her car, she slid inside, totally aware of him sitting in his truck, knowing that he was waiting to see her safely out to the street.

He didn't just see her out of the drive—he followed her home. And waited in front of the house, his engine running, until she was safely inside. Then, without so much as a wave, he drove off.

Abby wondered if she'd ever see him again.

# CHAPTER FOUR

FOR ONCE, Brittany Miller wasn't happy to see Dr. McIntyre. He interrupted her math lesson Friday morning just when she was finally beginning to understand how to find the derivative of a function of x when the function in question was defined implicitly.

"You want to go for a walk?" he asked, leading her away from the room where the rest of the girls were still working with their tutor, Tammy Brown.

Picking up Beanie, the four-pound mutt who was pouncing at the doc's feet, Brit shrugged. What she wanted was to get her math done. After everything the doc had tried to do for her, though, she could hardly be rude to him. And maybe, just maybe, he'd be able to make things right again. But she didn't think so.

"Charles told me what happened yesterday with Mrs. Leonard."

They were outside, walking across the huge, fenced-in front lawn. She could have put Beanie down, but he was so comfortably cuddled, she didn't. "It was no big deal." Brit was so used to hiding her feelings the lie came naturally.

"She made you cry."

*Damn* Charles and his do-gooder wife. Didn't a girl deserve a little privacy? Even a sleazy, immoral girl like her?

"I was just missing Jimmy."

The doc nodded, but Brit could hear him reading between the lines, almost as well as if he'd been speaking out loud.

"You think the things she said about you are true?" he asked.

"Doesn't much matter what I think." Because she couldn't take back things she'd done, bridges she'd burned. She couldn't take back her virginity.

"I think it does."

"Why?"

"For one thing, they weren't true."

Right. Try telling her daughter that when she wanted to know if her mother had really been pregnant at seventeen, Brit thought, walking silently beside the only man she'd ever trusted—other than Jimmy, of course. No matter how she tried to sugarcoat it, she was nothing but an unmarried and pregnant high-school girl.

"You made one mistake, Brit."

But it was the one mistake a good girl didn't make.

"You're a wonderful young woman with a generous heart who'd never hurt another soul if your life depended on it."

Maybe, but she'd broken God's law. Her stepfather had made sure she got that message loud and clear before he'd thrown her out.

Holding Beanie close, Brit remained silent, walking slowly, her head bent against the bright California sunshine. Shame engulfed her, almost suffocating her under a weight she knew she'd carry for the rest of her life. What had ever given her the idea that she could keep the baby she and Jimmy had made? How had she ever believed that a child conceived in love wouldn't be hurt by the inappropriateness of that conception?

"Are you having second thoughts about Jimmy?"

"No!" Brit said, raising her head to stare at the doc. She'd thought he understood. He was smiling down at her, his eyes making her feel warm for the first time since that awful Mrs. Leonard had cornered her the day before.

"I didn't think so," he said softly.

He pulled her to a stop beside him. "You and Jimmy share a very unusual love, Brit," the doc said. "It came to you at an age most people consider too young, an age that for most people *would* be too young—except that the circumstances of your life, and Jimmy's, made you both ready."

Brit swallowed, unable to tear her eyes away from the doc's, even though she'd warned herself not to get sucked in again, not to believe she could have the impossible. She couldn't understand why the doc didn't judge her the way almost everyone else did.

"And beyond that," the doc continued, "it's a love that the majority of the world will never experience and therefore won't understand."

"You're trying to tell me I'm not wrong to believe in something no one else even acknowledges."

"You have to see yourself from the inside out, Brit, not from the outside in the way other people see you."

She knew what he was getting at. And wished it really was that simple.

"Mrs. Leonard looked at me and saw an immoral pregnant teenager." Brit could barely get the words out. Because seeing herself through the other woman's eyes, a woman who had no personal investment in her, no reason to lash out in disappointment, had shaken Brit up more than anything else that had happened in the past six months. Was she really that girl? The one who, simply by existing, would tarnish the life of an innocent baby?

"Is that what *you* see? An immoral teenager?"

Brit couldn't answer. She just didn't know anymore.

Dr. McIntyre stood quietly in front of her, watching her with those eyes that made her feel like he saw everything inside her.

Lowering her own eyes, Brit shook her head. She knew she loved Jimmy with all her heart. And what was more, she knew Jimmy loved her, too. They were both so much older than their years in every way other than physical age, and their bodies had simply followed suit. Neither one of them had knowingly done another immoral thing in their lives.

"Mrs. Leonard is ignorant, Brit, and hurtful in that ignorance."

Brit nodded. But truthful, too? No matter what Brit knew about herself, would her baby suffer because of her mother's sins?

"She was also fired this morning."

Brit nodded again. She wasn't surprised. The doc ran a first-class place, and he really cared about all of them. Maybe it was time for Brit to quit fooling herself and do what the rest of the girls were doing. Maybe it was time to find a good home for the baby she already cherished with all her heart. Maybe it was time she quit believing she was different.

"Doc, if you were Jimmy and you found out that I'd buckled, that I'd kept your baby from you because my stepdad made an unfair demand, would you hate me?''

"Not if I understood you had no choice.''

"I had a choice. We always have choices. Isn't that what you teach us?''

"Your stepfather refused to have you in his home, Brit. Without his help you were facing, at best, a home for pregnant teens funded by the welfare system, a home where you'd get no education and minimal care, a home where who knows what kind of rough housemates you'd have.

"But your stepfather signed the papers necessary for you to come here—on the condition that you break off all contact with Jimmy, at least until you're eighteen and no longer his legal responsibility. Brit, he's even agreed to let you live with your aunt after the baby's born, so you can finish high school. From where I'm standing you had only one choice.''

"By being loyal to a man who's never loved me, instead of the only person who ever has?''

"You're being loyal to Jimmy, Brit. By taking care of his baby, of yourself and your future, you're being loyal to the love you share with Jimmy.''

"Jimmy would have taken care of us, if he'd known.'' Brit hated even to say the words, hated to think of what she might have traded away for a mean old man's signature.

"He'd have done his best, Brit, but face it, Jimmy's a kid, too, with no health insurance. He was barely supporting himself. How could he possibly have provided the care you need? The care your baby deserves? And even if he had, it would've been at the expense of his scholarship, his future, which means your future, too. And your baby's.''

Blinking back tears, Brit wished she felt half as sure as the doc sounded.

"Have your baby, honey, and let your stepfather's insurance cover your medical expenses. Your bargain with him is binding only until you're eighteen. That's not so long to wait."

Brit buried her face in Beanie's neck. She wouldn't be eighteen for another five months.

And in spite of what the doc said, there was no guarantee Jimmy would even want her when he found out what she'd done. She knew, if the situation was reversed, she'd be mighty hurt if Jimmy had kept something this monumental from her. For whatever reason.

"Anything else you need to talk about?" Dr. McIntyre asked.

"Uh-uh." Brit shook her head. Maybe if the doc were a woman, she could say what she was thinking. Could ask if, deep in his heart, he meant everything he'd said—or was it just therapy, stuff he thought he was supposed to say? With a woman she could ask if there was something wrong with her for being so turned on by Jimmy's body that sharing *her* body with him had felt not only right but necessary. Did that make her a slut, like her stepfather said? But the doc wasn't a woman, and the one who'd been hired to talk the girls through times like these had just been fired.

Which was about par for the course when it came to Brit's life. No matter how hard she tried to be good, to do what was right, to do what was expected of her, whatever she needed always seemed to be beyond her reach.

And maybe she didn't really need to talk to anyone

at all. Maybe the night she'd just spent, wide-awake in her bed, had been what she needed. Maybe she already knew what she was going to do.

Because if she and Jimmy didn't find each other again, or if they did and things had changed—even if he offered to marry her anyway, for the sake of the baby—then the baby would suffer, the way Mrs. Leonard said. And besides, how could she ever hope to convince her baby girl that she wasn't illegitimate, a bastard, when that was exactly what she was?

"ABBY, IT'S your mother, dear."

Abby grabbed the phone when she heard her mother's voice on the answering machine late Saturday evening. "Mom?" She'd been waiting to hear from her parents since Wednesday. Doug Blair had been waiting, too.

"Oh, good, you're there. Your father and I just got back from New York and we have to leave for France first thing in the morning, and I wanted to be sure and talk to you about this offer you've had before we go."

Abby's heart sank. "France?"

"The new scent's finally ready, and we're pulling out all the stops to get it packaged in time for the holidays," Lorna Hayden explained.

"But Thanksgiving..." Abby trailed off. What was she doing? She'd long since resigned herself to her parents' ambivalence about anything other than work—including holidays. The Haydens were becoming quite successful perfumiers.

"That's not until next week," Lorna assured her. "If things go well, we should make it back."

"It's this coming Thursday."

"Ohhh." Lorna's voice sounded truly pained for a moment. "I hate to leave you here alone, especially with Anna away."

"I know, Mom," Abby said, the heavy weight returning to press on her shoulders, her chest. Under the circumstances, they'd probably stay if she asked. "But we all know the best thing to do is carry on," she said. "It's not as if your being here is going to bring Anna home."

It wasn't their fault Anna was gone. It was hers. "You should go," she finished.

"You're right, of course, Abby," her mother said, her voice filled with relief. "But we'll stay if you'd like us to."

One. Two. Three… "No, Mom, really, I want you to go."

And part of her did. The part that automatically tended to those she loved.

"If you're sure…"

"I'm sure."

"Well, then, tell me about Doug's offer. I take it he made a good one?"

"Too good to pass up, I'm afraid," Abby said. She'd been thinking of the business, among other things, for most of the evening as she'd sat alone in her quaint little cottage on the beach and let the darkness fall around her. It hadn't seemed worth the effort to get up just to turn on a light.

Lorna was more than a little excited when she heard the terms of Doug's offer, and insisted Abby fax her the contract that night. "I'll read through it and have it back to you before I leave town in the morning."

"I can send it over just as soon as we hang up,"

Abby promised, feeling an odd sense of comfort after all. It might have taken twenty-eight years, but for the first time, Abby was going to be the reason her mother pulled an all-nighter. She'd be the beneficiary and not the victim of Lorna's workaholic tendencies.

And if Lorna completely missed the reluctance in Abby's voice when it came to selling the shop, well, Abby had expected as much.

"Have you canceled your lease?"

"Yeah," Abby said. She'd told Jeanine and Maria the day before, and had been regretting it ever since. "The ladies are staying on long enough to sell what we can of the current stock. We have to be out by the end of December."

"Good," Lorna said. "No problems getting out of the lease?"

"None." Abby regretted that, too. "They've already got it rented. To Raymond next door. He's been wanting to expand for more than a year."

"Wonderful!"

Yeah. Abby supposed it was.

"So, you'll fax me the contract?"

"Of course, but first, is Daddy there?" Abby asked quickly before she could change her mind.

"He's in his office. I'll buzz him."

Her mother put her on hold and Abby tried to amuse herself watching the moon flicker over the ocean in the distance. She used to love that sight. Back before the beach had become something to fear—

"Abby, honey, congratulations!" Lincoln Hayden's voice boomed. "Your mother told me about the offer," he continued. "I must say I'm not surprised. After all, you're a Hayden."

"Mom said she'd look at the contract tonight," Abby told him. It was almost worth getting the offer just to hear the pride in Lincoln's voice.

"So she said. I'm not supposed to keep you so you can fax it over."

"I know, but..." Abby paused. Maybe she was being ridiculous.

"What?"

Should she bother telling him? Or was she making a big deal out of nothing?

"Something wrong, baby?" Lincoln's voice sharpened.

Blinking back tears, Abby shook her head. "There was a little incident on Wednesday, but everything's fine."

"What kind of incident?" She had her father's full attention and still wasn't sure she wanted it.

"Some kid tried to grab my briefcase outside the shop."

"What kid? You were mugged?"

Abby shrugged, concentrating harder on the moon's reflection as it danced across the waves.

"That's what the policeman called it."

"Police? Abby, tell me exactly what happened."

Abby did. Every detail—right up to the part where Nick McIntyre had asked her out for dinner. She couldn't ever remember her father having used that tone with her.

"I've told you before not to wear that briefcase over your body, Abby," he said. But if he had, Abby didn't remember. "Much better to lose it than to lose you."

Abby twirled the phone cord around her finger. "He was strangling me, Daddy," she said softly, quickly, trying not to cry. Her father wouldn't know what to do with tears.

"Probably panicked when he couldn't get the briefcase, Abby. Are you sure you're all right?"

"I'm fine." The ugly welts were almost gone.

"Just the same," Lincoln said, "I think it'd be best if you moved in here for a while. It's not like we don't have the room, and I'd feel better having you here with the gates and the security system."

"I have a security system." Lincoln had had it installed after Audrey was killed.

"You're still not as safe out there as you would be here."

"Daddy..."

"Besides, your mother and I are going to be away. It'd be nice to have someone here while we're gone. We wouldn't have to worry about the plants."

"Clara waters your plants, Dad." Clara had been keeping house for the Haydens since the triplets were in high school.

"Well, Clara could use the company...."

The fear Abby had been trying to hold at bay almost choked her. "You think there's some connection between Audrey and the attack, don't you?"

"No!" Lincoln sounded honestly surprised. "The thought never even crossed my mind, Abby. The psycho who murdered your sister was after more than a briefcase."

Investigators concluded that the guy had been after Audrey's body—until she'd made him angry by trying to escape. Abby wasn't so sure; Audrey was the type to crumble, not resist.

"Then why this talk of me moving home?" Abby

asked, glancing over her shoulder into the shadowed hallway. "You're scaring me."

"I'm sorry, baby." Lincoln said, his robust tone a little gentler. "I overreacted a bit. I've lost one daughter. I'm not going to lose another."

"I know, Daddy," Abby said, gazing out at the ocean again. "I'm sorry, too. I'll be more careful in the future."

"Well, now, there's no reason to live your life in fear, girl."

Abby trusted her father. She wanted to believe him.

"We can't let what happened to Audrey paralyze us, Abby."

"I know."

Lincoln grunted. "Just the same, it doesn't hurt to be smart—and careful...."

His words frightened Abby all over again.

BY SUNDAY, Nick still hadn't found a new housemother. Nor had he managed to get caught up on the paperwork left over from the week—his usual Sunday afternoon chore.

It was possible that he'd had more paperwork than usual last week. It was also possible that his mind wasn't completely on his work. Every time he tried to concentrate on a case, Abby Hayden's tortured eyes were there, haunting him.

He didn't understand it at all. He saw pain-filled, disillusioned eyes every day of his life. But he didn't bring those patients or their stories home with him; he couldn't. He'd be of no use to them if he afflicted himself with their conditions. There was absolutely no reason Abby Hayden should continue to linger in his subconscious day after day.

Or—maybe—he just wasn't willing to understand why he couldn't let her go. Maybe he wasn't willing to listen to a part of himself he'd long since sacrificed to the life he'd chosen—the life he wanted.

Finally, desperate to get his life in order again, he picked up the phone early Sunday evening and called Heather.

"It's Nick," he said as soon as the neurosurgeon answered. "You on call?" he asked.

"Nope."

"Busy?"

"Nope."

"You want to have dinner?" They both knew that dinner wasn't really the point of their liaison.

"My placc or yours?"

The idea of Heather in his condo was suddenly distasteful, which made no sense, considering she'd been there a few times in the years they'd known each other.

Still… "Yours."

"Give me half an hour," she said, hanging up the phone before he could ask if she'd like him to bring some wine. Married to her career, as he was to his, yet still prone to the needs of the flesh, Heather didn't require presents or flowers. She didn't want romance. She just occasionally wanted Nick.

On his way out, he grabbed a bottle of wine from his refrigerator, just in case. Heather usually enjoyed a glass of chardonnay over the snack they'd probably share. And tonight, he could use a drink himself. To relax. To mellow. And to forget a pair of big brown eyes that held too much sorrow.

WITH MACY'S Thanksgiving Day Parade playing in the background, Abby sipped from a glass of wine as she divested her poor turkey of its innards, hoping all the while that it hadn't suffered too much before the trip to the supermarket. She made enough boxed dressing to stuff the bird, and as soon as she'd placed it in the oven, started on a couple of pies. Turkey, dressing and pies. That ought to do it. Lord knows, with her lack of finesse in the kitchen, the finished products probably weren't going to be edible, but she couldn't not have a Thanksgiving dinner.

And throughout the morning, while she watched the clock and waited for it to be late enough to call New York, she also stole glances at the portable television set in the corner of the kitchen. She wasn't looking for glimpses of Anna in the crowd of New Yorkers lining the parade route. At seven months' pregnant, Anna wouldn't be there.

And even if she *was,* the possibility of spotting her among the millions of faces in the crowd was nil.

But still…she looked.

Sliding the pies in the oven beside the bird, she wondered what kind of dinner Nick's girls at Home Away From Home were having. Did they pitch in with the cooking, help set the table? And, she wondered, not for the first time that week, about the woman Nick had hired to mother those girls. She didn't want the job. Panicked, actually, at the mere thought of letting herself care like that again, of being responsible for another life. But she envied the phantom woman just the same.

Football played in the background later that morning, filling the kitchen with shouts and cheers while Abby carved her turkey. The pies had been a flop, but she was going to get several meals out of the bird.

Detroit scored. Abby glanced up to see a bunch of grown men, giants more like, dancing around, hugging and swatting one another's butts. Was Nick watching the game? Did he even like football? Did he want Detroit to win?

Where was *he* eating Thanksgiving dinner?

And with whom?

There was an injury on the football field and the announcers took a break, going by satellite to Chicago to interview the coach of the Chicago Bears. Abby made sense of only one line of the interview. It was one o'clock in Chicago and the coach was just getting ready to sit down to Thanksgiving dinner with his family.

Licking juice from her fingers, she put down the electric knife. One o'clock in Chicago meant two o'clock in New York. She picked up the phone.

Her fingers shook as she dialed the number, anxious to speak to Jason, to connect in the only way she could with the sister who was one-third of her soul. And Jason... Very dear to her heart, he'd once been as close as a brother to her. Until she'd snatched away his one chance at happiness, taking from him the love he'd been searching for all his life.

The previous spring Jason had had the job offer of his life—a chance to be lead anchor for the evening news at a major New York station—and asked Anna to marry him, to move across the country with him. And instead of setting Anna free, Abby had held steadfastly to her belief that Anna would be miserable so far away from home. Away from Abby. Jason had gone to New York alone. Then, some months later, Anna had gone; Abby hadn't known where. In spite of the hurt he'd suffered at their hands, Jason had come to Anna's side when she suddenly turned up on a New York newscast as Anna Doe. Only partially identified by the necklace she was wearing. She'd been a victim of one of the most horrendous subway crashes in history. He'd identified her. He'd taken care of her. Even after the discovery that Anna was pregnant—with another man's child.

The pause while she waited for her call to go through was interminable. And then, finally, when her stomach was no more than one huge knot, tightening painfully around itself, she heard the first ring. And then the second.

Surely she hadn't waited too long, wasn't too late. Crushing disappointment tumbled over her, weakening the resolve she'd mustered to get through the day. She'd been waiting for hours just to have two minutes of conversation with the man who should have been her brother-in-law.

By the fourth ring she could feel the tears building behind her eyes. The heavy aromas of Thanksgiving dinner were gagging her.

"Hello?"

*Ohh, God.* Abby's entire body jerked to attention. And ached. That soft feminine voice wasn't Jason's. Her hands shook so badly she almost dropped the phone.

"Is this…" Shocked, before she could think, she rattled off Jason's number. She should have hung up, disconnected the line.

"Yes." Anna was tense. Abby could hear the strain in her sister's voice.

And the confusion.

"Is Jason there?" Frantic, she couldn't hang up now that she'd spoken, not without alerting Jason to the horrific situation, warning him. Anna had just heard Abby's voice for the first time since the accident. She might have recognized it, could at this very second be remembering. Or Abby's voice might have sent her even further into the void she'd created to protect herself. Months of work might have been wasted as though they'd never been.

"Who's calling, please?"

And that was when Abby, the strong one, lost all her strength. Completely stunned, she felt the life drain from her body. Understanding the conditions of Anna's amnesia had in no way prepared her. Hadn't brought home what Anna had lost—and how completely alone she herself really was.

*Anna didn't know her.* Even speaking to Abby, hearing her voice, brought forth no recollection. Her identical sister had completely blocked out her existence.

"Is he there?" She forced the words, tears running slowly down her face as she slid to the floor. She wanted to die. To lie on the floor they'd all chosen together—the floor Audrey had spilled on when she'd cooked, the floor Anna had cleaned—and die.

But she had to warn Jason first.

Anna might not remember anything, but Abby could tell that her sister was badly upset by the phone call. Even now, when Anna didn't know her, Abby still felt the connection. Still felt Anna's fear as clearly as if it were her own. And in a sense it was. The three of them had been experiencing one another's sorrows—and joys—all their lives.

Anna wasn't answering. She couldn't. Abby understood that.

"May I speak with him, please?" She had to keep

her voice strong. To make Anna put Jason on the phone.

God alone knew what damage she had done, exposing herself to Anna. Had she sent her sister into permanent memory loss?

Holding her arms tightly against the excruciating pain in her stomach, Abby felt a criminal's trapped desperation. And a fear deeper than any she'd felt before. She prayed that she hadn't sentenced her sister to a permanent void, never remembering Abby but never remembering her love for Jason, either. She prayed she wouldn't lose Anna forever.

"One moment, please."

The distress in Anna's voice was acute. If Abby hadn't been suffering so completely with her sister, she would have smiled. Only Anna could be upset to the point of falling apart and still be polite.

The silence lengthened, giving Abby too much time to worry. Had Anna hung up on her? Or had Abby's phone call sent her over the edge of that final precipice she'd been teetering on for months?

Tears continued to fall unheeded down Abby's cheeks as she sat huddled on the kitchen floor. Arms around her knees, she cradled the phone against her shoulder and rocked herself slowly. The soothing rhythm gave her a thin grasp on control.

She thought of Nick. Of his eternal hope. And she wished with all her heart that the faith he had in happiness was more than just a man's foolish dream. She wished he *were* St. Nick, as she'd teased him last week. Then she could ask him to make things better and know that he could.

"Hello?" Jason's voice was curious, but so far not panicked.

"I'm so sorry…" Abby sobbed, beyond caring that she'd begun to cry.

"Oh!" She could hear his consternation and then, understanding. "Hi!" he said, as if Abby were the family to him she should have been. The family she'd once been.

"Is she still sitting there?" Abby asked, still crying.

A pause. And then, "Uh, yeah," not nearly as enthusiastically.

"Is she okay?"

Another pause. "I don't know. She just ran for the bathroom."

"I made her sick."

"Did she remember you?"

Abby's "No" was little more than a squeak through a fresh spate of tears.

"She looked like she'd seen a ghost when I came out of the kitchen."

"Oh, God, Jason. I'd die rather than hurt her, so why do I keep doing it?"

"It was bound to happen sooner or later, Ab," Jason said. "We can't keep coddling her forever."

"I thought you'd answer the phone," Abby said, and then continued without giving him a chance to reply. "You always answer your phone." She was afraid to let him talk. Afraid to hear what was going on in his apartment. "Is she still in there? Can you tell if she's okay?"

"The water's running," Jason reported, leaving unsaid the fear that palpitated between them. What would he find when Anna came out of that bathroom? "I was in the kitchen, dealing with the turkey. I didn't hear the phone ring. So she answered it.…"

"You'll call me later, when you get a chance?"

"Of course," Jason said, his voice warming Abby's frozen heart. "She usually naps after she eats. I'll call you then."

"I miss her so much…" Abby's voice faded. She just couldn't bear to lose this tiny connection and be all alone again.

"I know," he said, his voice filled with regret.

"You, too," Abby finally whispered. "I miss you, too." In all the months she and Jason had been talking, they'd only skated around the relationship they'd both once taken for granted.

"I miss you, Ab," he said softly. "A lot."

"Call me…" Abby choked, hanging up the phone as the tears overwhelmed her.

But she didn't get up. She sat for more than hour, crumpled on the kitchen floor, her Thanksgiving turkey getting cold on the counter above her. And waited for Jason to call her back.

# *CHAPTER FIVE*

NICK MADE IT—barely—until the morning after Thanksgiving before he finally called her. He'd spent the holiday rushing from one place to the next. Home Away From Home, a stop at Sally's, having a bite to eat with Kaylee and her mother and little brother out in Mission Viejo, the house of one his colleagues. Had he ever been in one place long enough, he'd have called Abby for sure. She'd been on his mind the entire day.

And much as he told himself not to, he picked up the phone first thing Friday morning. More than a week after the mugging, he wanted to make sure she'd recovered completely.

"Nick! How are you?" she greeted him as soon as he'd identified himself.

"Fine." He hadn't expected her to sound so glad to hear from him. "Busy."

"Out conquering bad guys?"

"In my spare time." Nick chuckled. So maybe he occasionally took himself a little too seriously. "Speaking of bad guys, you all recovered?"

"Good as new. Except…"

He sat up straighter, the pen he'd held dropping to the desk. "Except what?" he asked. "Something's wrong?"

"Only that I never thanked you properly," Abby

said in a rush. "How about letting me cook you dinner?"

She was fine. That was all he needed to know.

"When?" he heard himself ask. He had no time. And no intention of carrying this any further. For Abby's sake as well as his own.

"Tonight?"

His refusal stuck in his throat. She sounded lonely.

"I have an appointment with a couple in Beverly Hills at six," he said, reading from the calendar in front of him. "Marriage counseling."

"Oh," she said, uncertainty clouding her earlier cheer. "Well, another time...."

"We could do it after that, if you wouldn't mind eating late." The words were out of his mouth before he could consider their harm. Or stop them.

"Late's not a problem," Abby was quick to agree. "With the shop not closing until six, I'm used to eating late."

"How's eight-thirty?" He could just about make it out to the beach from Beverly Hills by then. As long as his session ended the second it was supposed to.

After ascertaining that he liked lasagna and hadn't eaten it recently, Abby issued a warning to drive carefully and rang off. Nick sat at his desk, looking at the phone still in his hand, wondering what had just hit him.

BRITTANY ALMOST CRIED the first time she saw Kaylee McDonald. A year younger than her, Kaylee looked just like pictures of Brit's mother at that age, her blond hair almost golden, her round face so innocent. And there the resemblance ended. Because the shame Brittany noticed in the other girl's eyes reminded her of what she'd seen in the mirror when she brushed her teeth that morning. But this girl was too young, too sweet, to be suffering the agony Brit had been putting herself through.

She waited until Kaylee was shown to her room, until the other girl was alone, unpacking, before she went to introduce herself. She knew how hard it was to meet new people when you couldn't even bear to meet your own eyes in the mirror.

"Hi," she said, knocking lightly on Kaylee's open door. She envied the girl her short, sassy blond hair. Brittany's own long, dark locks were like a cloak of shame. Her stepfather had held such iron control he'd even dictated how she wore her hair. Maybe she should think about cutting it now....

"Hi." Kaylee didn't look up from the jeans she was taking from her suitcase.

"You want some help?"

"I'm almost done," Kaylee mumbled. "But thanks."

Brittany would've taken the hint and left if she hadn't recognized the turmoil of emotions that chased across Kaylee's face. If she hadn't just suffered through the same thing herself a few months back.

"I'm Brittany," she said, coming in to sit on the edge of Kaylee's bed.

"Hi," Kaylee said again. Her face turned all red.

"That's Bones." Brit pointed to the lazy dog curled up in a corner of Kaylee's room. She'd noticed that Bones greeted each newcomer to Home Away From Home in the same way.

Hardly glancing at the dog, Kaylee nodded.

"It's okay, you know," Brittany said softly. "Everyone's really nice here."

Kaylee nodded again, her blond head still bent as she shut the drawer on the last of her clothes. Brittany saw a tear slide down the girl's face.

And felt her own throat choke up. "You scared?" she asked.

Kaylee shrugged.

Of course she was. Just the physical side of having a baby at sixteen was enough to scare you to death. Let alone all the other things that came with teenage pregnancy. Being ostracized from your family, having to leave your friends, knowing you'd never fit in again. That you'd never be the same. You'd never be a kid again.

Brittany remembered her own first day at Home Away From Home, the frightening barrage of emotions that had attacked her until she'd thought she'd die.

"They'll all like you," she said, thinking about that first fear, which had quickly been put to rest.

Kaylee looked up then, and Brittany knew she'd guessed at least one thing right.

"And not because the doc tells them they have to, either," she added.

Kaylee sat down on the opposite edge of the bed, her back to Brit.

"They're all okay, except Diane." Brittany directed her words to Kaylee's reflection in the mirror on the dresser in front of them. "She's got ADD or something and drives us all nuts, but she's not mean or anything."

Kaylee glanced briefly toward the mirror and nodded. "And then there's Becca. She's a real airhead, but she's funny. And nice...."

Brit thought about the other girls, feeling some

kind of affinity with each one of them. "Deb's pretty bitter," she said, only so Kaylee wouldn't take the other girl's attitude personally.

Kaylee didn't look up again, but she nodded. She was listening.

So Brittany told Kaylee about the rest of the girls currently living at Home Away From Home, all except their reasons for being there. Each girl had her own story, her own heartache. And while in some ways, the stories were surprisingly the same, they were all very different, too. And their own to tell.

Including Kaylee's. Brit was almost afraid to know the other girl's story. Kaylee was too innocent, too broken, to be in love. And Brit knew of no other happy reason to make a baby.

'Course, what was love anyway? She wondered if she could still believe in it when she'd been so wrong about other things.

IT HAD BEEN so long since Abby had prepared a meal for anyone but herself she miscalculated the time she'd need. When Nick arrived the lasagna was half an hour from being done, and Abby was just yanking a pair of jeans over her hips. He was fifteen minutes late.

Pulling her fingers through her hair in lieu of a brush, she took one last skeptical look at the vee neck of Audrey's purple angora sweater and ran for the door. She had to remain calm. Act natural. He didn't need to know that her nerves were taut enough to break at the thought of having someone here, inside her house. Could she do this? Could she be like any normal, reasonably attractive twenty-eight-year-old woman and just enjoy herself?

He looked so good, his professional attire in contrast with the hair hanging over his collar.

"Hi."

"Mmm. Smells great." Nick smiled, handing her a bottle of zinfandel.

Thanking him for the wine, Abby hung his jacket on the tree beside the door. "Dinner's not quite done," she apologized.

"I'm sure it'll be worth the wait."

Abby just smiled. Truth be known, lasagna was the only thing Abby made well. Audrey had been the cook.

He followed her into the living room, perused the off-white leather furniture, the entertainment center, the large screen television. And seemed to approve of what he saw.

"Can I get you a glass of wine?" She needed something to do. His presence was overwhelming—in a home that had been ruled by emptiness for so long.

"Sure." He nodded. "You must have a fantastic view," he said, crossing to the wall of windows hidden behind thick white curtains.

"Mm-hm." Abby agreed, forcing aside memories of white sand soaked with blood. Policemen. An ambulance. She hadn't opened those drapes since. "It's even nicer from the kitchen. You see more of the ocean." And nothing of the stretch of beach where Anna had found Audrey's body.

"Here." She handed him his wine, taking a long sip from the glass she'd poured for herself. She'd been wrong to invite him here. To think she was ready.

She sank onto the couch, and loosening his tie, Nick sat beside her.

Abby could feel the warmth emanating from his body like a tangible thing.

"You okay?" He dropped his arm along the back of the couch behind her.

Abby nodded. Or at least hoped jerking her head up and down looked like a nod. "Fine."

The room fell quiet again. His fingers were only inches from her shoulder. Abby wanted to be held so badly she ached. She could concentrate on nothing but those fingers hovering just behind her.

"I sold my business," she blurted, fighting the urge to jump up, to put the room between them. Or to curl into Nick's body and weep until her heart had no more tears.

He was watching her. "You're happy about it?"

"Mostly."

"And you've found something to fill all those free hours?" Nick asked, still watching her. His gaze wasn't probing, clinical. He just seemed interested.

Abby finally looked away. "There haven't been any free hours yet. Just the opposite, in fact." She pulled her legs up and hugged her knees to her chest. "I've had a ton of arrangements to make, and we're still filling holiday orders."

The two ladies who worked for her would be filling orders until the end of December. Abby had finished up most of what she had to do at the beginning of the week.

But she had a fall line to design.

IT DIDN'T OCCUR to Abby until halfway through dinner that she was wasting a perfectly good opportunity.

She'd been so busy worrying about whether Nick's interest in her was more personal than clinical that she'd missed the bigger picture.

She'd forgotten the one important question she could ask. *How can I help Anna?*

Her adored sister was suffering from a psychological disorder and here she was, sitting with a man who had a medical degree in psychiatry. Maybe he could tell her how to help Anna. Have a different take on the situation. Maybe there was something else they could be doing to release Anna from her self-imposed isolation.

Yesterday she'd spoken to Jason twice more, and while Anna had not remembered anything, she'd clearly been agitated. So was Anna *starting* to remember? Had Abby's voice touched a chord deep inside her? Were they on the verge of discovery? Or was her sister merely on the verge of escaping permanently into the nothingness she'd created to shield herself from the vagaries of a world she no longer trusted?

"This is excellent." Nick smiled at her over his nearly empty plate.

"Thanks," she said, almost losing her nerve.

Putting down her fork, she pushed back from the table far enough to bring one foot to the edge of her chair, holding her knee against her chest. She'd had very little appetite these past months. Right now she had none.

"Tell me about hysterical amnesia." She forced the words out of a suddenly dry throat. Other than her parents and Jason, Abby had discussed Anna's condition with no one since the day Dr. Gordon had called from New York to tell her her sister was in the hospital. Not because she was afraid to speak of the condition, but because she was afraid she couldn't speak of Anna without breaking down.

Jason put down his napkin, his gaze focused on her. "Why do I think this isn't casual dinner conversation?" he asked.

Uncomfortable under that knowing stare, Abby glanced away. "Do you think such a thing exists?" she asked.

"I know it does."

She'd expected to feel relief, at the very least, to hear his confirmation. But she didn't. She'd known all along that hysterical amnesia was a valid diagnosis. Because she was the other part of Anna. She could *feel* her sister's confusion, her fear. And for the first time since they were born, she couldn't feel her love.

"Is it permanent?" Heart thudding painfully, Abby waited for his answer, holding her hands wrapped around her knee.

"Sometimes."

Her heart stopped. Her breath stopped.

"Not usually."

Abby nodded. It was all she could manage.

"You okay?" Nick asked. Ever aware.

Nauseous. Light-headed. Afraid she was going to cry before she got through this. She nodded again.

He didn't believe her. She could see the doubt in his eyes.

"How do you treat it?" She didn't know how the words kept coming. But after the past twenty-four hours of frantic worry, she was desperate for answers, for reassurance.

"Case by case." Nick's tone held more question

than answer. "Usually by allowing the mind to heal itself."

"And if that process is…interrupted?"

"Then the damage could become permanent."

Abby's blood froze in her veins. Oxygen refused to flow to her brain. He wasn't reassuring her. He was confirming her worst fears.

"H-how would you know if that had happened?" she asked, her voice thin, frightened. Had she loved her sister straight to permanent hell? Her own selfish need to connect once again ruining Anna's life? Would she never learn?

Nick's eyes were full of concern. "Again, that varies from case to case," he said slowly. "Oftentimes the patient merely becomes complacent, content with the void."

Hugging her knee so tightly it hurt, Abby stared at him. "And if the patient becomes agitated, instead, could that be a sign, too?"

Nick shook his head. "Agitation is almost always a sign of brain activity—not complacency," Nick said.

Her relief was so acute she went limp, her head falling down to her knees.

"Are you going to tell me who we're talking about?" Nick asked softly from across the table.

"My sister." The words were barely a whisper.

NICK STARED at the woman across from him and swore silently. She was so beautiful. And strong. Intelligent. He wanted to make her happy. But obviously, whatever trauma had sent her younger sister, a sister she'd raised, into a state of emotional breakdown, had touched Abby, too.

He knew intuitively that he couldn't fix this with words. Something was very wrong, more than a little counseling would make right. This was more than hurt feelings and misunderstandings. Watching Abby, understanding only a fraction of what was going on inside her, he sensed that the pain she was feeling was soul-deep. And he wasn't qualified to fix souls.

But neither could he walk away.

"Tell me about her," he coaxed. As badly as he wanted to round the table and take her in his arms, he already knew Abby well enough to figure out that would be a mistake.

She looked up at him, tried to smile. Her attempt failed, but Nick pretended it hadn't. He smiled back at her, encouraging her to talk to him. To trust him.

"She was in a subway crash in New York back in June."

He'd heard about the crash. A terrible accident. But thankfully the fatality count had been lower than expected.

"When she regained consciousness the next day, she didn't know who she was."

"They did neurological tests? A CAT scan? A PET scan? An MRI?" he asked, ever the doctor, though he knew there had to have been a battery of tests.

Abby nodded, gazing out over the table, but seeing, Nick suspected, nothing of the leftover food, the dirty plates in front of them. She was someplace else. Alone.

"She had a slight concussion, but otherwise she was fine."

"Who's her doctor?"

"Thomas Gordon. He's a neurologist."

And a fine doctor, Nick was certain, but made a

mental note to place a couple of phone calls just to check.

"Dr. Gordon's conclusion was that Anna's been running from something she subconsciously wasn't prepared to handle." Abby's voice was wooden. "He recommended that we give Anna whatever time she needs to gain the confidence in herself to come to terms with whatever's bothering her."

"And you know what that is?" Nick was sure she did. He could see the pain of truth in her eyes.

"Partially."

Abby fell silent, gone from him again—garnering her strength. He let her go, waiting for her to come back to him when she was ready. And hoped to God she would.

"Our other sister, Audrey—" Abby's voice nearly broke "—was murdered a couple of years ago."

She stopped. Nick saw her fighting tears, and looked away. But only because he could understand how much it bothered Abby that he was seeing her this way.

"Anna found her."

*Oh, God.* Nick stared at Abby. She was no longer fighting tears. She was frozen, armored with ice. The same armor that had surrounded her the day of the attack. Her eyes were dull, lifeless. Cold. Resigned.

"Where?" he asked. But suddenly he knew. And broke out into a cold sweat.

The desperate look on her face when he'd mentioned the view from the living-room window earlier hadn't escaped him. Nor had the fact that she hadn't offered to open those drapes and share the view with him.

"Outside." She confirmed what he'd already guessed. "On the beach."

It was like living in her sister's casket....

"Did they catch the guy?"

She shook her head.

"Damn." Dr. Nick McIntyre, the detached professional, had disappeared. Nick didn't know what to do with the man who'd been left in his place. He hurt for Abby. Really hurt for her. And burned at the thought of someone who'd created such destruction running free.

"They said it was a random mugging," Abby recited. "That Audrey resisted."

"Had she been raped?"

Abby shook her head.

His relief didn't last. Audrey might not have been raped, but there was more. He saw the horror in Abby's eyes. In the stiffness in her shoulders. Her knuckles were white where she was clutching her knee.

"She'd been attacked with a knife." Abby paused. Swallowed. "The funeral was closed casket."

"And your sister found her?" The doctor in him was back as Nick considered the potential damage to a woman who had seen...

Abby inclined her head. "Audrey was facedown in the sand, but there was so much blood around her." She closed her eyes. "Anna screamed. And just kept screaming."

Abby was gone again. Reliving untold nightmares. And Nick knew who'd heard Anna's screams.

Knew, too, that he wasn't going to learn how Abby had felt when she'd heard her sister's anguish. Abby was talking to him for one reason only.

Anna.

Or, at least, Nick was fairly certain *she* thought that was the only reason. That Anna was the reason she'd given herself for confiding in him. He wasn't so sure.

Which could have been just wishful thinking on his part.

"How was she afterward?" he asked. If he had to help Abby through Anna, so be it. But he *would* help her.

"Distraught, at first," she said, lifting her other knee to her chest, rocking slowly on the dining-room chair. "We all were."

"Were your parents here?"

"For the funeral."

But not afterward. Nick didn't even have to ask.

"And Jason was around, too," Abby said, surprising Nick. "He was a rock."

*Jason?* Who was this guy who brought such a warm look to Abby's eyes? Where was he? And why did Nick suddenly not like a man he'd never even met?

"He and Anna were practically engaged to be married."

"Were?"

"They broke up." Abby's voice was emotionless again, her face devoid of expression. "About a year after Audrey was killed—" she took a deep breath "—Jason moved to New York."

"Where Anna is now?"

Abby nodded.

"Any correlation?"

She shrugged. "You'd think so, wouldn't you?"

"You don't?"

She looked at him then, her eyes dull, lifeless.

"Anna's seven months' pregnant. Jason left eight months ago."

"The baby's not Jason's?"

Abby shook her head.

"Whose is it?"

"That's the six-million-dollar question, Doc," Abby said, almost bitterly.

"You don't know who she was seeing before the accident?"

"No one does."

"Why was she in New York?" Nick leaned forward, reaching for a pen that wasn't there to take notes on a patient who wasn't his. "Is there anybody there who'd know? This Jason, maybe?"

"Apparently not, least of all Jason," Abby said. Her hair fell over one shoulder as her head once again drifted down to her knees. He itched to touch her golden hair, to cradle that head in his own arms.

"The first Jason heard of Anna being in New York was when he was looking at footage of the crash, preparing to do the six o'clock news," Abby continued sadly.

"He's a newscaster?"

Abby nodded wordlessly, her cheek rubbing against her knees.

"After the initial horror of Audrey's death passed, did Anna resume her normal life?"

"For the most part. She was happy with Jason."

"But she never spoke of the murder?"

"Anna's always been one to keep things to herself. She seemed to think that if we weren't a bother, our parents would stay around more."

So who'd Abby talk to? Grieve with?

As Nick watched her, as he replayed all that she'd

told him, both tonight and in other conversations, as he began to piece together everything she was and wasn't telling him, his concern for her grew. And his ability to walk away dwindled even further.

# CHAPTER SIX

COMPELLED BY NEEDS, by feelings, he didn't want to consider, Nick took Abby's hand, drew her from her chair and led her back to the couch in the living room.

Uncharacteristically, she just followed him, even settled in easily as he pulled her down next to him. He placed his arm on the couch behind her.

Nick suspected that if Abby didn't get some emotional nourishment soon she was going to shrivel up and die.

"So, why didn't you know what Anna was doing in New York?" he asked softly.

Even expecting the flinch he felt, he wasn't prepared. Her pain tore through him, reminding him that this had become far more personal than he could afford it to be.

"I'd smothered her." The voice wasn't Abby's. It wasn't strong. "She'd asked for a year away—to figure out who she could be by herself, she said. She made me promise not to contact her, or even try to find her, until the year was up."

That reaction was typical for a young person preparing to strike out on her own. But although she'd raised her younger siblings, Abby was only twenty-eight—an age to be having babies, not letting them go.

Giving in to impulse, he touched a strand of Abby's hair, running the ends along the edge of his thumb.

"A youngster needing to test her ground is perfectly normal, Abby," he said confidently. "You can't blame yourself."

She smiled. Sort of. The expression was a travesty of what he knew her smile could be. She wasn't listening.

"How long had she been gone before she was hurt?" he asked.

"Two months."

"And she was, what, about eight weeks' pregnant at the time of the crash?"

Abby nodded, bringing one knee to her chest again.

"So he could have been someone from here."

"Or not."

Considering Anna's current condition, there was one possibility very obvious to Nick. But surely Gordon would have thought of it.

"Is it possible she was raped?" he asked softly. If Abby were someone else he probably wouldn't have asked, but her strength demanded that he not coddle her, not hide the truth from her.

Still, he was relieved when she shook her head. "Anything's possible, of course, but Dr. Gordon doesn't think so. There were no physical signs of abuse, and no emotional ones, either. She doesn't act threatened or afraid for her safety so much as emotionally bruised."

Frustrated with his inability to see Anna himself, to examine her, to reassure Abby, to give Abby the answers she so desperately needed, Nick continued to ask questions—about Anna, her progress, the small, insignificant things she was remembering. Abby's an-

swers gave him a clearer picture of the situation—
Anna's situation, but Abby's, too.

She was virtually alone. Without emotional re-
sources. And she was still holding back something
about all of this. Something that was bothering her.

"When was the last time you spoke with Jason?"
he asked. Abby had said her sister's doctor had ad-
vised that she not contact Anna just yet, as Abby was
part of what Anna had consciously decided to leave
behind. She'd also said that Jason kept in touch.

"Yesterday," Abby said.

Thanksgiving. He'd thought about her all day. Had
wanted to call her. And decided that precisely because
he so wanted to, he couldn't.

"Did your parents talk to him, too?" Nick asked.

Abby shook her head. "They're in France."

She'd spent the day alone. He'd known it. Somehow he'd just known it. He should have called.

"You asked about agitation earlier," Nick said, determining to deal with himself later. "Did Jason say
Anna's getting agitated?"

Abby's other leg came up. She lowered her head
to her knees and nodded.

His hands itched for his notepad. "Does he have
any idea why? Did something happen?"

She was quiet for so long Nick knew she'd told
him all she was going to. He'd be no more help to
her if he continued to push.

"I'm the reason."

Her words were almost a whisper—and so loaded
with condemnation Nick's stomach dropped. "She's
remembering you?" he asked.

Abby tried to shake her head, but her knees got in
the way. She started to shiver. And Nick gave up

analyzing anything. Moving purely on instinct, male instinct, he pulled her into his arms and cradled her against him as he'd been wanting to do since he'd walked in the door.

"Not a bit," Abby said. "She remembers nothing about me." Her voice was choked but dry. And as much as he admired her control, her strength, Nick wished she'd just let go and cry. She was wound so tightly, one of these days she just might snap.

"I called Jason yesterday," she said a couple of seconds later. "Anna answered his phone."

Nick experienced two simultaneous reactions. The doctor was back in a flash, digesting the possible ramifications of Abby's revelation, the significance of Anna's agitation. But all the man could do was imagine how devastating it must have been for Abby to finally speak to her adored little sister—and not be remembered.

He should have called.

ABBY WAS in the kitchen early Saturday evening, wearing another of Audrey's outfits, a designer jogging suit in black silk, and vacillating between horror and a strange kind of comfort as she relived her conversation with Nick the evening before. When she thought of the things she'd told Nick, and the things she hadn't said but was afraid he'd surmised, she wanted to leave town and never see him again. Vulnerability frightened the hell out of her. It sapped her energy, took away her ability to maintain control.

And yet, when she remembered the warmth in Nick's voice, the concern in his eyes, the way he'd wrapped that strand of her hair around his fingers, she smiled from the inside out. He made her feel alive. And the feeling was addictive.

Like most addicts, Abby didn't have the strength to say no.

Which was why she was seeing him again. Late that evening. They were going to roast hotdogs on the beach. Nick's suggestion, not hers. Tonight she was ready—probably because all she'd had to do was put some wieners and buns on a plate, dump precut veggies in a container, grab a bag of chips and open a bottle of wine.

Aside from Audrey's black silk jogging suit, she was all Abby tonight. She hadn't bothered with extra makeup and had left her hair long and straight around her shoulders. If Nick was going to like her, she wanted him to like the *real* her.

And she wasn't Audrey.

Jason had installed a gas grill out back the summer before he'd left, and Abby was relieved to find it still had sufficient gas to start when Nick tried it half an hour later. She hadn't touched the thing since Jason moved to New York.

"Okay, it's your turn," Abby told him, perched on top of the picnic table next to the food, wineglass in hand. She watched Nick carefully arrange wieners on the grill, then adjust the heat.

"Excuse me?" He half turned, cocking his eyebrow at her.

"I gave it up last night." And she had, figuratively speaking. "Now it's your turn to tell me your dark secrets."

He turned back to the grill. "I don't have any."

"Come on, Nick," she cajoled. "Everyone has a story to tell."

"Not me. I spend my life listening to other people's stories." He continued to give her a view of his backside. And a very nice view it was. For the first time since she'd met him, he wasn't dressed for business. The form-fitting jeans and Cal State sweatshirt were much more impressive, to Abby's way of thinking.

"What about that house you run, Home Away From Home?" she asked casually. She might not want anything to do with the place herself, but she couldn't help being curious.

"What about it?"

He wasn't going to make this easy for her. But that was okay. Railroading other people was her specialty.

"How'd you get involved with it?" she asked, swinging her feet as she stared at his back. And it struck her suddenly that she'd been out on the beach for more than twenty minutes and hadn't once looked at the spot where Audrey had been killed. The man was definitely good for her.

GLANCING OVER his shoulder Nick caught sight of those swinging feet—and opened his mouth.

"I was abandoned by my mother when I was two years old," he said, uncomfortable when he actually heard the words. He hadn't spoken of his childhood in years.

"She gave you up for adoption?"

He shook his head, turned the hotdogs and faced Abby. "She wasn't that kind. I was sent to a different foster home each time she disappeared, while I waited for the state to locate her again."

"And they'd let her take you back?" Her feet

stopped swinging; her eyes filled with compassion. She'd put down her wineglass; Nick picked his up.

"Only the first couple of times. But it didn't matter whether I lived with her or not, she still wouldn't sign the papers to give me up."

As the hotdogs cooked, he told her what little he remembered about those four hellish years—and the way they ended.

"She died when I was six," he said. The memory of the day that social worker had come to the door to tell him about his mother's death was as clear as it had always been. It was the last time he'd cried. He'd loved his mother, in spite of her failings—had believed in her, believed she'd somehow straighten out her life, that she'd come back to get him and make a real home for him.

Realizing he'd fallen silent, Nick glanced up to see tears welling in Abby's eyes. And somehow the rest came pouring out—the cruel things his older foster brothers had said about his mother's suicide. The way they'd termed her death "no great loss." And the anger that had built inside him until he exploded. The fights. The running away. The labels placed on him. And the detention home he'd been sent to at the age of seven.

He'd long since removed the hotdogs from the grill and they were cold on the table between them when his voice finally droned to a stop.

"I'm so sorry," she said softly.

The need to take her into his arms, to possess her, to make her a vital part of his life, was so strong. Too strong.

"It was all a long time ago." Nick got up from the

table to put the hotdogs back on the grill. "I'd almost forgotten about it."

"So, how'd you make it from juvenile delinquency to a medical degree?"

"I was adopted." That was the easy part. His sad story had a fairy-tale ending. "My parents were unable to have children of their own, but that never made any difference to them. The day they took me home with them changed my life forever. No biological child was more loved than I was."

"Where are they now? Here in L.A.?"

"Florida." Nick scooped three hotdogs into buns, turning the heat down on the grill to keep the others warm. "They retired about five years ago."

And though they'd fought him the whole way, he'd bought them the resort home they'd always wanted. "My dad plays eighteen holes of golf a day."

Abby squeezed ketchup into the bun he handed her.

"So that's why you started Home Away From Home?" she asked softly, sliding down from the table to the bench across from him. "To give those babies a chance?"

"And the mothers," Jason told her, back in control as he talked about what he did best—helping others. "My mother would probably have allowed me to be adopted if she hadn't spent the first two years of my life loving me. And without me, she could have finished school, gotten a real job, had a life...."

The hotdogs were a little overdone, but good nonetheless. And the night, even better. Nick was more relaxed than he could remember being in months, sitting out on the beach behind Abby's cottage as darkness fell around them. Almost deserted, the stretch of sand between her house and the ocean was illuminated by the single light in her yard, a moon that had barely crept above the horizon—and a million stars.

He could get used to this.

And to her.

Abby smiled as he told her about the littlest of his menagerie of stray pets that also boarded at Home Away From Home. Beanie, as one of the girls had named him when Nick brought home the four-pound puppy two years before, believed he was the resident baby. And the fact that the four pounds he'd brought with him were all he had now helped him perpetuate his misconception.

"He won't go out the doggie door, even though it's carpeted?" she asked, still grinning.

Nick shook his head. Just another of the problems he had yet to solve. "He lies in front of it and emits strange sounds until someone lifts the flap for him."

Abby burst into laughter. "Strange sounds? You mean he whines?"

Abby's big brown eyes were glowing with mirth, and her generous lips, still moist from the sip she'd taken from her glass of wine, smiled at him. Nick forgot what they were talking about. Where they were. Consumed with want, he stared at her.

"Or does he bark?" Abby asked.

"Neither." Nick shook himself. He'd better get a grip. Or get out. "It's a mixture of whining and growling that ends up sounding like he's talking to you."

"And someone lifts the flap?"

"Of course."

She stood up, putting the cap back on the ketchup bottle. "He sounds precious." Her voice was soft, warm.

"He's a brat."

"But you keep him around anyway," she said knowingly.

Nick gathered the grill utensils and closed the lid. "For now. He's good for the girls," he said. "Pet therapy has proven very effective."

Abby nodded, still smiling, and helped him gather up the remains of their dinner to take to the house.

"Besides," he added, "I haven't found a home for him yet."

A lone couple, strolling hand in hand down by the water, stopped suddenly, turning into each other's arms for a kiss that wasn't meant to be witnessed. Following Abby inside, Nick envied them.

HE HAD TO LEAVE. Because if he didn't, he was not only going to risk everything his life was about, he was going to hurt Abby. And she'd already been hurt far more than one woman could take.

"You want to go back outside while we finish these?" she asked, holding up their half-empty wine goblets.

"Sure."

But when he left, he still wouldn't know what that silky jogging suit felt like sliding through his fingers. Still wouldn't know the touch of her skin, the feel of her body...

Nor any other woman, he was afraid. Heather had called on Thanksgiving, and Nick had heard himself ending their liaison before he'd even made a conscious decision to do so. He wanted Abby.

Nick wasn't quite sure what caught Abby, what sight or smell or sound returned her to the realities of her life, but he felt the change the moment it happened. Just as they were settling on the sand, she withdrew. She was in pain; no mistaking that.

Maybe the sand had done it. Her sister had been found in the sand....

Sitting beside her, legs bent, he rested his forearms on his knees and stared into the distance, to the water that held far more mysteries than it revealed.

"My mother couldn't swim," he said, the darkness giving the night a dangerous intimacy. "The night she died, she just walked into the ocean. And kept going until the water took her away from a life she no longer wanted."

"Oh, my God." She was hugging her knees to her chest as she sat on the sand beside him. Nick had never been more aware of a woman in his life. Aware far beyond the physical desire he felt for her.

"I blamed myself."

"Oh, no, Nick!" Her head shot around, her gaze locking on his profile. "You were just a little boy. You couldn't possibly have had any control over the decisions she made."

"Of course I realize that now, but then..." He caught sight of the couple he'd seen earlier; they were heading back down the beach the way they'd come— still holding hands. Probably lived in one of the other cottages scattered along this private stretch of beach. Or maybe they were honeymooning....

Abby, he noticed, was watching them, too. And then she wasn't.

"You couldn't have stopped her from walking into the ocean if that's what she'd made her mind up to do," she said.

Of course he couldn't have stopped her at that point. But... "I never got mad at her all those times she took off, never blamed her," Nick said, telling her something he'd figured out years before—but never spoken of. "Each time they found her, every time they brought her back, I was so damn glad to see her."

"She was your mother. You loved her."

And suddenly Nick understood why he was talking to Abby. Or part of the reason, anyway. She knew. Her mother and father were lousy parents, but she loved them anyway. Just as he'd always loved his mom.

"I think if I'd rejected her, she'd have been able to leave me behind," he finished. "And maybe make a life for herself."

Abby was silent for so long Nick turned his head to look at her. She was staring out at the ocean as though it alone could offer the elusive peace, the answers, she sought. The moon, which earlier had been merely a shadow in the sky, cast an ethereal glow across the water.

"I'm to blame for Audrey's death, as well." Her words dropped between them.

"What?" He didn't know what he'd been expecting, but it wasn't that. She'd been responsible for a random attack?

"I never taught her how to fight her own battles." Her voice was as devoid of expression as her face. "I was always too busy fighting them for her myself." She paused, still gazing at the ocean, but Nick suspected her mind's eye was looking at that stretch of beach behind and slightly off to their right. Her muscles were tensed, as if she were trying to ward off the shadows lurking there.

"She didn't know how to defend herself," she

said. "The police think she was killed because she resisted the attack. I don't. She would've begged, cried—she wouldn't have fought. But even if they're right and she did resist, she didn't stand a chance. She didn't have any survival skills. Nothing to ensure that her resistance would be successful."

And that piece of beach was a constant reminder.

"Why do you stay here?" Nick had to ask.

"It's my home." She wouldn't look at him.

"It wouldn't be if you lived somewhere else."

The night air was cool, falling silently around them.

"The three of us were so excited when we bought this place," she said softly. "We had more fun fixing it up together. We spent an entire week painting. Anna sewed window treatments. It took us days to decide on the tile for the kitchen. That whole first month we were consumed with the place—making it perfect."

"But it's not perfect anymore." He shouldn't pressure her. He didn't have that right. But after all they'd come through together in the past couple of days, the emotional scars they'd exposed, he couldn't just sit silent.

"My happiest memories are here."

And so were the most horrible. "But they aren't making you happy."

She shook her head, eyes glistening with tears, but he knew she wouldn't shed them. Not for herself.

"The place isn't mine to sell even if I wanted to," she finally said. "Anna's half owner."

"With no recollection of ownership." Obviously, Anna wouldn't remember the house if she didn't even remember Abby.

Abby nodded.

So did that mean Abby waited, possibly forever, for her sister to return to the life she'd left behind?

What if Anna never remembered? Was Abby going to grow old, wasting her life away on what had once been?

Abby rocked slowly, back and forth on the sand. "Anna may never want to come home, but it would be cruel to sell this place out from under her when she's not even aware it exists."

"She'd already left it, of her own free will, before the accident, right?"

Abby shrugged, glancing at him and then back over the ocean. He could hear the whisper of silk as she hugged herself tighter.

"And signed over her power of attorney?" He reminded her of something she'd told him earlier.

"I just sold the business. I can't give up the house, too."

Nick didn't say a word. He couldn't. Not and keep her friendship.

# CHAPTER SEVEN

"HOW WAS YOUR DATE Friday night?" Abby looked up as the back door of the shop opened on Sunday morning. The shop was closed, and Maria wasn't due in until tomorrow.

"It wasn't a date," she answered. She spoke to her seamstress and friend in Spanish.

Maria's face fell as she stopped just inside the door and dropped the bag of sewing she'd brought in with her. "He didn't show?"

"He showed. And what are you doing here on your day off?"

Maria worked too hard, which worried Abby. Who was going to watch out that her friend didn't sew herself into an early grave when she went to work for Doug Blair?

"Don't change the subject," Maria insisted, treating Abby to a spate of Spanish that had no clear English translation. The gist of it was that if Abby blew this one, she might as well bury herself now and save her parents the trouble.

"I didn't blow anything," Abby told her friend. But she wasn't sure she was telling the truth. You certainly didn't attract a man by pouring the sordid details of your life at his feet. And psychiatrist or not, you probably didn't turn him on by showing him what an emotional cripple you were.

Whatever the reason, she certainly hadn't brought Nick panting to her side. Two nights in a row they'd been alone together. And two nights in a row he'd left without so much as a kiss good-night.

She and Maria worked hard for most of the morning, Abby packaging the last of the orders Maria and Jeanine had sewn, tying up the loose ends of a business that had consumed her life for so long she didn't know what she was going to do without it.

She was thinking about that as she drove home later in the day. She'd finished up most of what she had to do. Her trunk was full of the things she'd still had at the shop. Maria and Jeanine would be there until the end of December, cleaning, meeting the people coming to pick up the racks, cash register and display cases she'd sold, filling orders, packing up samples and leftover stock, and then, when the lease was up, they'd turn in the key. There was really no reason for her to go back.

Other than Thanksgiving, there hadn't been a day since Anna had left that Abby hadn't spent in the shop. And if Thanksgiving was any indication of how she coped with days off, she didn't want another one. The week ahead stretched before her in its emptiness, the rest of her life right on its heels.

She was about halfway home when she noticed the blue car behind her. It seemed familiar. Glancing in the mirror again, she ran through a mental checklist of people she knew and the cars they drove.

She didn't know anyone who drove a blue sedan. An expensive-looking sedan. And then she remembered where she'd seen the car before. Or one like it. The night she'd been waiting at the shop for her date with Nick, a blue sedan had driven slowly by. And like an idiot she'd panicked.

She was over that now.

She wondered if Nick would call later. After two nights in a row, sharing the evening hours with him seemed like habit. Or at least like something she wanted to do again.

Maybe.

And maybe not. What was the point of pursuing something that could never be? Why tempt herself to love again when she knew the grief that would surely follow?

Exiting the highway, Abby passed Anna's favorite fast-food spot, remembering the last time they'd been there. With Jason. It had been springtime, but Abby hadn't felt the promise in the air. What she'd felt was threatened. Excluded. Anna and Jason had been sharing their words with her, but their real communication had been with each other—their special looks, their little touches. And those she couldn't share.

But she'd been happy for her sister, too. Really happy. And relieved. She'd felt so worried about Anna since Audrey died. Her middle sister had never seemed to grieve, never spoken about those minutes when she'd been alone with Audrey's body on the beach....

Abby stopped at a light a couple of miles from the cottage and glanced in her rearview mirror. The blue car was still there.

Odd that in a city the size of Oxnard someone would be leaving the 101 at exactly the same time and traveling all the way out to the beach.

Trying to see who might be driving, wondering if it was someone she knew after all, Abby studied the image in her mirror. But with the sun's glare she couldn't make out anything other than a pair of sunglasses and the barest outline of a face. She couldn't even tell if the driver was a man or a woman.

And she didn't want whoever was behind her to know she'd been curious. That she'd been looking. Staring straight ahead, she accelerated as soon as the light turned green, taking a couple of extra turns to lose the mysterious blue car.

Except she didn't. Whatever turns she took, the other car took, too. If she sped up, the car sped up.

Abby adjusted the air in the car, suddenly unable to breathe. She told herself she was being ridiculous, and yet her heart began to pound heavily. Another turn. Another five miles an hour faster. And still the car was behind her.

She was being followed.

AN HOUR LATER, safely locked in the cottage, Abby hadn't stopped trembling. Or admonishing herself. The blue car had merely been going to the neighborhood adjacent to the beach. Probably for a Sunday-afternoon family dinner, or cookout with friends.

Oh, God.

She needed Anna.

She needed something to do, to occupy her mind before her irrational fears took over and drove her beyond rational thought. Drawing wasn't really work to her. She needed to be *needed* again. If only from a periphery. To make certain Anna's ankles weren't swollen. To buy baby clothes and extra bottles.

She needed to talk to the one person alive who really knew her. Who'd understand. Who'd been there during every crisis Abby had ever had.

She didn't know how to get through this alone.

ABBY SAT UP in bed, her nightshirt glued to her skin with sweat. Eerie grayness hung over her bedroom with the first light of Monday's dawn. She didn't think she'd slept all night. She'd lain awake for hours, listening to every sound in the cottage, trying not to think about life—about the future—about how disappointed she'd been that Nick hadn't called.

But she must have finally drifted off because, for a second there, she'd heard Anna calling out to her. Something about Audrey. Not heard with her ears, but with senses that had always existed only for the three of them. Yet those senses had been dead for months. Ever since Anna's accident, since her sister no longer knew her, no longer needed her, no longer communicated without words.

She must have been dreaming.

It was probably the cruelest thing that had happened to her since her sister had walked out. This fiendish teasing of the most vulnerable part of her. The part that existed, not on its own, but as one-third of a greater entity.

Falling back to her pillows, Abby burrowed beneath her covers, cradling her knees to her chest, and held on. Just held on. She didn't know what else to do as the tears came—and just kept coming.

NICK KNEW he couldn't see Abby again. Not like he'd seen her over the weekend. He wouldn't be able to walk away a third time.

But as the next two days turned into three, he made himself nearly crazy, thinking about her at the cottage all by herself, without even her shop to keep her busy. It wasn't healthy.

But more, it pained him to think of her so unhappy. She was too vibrant, too strong, too special to be all alone.

"You find anyone for Home Away From Home yet?" Sally asked him Tuesday morning. He'd been at his desk for a couple of hours already by the time she came in at eight—trying to catch up on all the work he'd put aside to spend the weekend with Abby.

Nick shook his head. "Marianne's doing what she can, but with the holidays coming..."

"She can't possibly keep up that big old house and watch out for six girls, too."

"Seven."

Sally frowned. "Oh, right. Kaylee McDonald moved in last week, didn't she?"

Nick nodded, looking over the notes he'd written at his marriage counseling session Friday evening before going out to Abby's. He should have written this report Friday night while the session was still fresh in his mind.

"How's she doing?" Sally asked, taking a seat in front of his desk.

"Hmm?" Nick glanced up. "Kaylee?"

Sally nodded.

"As well as can be expected, I guess," he said. "She's wounded."

"Of course she is," Sally said, indignant. "Her trust was shattered."

"I think it's more than that," Nick told her. He just didn't know what. He'd spent an hour with Kaylee the day before, but in spite of his years of training, in spite of everything he'd learned since, he couldn't get Kaylee to talk about the night she'd conceived. She'd answered in monosyllables, volunteered nothing, refused to meet his eyes.

Thank God for Brit. At the moment, she was the only person Kaylee was talking to at all.

Although Brit wasn't in great shape herself at the moment. She'd helped Nick bathe Beanie the other day, laughing with him over the watercolors staining the curious little guy's nose and ears. Beanie, who'd been sitting on Becca's lap, had tried to "help" Becca paint a poster she was making for geography. Brit had found humor in the situation, but there'd been no joy in her laughter.

The strength that love had given her seemed to be on the blink.

And for once, she'd shut him out. Not entirely, of course. They'd become friends during the months Brit had been at Home Away From Home, drawn to each other by their shared optimism, by their faith in good over evil, in a love that conquers all.

So she'd told him about missing Jimmy. Asked him again if he thought she was crazy for wanting to have Jimmy's baby, wanting to keep it.

She'd nodded when he told her she wasn't crazy to trust her heart, smiled when he'd reiterated that she was one of the sanest young women he knew. She'd seemed satisfied with his answers. But he hadn't been able to bring that lift of confidence back to her step. Or the sparkle to her eyes. His words weren't enough anymore.

It seemed only a few hours later that he heard Sally say, "It's almost seven. Time to leave." Sally was back in his office and it was evening already.

"You go ahead," Nick said, glancing at his secretary. "I'll be out of here soon." They'd put in another long day, but Sal never complained. And as he did so many days, Nick thanked God for the day he'd found her.

"There's a sandwich in the fridge if you get hungry," she called out a couple of minutes later. Her words were followed almost immediately by the closing of the outer office door.

Together, in one day, he and Sally had cleared up the weekend's backlog and made a good start on the week, as well. He'd even managed to get caught up on client reports. He'd managed, too, not to call Abby for three whole days.

He *wasn't* in over his head. He *could* control the attraction that had flared so instantaneously between them. Which meant that now that the day's work was done, he could call to check up on her without guilt. He could at least satisfy the doctor in him, if not the man. Maybe she'd heard from Anna again.

After his queries regarding Tom Gordon yesterday morning, Nick felt confident that Anna was getting the best care available.

Quiet hummed through the vacant office as he waited, phone at his ear, to be connected to Abby. Three rings later, the quiet was replaced by the tapping of his fingers on the desk. He was convincing himself that the tightening in his stomach was hunger pains and not anticipation when Abby finally picked up on her end.

She sounded pleased to hear from him. He was glad to hear her voice, too. To assure himself that she was okay.

"I'd ask what you've been up to, but I'm afraid

you'd tell me you'd written another bestseller or something since I saw you."

He grinned. "It's only been three days."

"You never know. God created the world in seven."

"Yeah, well, the only thing I've created is more work for my secretary."

"Too bad for your secretary."

Nick grinned again. Abby was good for him. "Think I should buy her a present or something? Tell her how much I appreciate her?"

"No way." Abby chuckled. "A picture's worth a thousand words. Give her a few Ben Franklins."

"Money, huh?"

"Definitely. Think of it as a Christmas bonus."

Feet up on his desk, phone tucked against his shoulder, Nick was still grinning. And enjoying himself far too much. This was, after all, supposed to be a professional call.

"I checked on your sister's doctor yesterday."

"And?"

"He's one of the best. No question of that."

"Thank God." Her relief was almost tangible.

"Have you heard any more from Jason?"

"He called yesterday. He says she's still restless, but he feels she's stronger, too. She's determined to take control of her life, one way or the other."

"Sounds like she's gearing up to return."

"God, I hope so." Abby sighed. "The waiting's interminable."

"The best thing *you* can do is keep busy." Nick reached for his pen, twirled it between his forefinger and thumb. "So, what have you been doing now that you're a lady of leisure?"

"Going crazy." She laughed, but there was an edge to her humor.

"Too much free time?"

"No, I mean really crazy," she said, suddenly serious. "I'm getting paranoid, Nick." Her candor surprised him.

"How so?"

"I'm scared."

Nick frowned, putting down his pen. "Of anything in particular?"

"It's the mugging." She tried to laugh again. "I can't seem to get over it. I keep thinking someone's out to get me. I even thought someone was following me the other day." The words came in a rush.

She was really upset, evidenced by the fact that she was telling him about this at all.

"I take it you weren't being followed?" he asked, his voice calm, soothing, as though he were talking to one of his patients.

"No."

"Your reaction is perfectly normal, honey," he said, disconcerted that the endearment had slipped out. He took a deep breath, then went on. "I'd be more worried if you continued to tell me you'd had no reaction to the attack. *That* wouldn't be normal."

"You're sure?"

"Absolutely."

"Then I guess I won't need to rent a room at the loony farm, huh?"

"No." He hesitated. He shouldn't do this. He had no right to pressure her. "But I know where there's an empty room that does need filling."

She'd given him an unequivocal no. But the solution was so perfect. For her. And for him.

"Where?" He could tell she knew what he was going to say.

"Home Away From Home. The position of house-mother is still open." He'd be helping her—giving her a houseful of needy girls to love. Giving her purpose. Giving her a reason to get up in the morning.

He'd be helping the girls, too. Brit, who was holding something back from him. Kaylee, who was hurting far more than she let on. Even Becca, who needed mothering....

The line was quiet for so long Nick took hope.

The solution was perfect, he thought again. He'd be able to see Abby...without *seeing* her. It wouldn't be personal, not at all. He could even spend part of the holidays with her and risk nothing. He could show her that loving wasn't a negative thing—that there was nothing wrong with her or with the way she cared.

"I can't, Nick." The words were a crushing disappointment. "I'm sorry."

"I've got seven girls who need a woman's care, Abby, especially now with the holidays approaching."

The girls were eagerly making plans for Christmas—how they were going to decorate, what they were going to buy. Still just children themselves, they were getting all wound up with secrets and excitement. The last time he'd been there, Nick had given each of them a fifty-dollar budget and suggested they draw names for gift giving.

"Aren't they going home for Christmas?" Abby sounded surprised.

"If they were wanted at home, in their condition,

they wouldn't be at Home Away From Home to begin with.''

"Oh.'' He'd never have believed the single word could say so much.

But it was all the incentive Nick needed to push her a little more. "You owe me one, Abby,'' he said, collecting on a debt he'd never considered a debt to begin with. "Just until after the holidays?''

ABBY CHEWED her lower lip. She wrapped the telephone cord around one finger, then moved to the next. She'd had a call from her mother that morning. Her parents were planning to be in France until at least the first of the year. Maybe longer. They'd rented an apartment there.

Ever since she'd hung up, she'd been obsessed with the fact that she'd be spending the holidays alone.

Even before she'd spoken to her parents, Abby had been dreading her first Christmas without Anna. She had no idea how she was going to get through it. But she'd always assumed her parents would be there with her, needing *her* help. Now, without them...

Twisting the phone cord around her little finger, Abby thought of not living alone for a while. Just until she was over the residual fear from her attack.

She tried not to think of the girls who'd be in her care. Tried to ignore the pull she'd felt on her heartstrings from the first time Nick had mentioned his project.

"You're sure it's just until January?'' Her throat was so dry the words stuck. "You can get someone else to take over then?''

"If that's the way you want it.'' Nick's voice was calm, as always. Reassuring.

Just until January. Four short weeks. Surely she couldn't hurt the girls too much with her unwise loving, her *smothering* in such a short time. Four whole weeks of going to bed without fear....

"All right." She said the words quickly, before they were snuffed out by the part of her that knew better. "But just until January...."

# CHAPTER EIGHT

SHE'D TAKE all her jeans, plus a pair of shorts or two, just in case. And one nice outfit for Christmas Eve. But that was it. She was going to be gone only four weeks. Two suitcases were more than enough. After throwing in several sleep shirts, underwear and her makeup, she zipped up the case. Anna would cringe to see her cramming makeup in with clothes. But Anna wasn't there. She wasn't going to be wearing the clothes. Or the makeup.

She hefted the second, smaller case onto the bed, then carefully packed a couple of sketchpads, a full supply of pencils, colors and charcoals. And the ornament she'd searched out late the night before, after hanging up with Nick. Anna's ornament. It had held a place of honor on every tree they'd had since Anna had sewn the angel in junior high. Abby wouldn't have a tree this year, wouldn't even celebrate Christmas here at home, but she couldn't let the holiday pass without at least looking at that ornament.

She jumped as the phone rang. She wasn't due at Home Away From Home for another couple of hours. And Nick had already given her a complete set of instructions....

"Hello?"

"Abby?"

Recognizing Jason's voice immediately, she turned away from the suitcase on her bed.

"Jason? What is it?"

"You okay?" he asked. "You sound funny."

"I'm fine." She couldn't tell Jason what she was doing. Couldn't bear to hear his recriminations, his warning about her tendency to control others' lives. His doubts. She'd spent the night with enough of her own.

"I called the shop," he said. "Maria said you're taking some time off over the holidays."

"Yeah." She hadn't told Jason about selling the shop. Legally, she had every right to sell the company, but morally, with Anna still gone…

"I'm glad to hear it," Jason was saying. "You taking a trip? Going to Europe to be with your folks?"

"No." She didn't want to tell him about the changes in her life. She wanted to tell Anna, when Anna was ready to speak to her again. And until then, she had to do things on her own, look out for just herself. "I'm staying right here in L.A. If you need me you can leave messages at the shop or at home. I'll be around."

"Yeah, Maria said she'd get a message to you if I didn't reach you at home."

Abby had phoned the older woman first thing that morning, giving her the number at Home Away From Home and asking Maria to call her there starting that afternoon—without telling anyone where she was.

She was probably being paranoid. As a matter of fact, she knew she was. But if part of her reason for agreeing to help at the home was to escape the fear that was still following her, she might as well take all

precautions and keep her whereabouts quiet. And it
wasn't like there was anyone in town she expected to
hear from. She'd spent her entire life caring for her
sisters, being their best friend. Other than Maria at the
shop, there'd been no opportunity to make close
friends.

"So how is she?" Abby asked, her mind returning
to the one thing that mattered. "Any change?"

"She chose a name for the baby."

Abby sank to the edge of the bed. Something in
his voice wasn't right.

"What is it?" she asked cautiously.

"Audrey."

She felt the blood drain from her face. Sinking
deeper into the mattress, she concentrated on filling
her lungs with air.

"She remembered."

"Not yet," Jason said.

And Abby was nauseated by the relief she felt.
Nauseated and ashamed. She wanted Anna to remember more than anything. Had been waiting for
months....

"Surely you don't think she just coincidentally
pulled that name out of a hat," she said.

"I think she's beginning to remember."

"Audrey." Abby blinked back tears. Anna remembered their baby sister. Somewhere in the dark re-
cesses in which she'd hidden herself, Audrey was still
important to her.

"I'm sure it's just a matter of time now," Jason
said softly.

Abby nodded, losing the battle with the tears that
slid down her cheeks. How much time? How long

until she could be certain that she hadn't lost Anna forever to the void that had consumed her life?

Or until she found out once and for all whether she'd lost her sister to conscious hatreds, instead?

"I'm scared for her to remember," she whispered, admitting the truth not only to Jason but to herself. Living without Anna all these months had been hell. But she'd consoled herself with the fact that her sister was ill. How would she ever cope if Anna remembered and still wanted nothing to do with her?

"I know," Jason said. "Me, too."

In some ways, he was as guilty as she. They'd both tugged at Anna until she'd had no choice but to escape. They were as much to blame for her amnesia as the subway crash was. But Jason had had these past months of living close to Anna, of sharing her pain, watching her grow, loving her, to make amends. Abby had nothing.

Of course, in the end, Jason, too, might have nothing.

"Still no word from the father?" Abby asked.

"None," he paused. "At least not *from* him."

"But you did hear something?"

"She'd been seeing someone, an older guy named Clark Summerfield. He comes from a good family. Lots of money."

She could feel Jason's pain with every word. "So where is he?"

"Europe." Jason bit out the word. "An extended business trip."

"You think he's the one?"

"Timing fits."

"You think he ran out on her?"

"More probably, he doesn't know."

Abby digested that possibility. And then, "How'd you find out about him?"

"I hired somebody."

"Like a private detective?"

"Yeah."

"He's good?"

"The best."

Knowing Jason, he would be. And suddenly Abby felt sick all over again. She'd hoped over the past months that something good would come out of all this—that her sister and Jason would find each other again, would finally be able to love each other as they were meant to love. Hoped that, if they were together, they'd both be able to forgive her.

She'd tried so hard to ignore the existence of another man in Anna's life. The man whose child Anna carried. Abby had so badly wanted the child to be Jason's, she'd almost convinced herself it was so.

"Oh, God." She swallowed. Wiped away another tear. "I'm sorry, Jase."

"Yeah, well, I haven't given up yet," he said, sounding more like the man she'd known and loved. "So don't you, either."

"No," she assured him. "I won't." But as she hung up the phone, she wasn't so sure.

HER BAGS WERE PACKED, her refrigerator cleaned out, the thermostat turned down and she still had half an hour before she needed to leave. Half an hour to do what she'd promised herself she wouldn't. Visit with her sisters one more time.

Walking slowly down the hall, drawn against her will, Abby entered Audrey's room first. Stale air. A few old pictures of favorite flames. Everything looking somehow faded. Bleak. Like the room of someone who'd died. Funny how she'd never noticed that before. When had it happened? When had the room taken on this alien emptiness instead of the comforting aura of Audrey?

Abby hated the feeling—and the room.

Anna's was across the hall and Abby was almost afraid to go in. Had Anna's room died on her, too? Was there nothing left but the bitter ashes of lost memories? Possessions that no longer mattered?

She went in because she had to. And almost wept with relief. Anna's things still seemed to breathe. To have purpose. To be waiting.

For Anna.

Not for Abby.

In reality, Anna's room was as empty as Audrey's.

Reaching up to the chain around her neck, Abby unfastened the clasp. She'd been wearing the charm—one-third of a heart—since she was a baby. Their parents had given one to each of the girls shortly after they were born, with their names engraved so the older Haydens could tell their babies apart. But the necklaces had been more than name badges. Cut from one golden heart, the charms had been a symbol of the unique and unbreakable bond the girls had shared. But it didn't mean anything anymore. She'd abused the promise it held, broken the trust that had been placed in her. The necklace was a mockery, a symbol of a partnership that no longer existed.

Suffocating, certain that the walls were closing in on her, Abby hurried out, down the hall to her own room, to the armoire where she kept special, personal articles—like the valentine her father had sent her when she was ten. And the movie stub from the first real date she'd ever been on. She'd been twenty at the time, a senior in college.

Opening a small drawer, she went to drop in the chain with its charm. But she didn't. She closed the drawer and opened one of her suitcases, instead, then slid the chain into the little pocket inside.

She had to let go. And she would. She had no other choice.

But not yet. She just wasn't ready yet.

"OOHHH! Noooo! I'm not ready!"

Brit held Jessie's hand. Or rather, she sat beside the other girl and allowed her to squeeze the blood out of her hand. "It's okay, Jessie," she said softly, trying not to watch as another pain racked the girl, twisting her face.

Oh, God. She'd had no idea it was going to be this way. Poor Jessie.

Poor her, too. She'd never make it through her own labor if it was like this.

"I want my mama," Jessie cried, tears streaming down her face.

"Marianne will be right back," Brit said. The housekeeper had just gone to call for help. Brit hoped help came soon. Marianne was a great cook, but she wasn't a very calm person.

"No, I really want my mom," Jessie said, looking at Brit with tearful eyes.

Brit watched the freckle-faced, redheaded girl, wishing there was something she could do. Jessie was only fourteen. Before she'd come to Home Away From Home she'd lived with an aunt and uncle who were elderly—and very old-fashioned. Jessie's mother, the aunt's baby sister, was a model. Not someone Jessie's aunt and uncle approved of at all. Especially since Jessie's mother traveled all the time. The way Brit understood it, Jessie saw her mother only once or twice a year.

But plain little Jessie thought the sun rose and set on her beautiful mother. Personally, Brit didn't think a whole lot of a woman who pawned off her kid and didn't even come through in a crisis.

"I'm scared, Brit," Jessie said, still crying. Her big belly protruded through the sheet Brit had pulled up over her after that last pain.

This was definitely a crisis as far as Brit was concerned. Jessie's pains were just ten minutes apart. And seeing that they'd started only an hour ago, Brit knew that wasn't good. Where was Marianne?

"Just relax, honey," Brit said. "Everything's going to be fine."

Brit hoped God would forgive her if she'd just told a lie. She hoped He was around somewhere, that He could hear her silent cries of terror. That He'd help sinners like her and Jessie.

"Marianne's still on hold with the doctor."

Turning, Brit saw Kaylee standing in the doorway. Dressed in corduroys and a short-sleeved shirt, Kaylee didn't really look pregnant yet.

Brit didn't want Kaylee to see Jessie. To see the horrible pain the girl was suffering. She didn't want any of them to see it. Including herself.

"Thanks," she said, trying her best to appear calm. "Why don't you and the others take Beanie and Bones out back so they don't get in the way," she said. "Remember to slide the thingie in the doggie door or Bones will come right back in."

The fenced-in backyard at Home Away From

Home was huge. It was too cold to swim in the pool, but the outdoor furniture stood in the sun. The girls could study out there. And be far enough away to not hear Jessie's cries.

"Is she going to be all right?" Kaylee didn't come in, but she stood on tiptoe, trying to see over Brit's shoulder.

"She's going to be just fine," Brit said again, squeezing Jessie's hand. Jessie gazed up at her from the bed, believing every word Brit said. "Take your books outside with you," she told Kaylee.

The other girl nodded and left. Brit was glad. She had more than she could handle convincing Jessie that everything was going to be okay.

"Ooohhhh!"

Brit's heart lurched, her stomach tensing as another pain took over Jessie's body. "I...want...to...go...home," Jessie cried through clenched teeth.

"Soon, honey," Brit promised. "Soon."

She wished help would get there. She was scared to death Jessie was going to die.

And she had no idea what to do.

She reached for a cloth to wipe the sweat from Jessie's face. Charles should be back from the store any minute. He could get them to the hospital. And the doc was due in another half hour or so.

"Hey, what's all the noise in here?"

Brit jumped at the unfamiliar voice, turning from Jessie's bed as the most beautiful woman she'd ever seen came into the room. Brit had no idea who the woman was. They were expecting the new house-mother, though Brit hadn't stayed around for the full announcement. Didn't even know her name. But this woman was way too young and way too beautiful to give up a personal life so she could hang out with a bunch of pregnant teenagers. She had to be someone else. But right now, Brit didn't care who the woman was as long as she helped Jessie.

"It hurts," Jessie cried, glancing up at the woman.

"I'm sure it does, honey, but you're making it worse than it has to be." The woman took Jessie's hand from Brit, sitting down in the chair Brit thankfully vacated.

"Just relax, now. Breathe," she said. "Didn't they teach you about breathing?"

Miraculously, Jessie's tears stopped as she stared at the woman and slowly nodded.

"Then show me how. Come on, breathe."

Brit watched as, in a matter of minutes, the woman had Jessie breathing regularly when she apparently hadn't even known how to do it herself. The next time Jessie had a respite between pains, she was calm enough to restore some of her strength for the next big hit.

"How far apart are they?" the woman asked, her voice still calm, her eyes never leaving Jessie's face. Following Jessie's lead, she breathed in rhythm with the girl.

"Ten minutes," Brit answered. She stood back, not wanting to be in the way but unable to leave just yet. She'd been watching out for Jessie for the past five months. She couldn't just walk out on her. No matter how badly she wanted to.

"Has somebody called the hospital?" the woman asked.

"Marianne's on the phone with them now."

"Did her water break?"

Brit shook her head, and then realized the woman couldn't see her. "No."

"We should be just fine," she said, smiling at Jessie.

And, unbelievably, Jessie smiled back. "I'm scared," she whispered.

"I'll bet," the woman said. "But before you know it, you'll be running around and turning somersaults again."

Jessie nodded, a little smile on her lips as she closed her eyes.

"You think I'm bad, not wanting this baby?" she whispered, eyes still closed.

Brit started to cry then, as she watched fresh tears slide down Jessie's face.

"I think you're very kind and generous to be giving a couple the chance to have a family of their own."

"The baby will hate me."

"The baby is going to grow up and be grateful that you cared enough to give him or her to parents who were old enough to look after a child properly."

"An ambulance is on the way..." Marianne hurried back into the room. "Oh!" she said, catching sight of the beautiful woman beside Jessie's bed. "You must be Abby," she said, shaking the woman's free hand.

Marianne knew her?

The woman nodded. "What a way to start a new job," Marianne told her.

"This is what I'm here for, right?" the woman called Abby asked.

"Yes, but we didn't expect your first day to be like this." Marianne wrung her hands as she walked around to the other side of Jessie's bed. "She's not due for another three weeks, but her pains are coming so fast, and she's—"

"You said the ambulance is on the way?" Abby interrupted just as the panic wrenched Jessie's features again. "Breathe, honey, you're doing just fine," she said in almost the same breath.

"Yes," Marianne agreed. "That's right. It's on the way." She looked like she thought Jessie might die before the paramedics got there.

"Then maybe you should go watch for it," Abby said calmly. "Give us a holler when you see it pulling into the drive."

Marianne nodded and with a last worried glance at the bed hurried out. Brit was really glad to see her go.

"Her name's Jessie." Brit pointed to the bed. "I'm Brittany."

"I'm Abby Hayden, Brittany," the woman said, her gaze holding Jessie's as though she was transfusing her own strength, her own calm, into the young girl with that look.

"Marianne said you're starting a new job?"

The only job Brit knew of at Home Away From Home was the one Doc had just filled. The housemother's job. But this woman wasn't old enough to be their mother at all. And she smiled.

"Yep," Abby said, never losing eye contact with Jessie. She breathed, in and out, long deep breaths. Jessie breathed, too. So did Brit.

"You're really the new housemother?"

"Mm-hm."

"The ambulance is here!" Marianne called frantically from downstairs.

Jessie started to cry again.

"Sh. None of that," Abby said, her voice warm but so stern Jessie stopped immediately. "Let's get you out of here."

"I'll carry her bag," Brit said, grabbing the small suitcase from Jessie's closet. Every girl at Home Away From Home had one just like it. The doc gave them the bags when they moved in. And insisted they keep them packed from that day forward.

Abby stayed right beside Jessie, holding her hand the whole time the paramedics worked on her, not even letting go when they transferred Jessie's awkward little body to the gurney. And when another pain hit just as they were moving Jessie, Abby made the girl focus on her—and breathe. Jessie got through the entire pain without yelling out once.

Kaylee and the other girls were watching from the bottom of the stairs as the paramedics carried Jessie down. Brit glanced around quickly, making sure Beanie and Bones weren't around to get underfoot. Both dogs had obviously been left outside. Deb's doing, Brit guessed.

"Is she going to be okay?" Becca asked loudly.

"Sh." Diane jabbed her in the ribs.

"Ow!"

"She's going to be just fine, girls," Abby said, her voice brooking no argument.

"Who's she?" Becca asked.

"Your new housemother," Marianne snapped uncharacteristically. Brit had never seen the housekeeper so tense.

Jessie groaned, and Brit got scared again. Jessie was awfully little to be having a baby. Seemed like a lot of things could go wrong.

''How does she know the runt's going to be fine?''
Deb murmured, the usual scowl on her face as she
looked at Abby. ''Is she a nurse?''

But Brit saw the fear in the other girl's eyes, as
well.

''No, I'm not a nurse.''

Brit glanced at Deb as Abby answered a comment
she hadn't been meant to hear. Deb actually blushed.

The paramedics wheeled Jessie out, while all six
girls, in different stages of pregnancy themselves, followed along behind.

''Don't leave me!'' Jessie cried as they lifted her
into the ambulance.

Abby climbed in behind the paramedic. ''I'm right
here, honey.''

Brit handed Jessie's bag to the driver.

''You girls stay close to the phone,'' Abby said
from the back of the ambulance. ''I'll call as soon as
I have the good news.''

All six of them nodded, and suddenly Brit's stomach relaxed a bit. If Abby was really expecting good
news, then maybe that was just what they'd get. She
seemed like such a no-nonsense woman she probably
wouldn't say something she didn't believe.

As the ambulance drove away and Marianne
shooed them all inside to the schoolroom, Brit
thought of something else.

Since Abby's arrival, little Jessie hadn't asked for
her model mother even once.

## CHAPTER NINE

IT WAS AFTER eleven o'clock that night when Abby finally made it back to Home Away From Home. Nick had had her car delivered to the hospital after stopping in to see Jessie himself that afternoon. He'd decided, with some urging from Abby, to wait at the home with the rest of the girls, rather than pacing the waiting room at the hospital.

Suited in sterile surgical greens, Abby had stayed right beside Jessie until it became obvious that the young girl wasn't going to be able to deliver the baby naturally. There'd been some trouble. Jessie's bone structure hadn't been mature enough. But they'd put her out and rolled her into surgery before any damage had been done.

Abby had called the other girls—and Nick—shortly after seven to tell them that Jessie had delivered a healthy six-pound five-ounce baby girl. And that both mother and child were doing fine.

The baby's new parents, a childless young couple from San Diego, had been at the hospital since early afternoon. Their placement agent had called them after hearing from Nick's office and they'd immediately driven down. After a late bite in the hospital cafeteria, Abby had spoken to them briefly outside the nursery, where they were gazing in awe at their new daughter. Abby had assured them, when they'd asked, that Jessie was just fine. The doctor had said she'd be ready to go home in a couple of days.

The baby would probably be leaving the hospital the next morning.

And then Abby had gone back to Jessie's room. There was no way she could've left the child to wake up alone. Not after the day she'd had.

"Hi." Nick opened the door just as Abby was climbing the steps to the house.

Her heart skipped when she saw him standing there. "I didn't expect you to still be here," she said, smiling tiredly.

"I meant to be here to welcome you today." He closed the door behind her and helped her off with the sweater she'd worn to the home that morning. "Charles took your bags up to your room."

Abby followed Nick into the large sitting room off the foyer. Even silent, with all the girls in bed, the room was welcoming. Looking at the couches scattered around, the large-screen television, she could easily imagine a wonderful evening of popcorn and movies and noise.

A large brown-and-white dog was curled up in a corner of one of the couches. Other than opening his eyes as they came in, he didn't budge.

"Down, Bones," Nick said, giving the dog's butt a gentle shove.

"Where's the little dog—Beanie I think you called him?" Abby sank onto another one of the blue tweed couches, scratching Bones's ears when he ambled her way.

"Probably snuggled up in bed with one of the girls," Nick said, reaching into a small refrigerator situated on a sort of wet bar counter in a corner of the room. "He's a grouch when he stays up past his bedtime."

Abby chuckled. "And when is that?"

"Any time someone goes to bed."

She'd keep that in mind.

"Everyone's okay?" she asked.

"Excited, a little nervous, but fine," Nick said, bringing her some wine in a paper cup.

"You keep wine in here?" Abby asked. That was the first thing that would change while she was there. Teenagers shouldn't be tempted with what they couldn't have.

"Of course not." Nick grinned. "I had it out in my car until the girls were all in their rooms."

Abby thought of the girl she'd met so briefly that morning—and been thinking about on and off all day.

"And Brittany? She's okay?"

"She was once you called," Nick said. "She told me you saved her from having to take care of Jessie by herself. You made quite a conquest there."

"Brittany was doing just fine," Abby assured him. She'd been touched by the young woman's bravery.

"She was scared to death."

Abby could understand that. She'd been terrified herself.

Bones nudged her hand with his nose as she stopped scratching him and Abby smiled, happy to fondle him to his heart's content. She'd always wanted a dog. But Audrey had been allergic....

"When's Brittany due?" Abby asked. The girl had appeared pretty far along, although she'd moved quickly enough when she'd followed the gurney out.

"The first of the year." Nick took a sip of his wine. "How was Jessie when she woke up?"

Remembering, Abby smiled again. "Better than she's ever been in her life." And, somehow, Abby felt better, too. Her shoulders ached. Her head was throbbing. But she hadn't felt so good in a long time.

At Nick's raised eyebrows, his silent question, her smile grew even wider. "Jessie's mother came tonight."

He snorted. "I'm surprised she bothered."

"Shame on you, Doctor."

He looked so good to her, lounging back comfortably, his suit jacket hanging open, the first few buttons of his shirt undone. He'd lost his tie somewhere between the hospital and now.

"Jessie adores the woman, and the woman gives her kid two days a year. If she's lucky." He frowned into his cup.

"The woman adores Jessie," Abby took pleasure in telling him, only because she already knew how much pleasure *he* was going to take in this story.

"Jessie's aunt is her mother's older sister and the only family Jessie's mother, Suzanne, has. She always disapproved of her modeling career and her lifestyle—culminating when Suzanne turned up unmarried and pregnant with Jessie." Abby could almost feel the pain Suzanne had felt sharing her story with Abby earlier that evening, all the while cradling a sleeping Jessie in her arms.

"The aunt agreed to help Jessie's mother, to support her while she was pregnant and unable to work, if she'd leave her the baby to raise in a so-called proper, moral home. The poor woman had been so beaten down for so long she honestly believed she was doing what was best for Jessie. The baby's father wasn't interested. She had no money. No education.

Modeling was all she knew. And traveling on the modeling circuit was no life for a child.''

Even though she'd known he'd have an open mind, Abby was still moved by the compassion in Nick's eyes as she relayed the other woman's story.

''Jessie's aunt only allowed Suzanne two days out of the year to see her daughter,'' she continued. ''She insisted that any more might influence Jessie to emulate her mother's ways.''

Abby nodded as Nick swore. She'd felt exactly the same when she'd heard the story earlier that evening.

''Jessie's mother didn't even realize Jessie was pregnant until today. I guess the aunt planned to hide the whole thing from her, but panicked when you called to say there were complications. She was afraid Jessie was going to die.''

''I never led her to believe anything of the kind.''

Abby shrugged, taking a small sip of wine. ''Guilt can do strange things to a person.''

After a moment's silence, Abby went on. ''Jessie's mom was in Oklahoma doing a shoot for Pepsi,'' she said. ''Suzanne told me she walked off the set and went straight to the airport. She doesn't plan to leave Jessie again for a long, long time.''

''Which breaks Jessie's heart, I'm sure,'' Nick said with a huge grin.

Abby smiled, too, thinking of the change in Jessie since she'd met the girl that morning. ''Like I said, she's happier than she's ever been in her life.''

''Thank you.'' His eyes were warm. Personal.

''For what?'' She couldn't look away, couldn't stop his warmth from flooding into her.

''For being there today.''

''Just doing the job you hired me to do.''

"And I'm just thanking you for doing it well."

But it was more than that. And they both knew it.

ABBY HAD another restless night. She was no longer afraid of who might be creeping through her house, but sleeping in a strange house, in a strange bed, unsettled her. Knowing that she was responsible for six sleeping bodies—eight if she counted the two dogs in residence—didn't help, either. Her new boss, however, had nothing to do with her inability to sleep.

As usual, her restlessness had her up before dawn. She'd barely glanced at the room with connecting bath when Nick had directed her there last night.

She'd waved goodbye and locked up after him, reminding herself that she had no reason to be disappointed when he hadn't kissed her good-night. He was her employer. And maybe her friend. Period.

Then she'd fallen into bed. But as she sat up the next morning, she took time to survey her new surroundings. And liked what she saw.

She was sleeping in a four-poster straight out of Audrey's fairy tales. The only other piece of furniture in the room, a large matching antique bureau, gave the room a warmth, a sense of age and continuity that had been missing from Abby's life.

From the bed, she could see herself in the bureau's large mirror. Except that the person staring back at her seemed almost foreign. This Abby bore little resemblance to the listless woman she'd seen in the bathroom mirror every morning for months. This new woman looked like she had a purpose; she didn't have to force her mouth not to frown or her brows not to furrow. But she practically had to force herself to quit grinning like an idiot.

That was when Abby threw back the covers and got out of bed. She had a job waiting for her. Girls to tend to. Unpacking to do.

These weren't reasons to feel quite so satisfied with herself, she thought sternly. Quite the opposite, in fact. She was going to have to clamp down on her controlling tendencies. No filling up her own empty places with other people's needs and dreams.

Unpacking took all of ten minutes. In the huge bureau drawers, there was more than enough room for the few clothes she'd brought. And she tossed her cosmetics into the vanity drawer in her new bathroom just as easily as she had at home.

Showered and dressed in black jeans and a USC sweatshirt, she set out to explore the rest of the house before everyone else woke up.

Except that somebody else was already awake. According to the layout Nick had described the night before, the second floor of the house, the floor her room was on, had four other bedrooms. Three of which were occupied. The fourth had been Jessie's.

There were four more bedrooms upstairs on the third floor. Three of them were currently being used. And if she wasn't mistaken, the sounds she was hearing were coming from one of those third-floor rooms.

Quietly climbing the stairs, Abby sought out the noise, trying to decipher just what she was hearing. It was barely six o'clock in the morning. No teenager she'd ever known was up at that hour. And although Thursday was a school day, these girls had school at home—and not until midmorning. Pregnant teenagers needed a lot of rest.

Abby's stomach tightened as she reached the top of the stairs. The sounds were louder now, more discernible—and more of a concern. Someone was whimpering. And scared to death. Surely there wasn't going to be another delivery so soon. She hadn't quite recovered from yesterday's.

Pinpointing the exact room from which the sound was coming, Abby knocked lightly on the door, then knocked again. There was still no response. After her third try, she went in anyway. If someone was in trouble, it was her job to know about it. To help.

The room was dark, except for a shell-shaped night-light by the bed. But it was enough to illuminate the sweating face of the girl lying there. Whether Abby was ready or not, it looked like she might be taking another trip to the hospital. If this kept up, she wasn't going to have to worry about caring for the girls. They'd all be gone in a matter of days and Nick wouldn't even need a housemother for the holidays.

Abby moved slowly into the room, tiptoeing, although she didn't know why.

"You okay?" she whispered to the girl. She wished there'd been time to at least be introduced to the kids in her care before she'd had to rush off the day before.

The girl didn't answer. She didn't even seem to have heard Abby, didn't seem to know Abby was there.

Abby drew closer to the bed. "Honey?" She said the word softly.

Still no response. Then, suddenly, the girl whimpered. The sound was almost animalistic, filled with panic—and completely unconscious. Abby stood at the side of the bed and stared. The young woman lying there was sound asleep.

Did people go into labor during sleep and not even

know it? Surely pains like the ones Jessie had experienced were too intense to sleep through. And yet…

The girl whimpered again. Abby frowned, trying to make out the girl's stomach, trying to see how far along her pregnancy might be. What she saw, instead, was an almost flat body. If this girl had gone into labor, she was having a miscarriage.

Just then the girl started to sob. Harsh, anguished sobs that racked her whole body. Sobs brought on by emotional pain, not physical distress.

Abby turned cold. She'd experienced enough nightmares to recognize the suffering.

"Honey?" She brushed her hand along the girl's cheek, sliding sweaty strands of pretty blond hair away from her face.

Whatever horrors were gripping her seemed to get worse. She thrashed, batting away Abby's hand and her covers at the same time. The girl couldn't be more than a month or two pregnant; she wasn't showing at all. Somehow Abby had assumed that *she* was the only newcomer to Home Away From Home. When she'd seen her pregnant charges clustered in the hall the morning before, she hadn't noticed this one.

"Sweetie?" she called, louder now. Abby couldn't stand to hear her anguish, ached herself with every shuddering breath the girl drew.

"Wake up," she said even more loudly. She was afraid to touch the girl again, afraid to make her nightmare even worse.

"No!" the girl cried, sitting straight up in bed. Then, almost indecipherably, she whispered "Oh," as her opened eyes focused on the room, on Abby.

She lay back down, turning her face away from Abby.

"Honey?" Abby was running blind. She hadn't had time to read the files Nick had left for her the night before, didn't even know all the girls' names. She'd thought she'd have the morning to learn them.

The girl didn't budge. She just lay there, unnaturally stiff, and stared at the opposite wall.

Should she run downstairs and get Marianne? Nick had said the housekeeper was still in the house, sleeping in quarters off the kitchen rather than in the guest house out back that she shared with her husband. Just until Abby got acclimated.

"Does your stomach hurt?" Abby asked.

Still no answer.

"Listen." Abby's voice, while still compassionate, was loaded with just enough steel to be effective. "I'm here to make sure you receive the proper care. Now, if you're in pain or need a doctor you have to tell me."

"I'm okay." The voice was softer than Abby expected. Almost childlike in its innocence. It didn't match the anguish she'd heard at all.

"No, you're not," Abby said. "But I'll take that to mean you don't need a doctor."

The girl shook her head.

"Good." But the news didn't do anything for the knots in her stomach. *Something* was very wrong.

"You going to make me wait until Marianne wakes up to introduce us?"

"I'm Kaylee. Kaylee McDonald." The girl spoke to the wall.

"I'm Abby Hayden." Abby knew Kaylee wanted her to leave. To pretend she'd heard nothing. But she couldn't. Walking away wasn't something she'd mastered yet.

She thought of all the times she'd had to coerce Anna into spilling whatever news she'd needed to tell. And the one time she *hadn't* forced her sister to talk—after Audrey's death. If Kaylee was left alone, whatever was haunting her dreams would only fester.

Of course Nick probably knew what was wrong. Most likely already had a handle on the problem. Staring at Kaylee's rigid back, Abby wished he were there. That she could turn this one over to him. He was strong and capable. Abby didn't feel either one of those things, not anymore.

She was afraid of getting too involved with this girl, of doing what she'd done to Anna.

But she couldn't leave Kaylee huddled alone among her covers. She'd been there too often herself.

Not knowing what else to do, she sat on the edge of Kaylee's bed and let her instincts take over.

"I have a sister who used to internalize everything," she started softly. "She thought our parents would love us more, that they'd actually hang around for an hour or two, maybe even remember a birthday, if we weren't any trouble to them." Abby had no idea where the words were coming from, but she could tell Kaylee was listening by the still way she held her head, as if she didn't want to miss a single word.

"What she never realized," Abby continued, "even when she grew up, was that the problem wasn't her. It was them. There was nothing she could have done to change who they are.

"Things got pretty rough for a while there. Someone…died. And she'd make herself physically ill trying to pretend nothing was wrong." Abby felt tears prick the backs of her eyes as she remembered her stalwart sister forging ahead through a life of turmoil.

Even after Audrey's death....

"Is she okay now?"

Oh, God. Abby felt as if she were ripping in two. How had she gotten herself into this? Why wasn't she home, safe, in her cottage?

Why did the agony in the young girl's voice tear into her so? She didn't even know Kaylee McDonald. But, in a sense, she *did* know her. She recognized a tortured soul.

"No," she answered softly. "She pushed things so far inside herself, she couldn't find them anymore."

Kaylee turned over, her eyes wide. "What?"

"She's suffering from something called hysterical amnesia. She doesn't remember anything about herself."

"Nothing?"

Abby shook her head, holding on to her control by the thinnest thread. "Not even her name."

"Does she remember you?" Kaylee whispered. "Or your parents?"

Abby shook her head a second time, knowing that if she spoke, she'd lose the battle with her tears.

"I'd die if I ever forgot my mom or Brian—my little brother." The girl's eyes filled again as she stared up at Abby.

"You've got something you've been keeping inside?" Abby asked. Her throat was so tight she could barely breathe. She was afraid Kaylee was going to tell her about that nightmare. Tell her something she wasn't ready to hear. She wondered where Nick was, if he was still at home. If she could call him.

Then, before she had a chance to do anything, Kaylee nodded, her lips quivering. Abby knew she didn't have time to call Nick. The girl was ready to explode.

And Abby was the only one around to catch the pieces as they fell.

"You can tell me about it, if you like," she offered, finding strength for her voice.

Kaylee opened her mouth, then closed it again.

"Back when my sister was your age, she used to say I was a great listener. That I could always make her feel better."

Of course, that had been back when Abby knew everything.

"Ohhh," Kaylee whimpered, the sound almost identical to those she'd cried in her sleep. Tears welled in her eyes, before spilling to fall slowly down her face.

"H-h-he said h-h-he'd smash Brian's face i-i-if I told."

Abby didn't want to be there. She didn't want to hear.

"Who did?" she asked softly, daring to brush the tears from Kaylee's cheek.

"H-h-he s-s-said it w-w-was my f-f-fault."

Was Kaylee in trouble with the law? Or did she know someone who was?

"I said no," the girl went on, her gaze locking with Abby's. She pulled the covers back up beneath her chin. "I said I didn't want to go."

"Go where, honey?" Abby wasn't qualified to do this. She couldn't explain. She couldn't advise. She'd lost all her answers somewhere along the way.

"I s-s-said, I s-s-said, I s-s-said nooooo." The last word was one long wail of anguish as Kaylee curled into herself and started to sob.

Sick to her stomach, Abby finally understood. The

girl was so young. So innocent. She fought the bile rising in her throat as she rubbed Kaylee's back.

"But he didn't listen, did he, honey?" she asked. Kaylee had come this far. Abby couldn't let her give up now.

Kaylee stilled, not even breathing as she lay there.

"Don't let him do this to you, Kaylee. Don't let him make you a prisoner in your own mind."

"It was after." She stopped, shuddered. "After the movie, he told me his parents were h-home," she finally said, the words muffled in the sheet she held. "I didn't want to go with him, but he said they wanted to m-meet h-his date." She glanced at Abby, her eyes begging for reassurance.

Abby nodded, though her neck was so stiff that even such a small movement hurt. She continued to rub Kaylee's shoulder.

"When we got inside, no one was hommmme." Kaylee started to cry anew, her eyes telling Abby of the horror that had awaited her.

Bad enough to be pregnant and abandoned while still in high school. But this...

"Afterward, he didn't want to see me anymore," Kaylee whispered several long seconds later. She looked at Abby. "He said all he'd wanted was to s-sleep with me, n-not date me."

Abby reached for Kaylee's hand where it was clutching the sheet, taking the girl's frozen fingers between her two hands, warming them.

"Did he hurt you, honey?" she asked. Not because she didn't already know the answer, but because she had a feeling Kaylee needed to finish what she'd started.

Kaylee nodded. Turned away. And then turned back.

"He said it wouldn't hurt if I didn't fight him, but it did." Fresh tears welled as she looked up at Abby.

"He was rough with you?"

Kaylee's pain was Abby's, too, as she relived that horrible night with the girl. Abby was weak with nausea, with the desire to cry.

She almost did cry when Kaylee shook her head. "Not once I quit fighting," she admitted. "He was actually really gentle, like he wanted me to…to enjoy what he was doing."

Thank God. At least Kaylee had been spared any brutality.

"I just wanted to die," the girl whispered.

That was a feeling Abby knew intimately. "But you didn't, Kaylee," she said, needing Nick more now than ever. "You have some pretty nasty memories, but you also have an entire life ahead of you to build better ones. And with time, if you let them, the nasty ones will begin to fade…."

Abby continued to utter complete nonsense until Kaylee calmed, until the girl actually grinned weakly at something she said.

"We have to tell Dr. McIntyre about this, honey," Abby finally told her.

Immediately, Kaylee started to cry again. But the instant denial Abby had expected didn't come. Kaylee simply nodded.

"You'll be there with me, won't you?" she asked.

Abby could no more have turned down the plea in the young girl's eyes than she could quit mourning the loss of her sisters.

"Of course," she said. "Now, how about you get

showered and give me a tour of this place before everyone else wakes up?''

"Marianne made cinnamon rolls yesterday," Kaylee confided.

Abby had no idea how Kaylee could even think about eating. But, then, Abby wasn't a kid anymore. Or pregnant.

"Well, let's go find them before they're gone," she said, smiling. She gave the girl a hand out of bed.

"You know," Kaylee said just as Abby reached the door of the girl's room.

Abby turned back. "What?"

"Your sister was right. I do feel better."

Abby had to leave then. The tears she'd been fighting had finally won.

# CHAPTER TEN

AN UPHILL BATTLE the day might be, but Nick wasn't complaining. He found the challenge invigorating. Starting with his standing Thursday-morning racquetball date with a buddy from med school at six, the day never slowed down. In between appointments, meetings and phone calls, he had another chapter to finish for his book.

And a keynote address to present at a conference of visiting CEOs at the Beverly Hills Hotel. The opportunity these speeches presented were important to Nick. People needed to understand that positive thinking was far more productive than negative, that dreams-come-true were actually the result of self-fulfilling prophecies. Letting go of hurt and anger, replacing vengeance with compassion—it was all part of his message. The more people who knew this, the more chance there would be of someday having a world at peace. Nick believed with his entire being that treating love as a verb—*acting* in a loving manner—was the only way to achieve that goal. Feelings were transient. Actions were lasting.

Nick figured that the country's CEOs were a great chance to get the message out. These were the movers and shakers, the people who were heard, who had the ability to change the world.

So he spoke to the room full of attentive millionaires and, when he was through, was humbled and heartened by the standing ovation his words won him. Half an hour later, still in Beverly Hills, he was counseling a couple who, at forty-two, were suffering through the terrible twos with a pair of adorable but highly active twins. After that, back at his office, he worked on the new book, while the tuna sandwich Sally had ordered him hardened on his desk. He returned phone calls. Signed a pile of papers Sally placed in front of him. Later that afternoon, he stayed longer than his usual stint at the family counseling clinic because he couldn't turn away the people who'd been waiting for hours to see him.

And he found a home for Bones.

Though they weren't expecting him at all, he'd meant to make it to Home Away From Home by dinnertime. Instead, it was almost eight o'clock before he was pulling into the drive. With the day he'd had, he should have been exhausted, but as Nick parked his Bronco, energy surged through him.

The house was ablaze, light pouring from every visible window, welcoming him. Nick smiled, imagining that this was how it might feel to have a home of his own to come to at the end of a long day.

Except that if the home was his own, he'd be greeted by the disappointed eyes of a tired wife who'd kept his dinners warming in the oven a few too many times and the voices of children whose needs he hadn't met.

Nick climbed the steps of Home Away From Home eagerly. Inside that house, he knew he'd be welcomed without question. His presence would be a nice surprise, not something that had been anticipated. And

Abby's smile would ask nothing more than that he smile back.

At least, he hoped she was smiling. Truth be known, Nick was a little nervous about Abby. She'd had a full day on the job, a full day of dealing with six very needy young ladies. Not only that, yesterday, at the hospital, had been long and exhausting. He'd be lucky if she wasn't packed and ready to walk out on him.

"Hey, Doc." Brit was the first one to notice him as he entered the huge living room. "What're you doing here so late?" She frowned. "Is something wrong with Jessie?"

"Jessie's fine," he assured everyone in the room. "I spoke with her doctor this afternoon." All activity stopped. The movie on the television screen paused in midsentence as seven faces turned his way, awaiting his news with bated breath.

Nick's gaze ran over the faces of his six pregnant charges, all showing varying degrees of fear, then settled on the eyes he'd been thinking about since he'd left the night before. Abby's. She didn't look ready to run.

In fact, in her hand was the television control—she must have been the one to pause the movie—and on her lap was a sketchbook. And Beanie.

"Jessie's due to be released the day after tomorrow," he told them all. "She'll be staying at a hotel with her mother until she feels strong enough for the two of them to go apartment hunting. And she'll be starting a new school in January."

The room broke into cheers so loud Nick grinned.

"I can't believe her mother really hung around," Deb said when the noise finally died down.

Nick's gaze met Abby's, though the relief he saw there had him feeling not quite as pleased as he'd been seconds earlier. She'd obviously been afraid Jessie's mother might run out, too.

"I knew she'd stay," Brit said, grabbing some popcorn from a bowl on the coffee table.

Pushing Bones aside, Nick settled on the couch perpendicular to Abby's. It felt good to be close to her.

"I've got some more news," he told them, looking from one eager young face to the next.

"Bones has a home."

"Cool!" Diane said. "Where?"

"A doctor at the family counseling center is going to give him to his kids for Christmas."

"It'll be good for him to be around kids," Brit said. Though she wasn't smiling, she seemed satisfied that the news was good. "Bones likes kids."

Nick glanced at Abby, mostly because he couldn't seem to *not* look at her.

Her hand lay protectively on Beanie's back, stroking his curly red fur. She'd set her sketchbook aside. "I thought this was his home," she said.

Nick shook his head. "He was a stray I found downtown," he explained. "He was half-starved and I brought him here just until he was healthy enough to find him a home."

"Yeah, nothin's permanent here, eh, Doc?" Deb said. In all his counseling with the dark-haired girl, Nick hadn't been able to break through her barrier of bitterness. And she was still wearing her oversize ragged overalls rather than the maternity clothes the home provided.

"Marianne and Charles are permanent," Brit piped up. "And Abby."

Nick turned toward Abby, hoping she'd let the statement lie. He didn't want the girls to know that Abby was only temporary. Not until after the holidays. Let them at least have a warm family Christmas to remember. For some of them it might be the last in a long, long time. For at least one of them, it would be the first. And maybe, just maybe, the memories would be something for them to hold on to—to strive for. They might be an example that would someday help the girls form healthy families of their own. Besides, by January he might have convinced Abby to stay.

But Abby apparently wasn't even thinking about her tenure at Home Away From Home. "What about Beanie?" she asked, her hand stilling on the little dog's back.

In that second, Nick almost gave her the answer she seemed to want. But he had an obligation to the charges in his care. Even to little Beanie. The dog deserved his own family, too, a permanent master, and he wouldn't find that here. Charles and Marianne lived in a guest house on the premises, not in the big house, the girls were all transient and not even Abby planned to stick around for long.

"He'll go, too, as soon as I find a home for him."

"But he's been here a long time," she said. "Two years." He'd forgotten he'd told her that that night on the beach.

Nick leaned forward, elbows on his knees. "Beanie's a little harder to place," he said, clasping his hands when he would have reached out to pet the little mutt. It didn't do to grow too attached.

Deb snorted. "Yeah, he pees in the house."

"Not much anymore." Brit leaned forward to stroke Beanie's tiny head. The dog's little tail flapped back and forth so fast it almost appeared motor-driven.

"He's a brat," Becca said. Her blond ponytail bounced as she spoke.

"Just 'cause he's so cute everyone spoils him." Diane grinned. "Whenever he wants something he does that whiney-talk thing until he gets it."

Brit smiled at the little dog. "He is rather persistent."

Abby lifted Beanie off her lap and held his small body in front of her face, her nose almost touching his. "I think he's adorable," she said.

"Wait until he's yipping at the side of your bed in the middle of the night," Deb muttered.

"I'd just pick him up," Abby said.

"Every time you lean over the bed he backs away," Rhonda added. Nick was surprised Rhonda even knew that, surprised the girl had even tried. As far as he was aware, she didn't do a thing for herself. And never had. A Beverly Hills socialite and too pretty for her own good, Rhonda seemed to view her pregnancy as a minor inconvenience—sure that once the baby was born, her daddy's money would make life all better again.

"Yeah, but if you try to go back to sleep, he keeps jumping at the side of the bed, begging you to pick him up." Diane was lying on her back on the floor, rolling her upper body slowly from side to side. Nick watched her, pretty certain the girl had attention-deficit disorder. She stilled for a moment. "He even bit my bedspread."

"Mine, too," Rhonda said.

Becca topped that, her ponytail bobbing. "He bit my dress one time."

Nick listened to the girls, satisfied, overall, with their interaction. Except for Kaylee. The girl hadn't said a word since he'd walked in the door. And when he glanced at her, she turned away.

Intercepting the exchange, Abby caught Nick's eye and shook her head. *Okay,* his eyes sent back the silent message. *I'll wait.*

"Oh! Omigosh!" Diane sat up, her hand splayed across her belly, her eyes wide as she gazed around at all of them. She resembled an elf with her big eyes and page-boy hair.

"What?" Abby was the first to respond. She jumped off the couch and crouched beside Diane. "Are you hurt?"

"Do we need the doctor?" Nick asked, standing. Diane's pregnancy was just becoming obvious. It was far too soon for labor pains.

"Nooo?" Diane dragged the word into a question, her hand still pressing against her belly.

The other girls kept their distance, all except Brit, who joined Abby on the floor. Everyone stared at Diane.

"There!" the girl said again, dazed. "Did you feel that?" She looked from Abby to Brit, seemingly unaware that she was the only one who could possibly have felt anything.

Brit reached over to touch Diane's belly. "Did it feel like someone punching you from the inside out?" she asked, concentrating.

"Yeah." Diane frowned, glancing down. "I

guess... Only lighter." She flinched. "There it is again."

Brit grabbed Abby's hand and pulled it toward Diane's rounded belly. "Her baby's kicking," she explained, grinning.

Pandemonium broke out as each of the girls, except Kaylee, wanted a chance at Diane's belly. Even the girls who'd been feeling their babies move for months were insistent on a turn.

"Let me feel the kid," Deb said, pushing her way in. As far as Nick knew, Deb hadn't felt anything from her pregnancy but morning sickness, though she was showing more than Diane was.

He stood back and watched, gladdened to see how much the girls valued and respected the wonder of life. In spite of their circumstances. Some miracles transcended morality, were above reproach.

"IT'S NINE O'CLOCK, girls," Abby announced half an hour later. "We'll have to finish the movie tomorrow night."

The room resounded with varying degrees of grumbling, Diane's loudest of all, but through a flurry of *Good night, Doc*s and *See ya in the morning, Abby*s they all filed out for the hour of quiet time they were required to have in their rooms before lights-out.

Suddenly Nick was alone with Abby, the huge house silent around them. Nick moved a little farther down his couch. A little farther from temptation. Abby picked up her sketchbook and pencil, obviously hard at work on her designs for Doug Blair.

"What's up with Kaylee?" he asked as he heard the last door close upstairs.

"She needs to talk to you as soon as you can spare

the time.'' Abby was studying the drawing in front of her.

"What about?''

She looked up, her eyes dead serious. "I think she needs to tell you.''

"Okay.'' Nick nodded. He'd make time in the morning for a meeting with Kaylee.

And tonight, he had to go. Before he did something he'd regret. Like push that damn puppy aside and climb onto his new housemother's lap himself. The way she was looking at him, the way she'd looked at him last weekend, with those big brown eyes so full of need, he had a feeling he'd be more welcome there than Beanie.

But loving her and leaving her was not the way to convince Abby to trust herself to love again. And today was a perfect example of why he could never do more than love and leave. Relationships took time. He knew that better than most. Spent his days teaching families how to put aside time for each other, if not during the busy hours of the day then at night or on weekends. And with his personal mission to serve, he could never have someone counting on his nights or his weekends. They just plain weren't his to give.

SLEEPLESSNESS WAS nothing new to Abby. That night, though, the reasons for it were brand-new. She was worried about Kaylee, about the ordeal the girl had ahead of her in the morning, admitting to Nick that she'd been date raped. She kept listening for the teenager's cries, for the sounds of nightmares coming from any of the six occupied bedrooms.

And when she wasn't worrying, she tossed and turned with the restlessness of a body that craved satisfaction. Why, after twenty-eight years, had she never felt this overwhelming desire before?

Other than that one brief kiss the night Nick had come to the shop, he'd never even touched her. And she didn't know why.

She was an able, consenting adult. Judging by the attention she and her sisters had garnered over the years, her looks attracted men. She knew they attracted Nick. At the cottage over the weekend, there'd been times she'd been sure he was going to take her in his arms, sure that his body was as much on fire as hers. Tonight, when she'd brushed against him as they'd risen from the couch, she'd been positive. So, why wouldn't Nick at least try to kiss her?

There was an obvious answer, and it drove her out of bed at five the next morning. He knew her too well, knew too much. Her body might attract him, but the person inside didn't. She'd confessed her sins, her selfishness. And she'd foolishly thought she'd found a measure of forgiveness with Nick's acceptance.

She'd actually thought that hiring her as housemother meant he trusted her not to ruin any more lives.

In reality, he must have known she wouldn't be there long enough to do any serious damage. And even if she'd agreed to the job permanently, nobody else was at the home long enough for her to take over their lives. Not even the dogs.

Twenty minutes later, showered and wearing a fresh pair of jeans and a long-sleeved beige sweater, Abby went quietly down the stairs for a cup of coffee. She was glad the new job didn't entail any cooking; she'd have been an immediate failure. But even she could measure coffee grounds into a filter.

Today, she didn't need to. Marianne was already in the kitchen, rolling out a fresh batch of cinnamon rolls. Dressed in light-blue polyester slacks and matching tunic, with a flowered apron tied at her waist, the little woman looked like the grandmother Abby had never had.

"Good morning," the older woman said cheerfully. Marianne was much more peaceful in her kitchen than she'd been handling Jessie's crisis two days before. "Sleep well?"

"Mm-hm." Abby poured herself a cup of hot coffee. She'd dozed on and off throughout the night, but at least she'd stayed in bed. For her that was good.

Marianne continued to move the rolling pin back and forth across the huge slab of dough in front of her. She was working at an island in the middle of the kitchen.

Leaving the long counter by the double sink and eight-burner built-in stove, Abby walked around the island to the huge antique table that took up the other half of the room.

"This is such a lovely place," she said, absorbing the homey feel, letting it chase away some of the cold the night had brought.

"Used to be a boarding house." Marianne was busily brushing butter over every inch of flattened dough.

"Well, I think it's perfect. The girls are lucky the state found such a nice place for Home Away From Home." The house really felt like a home. Not like an institution at all.

Marianne's buttery brush hung suspended above the dough. "Oh, it was far from perfect," she said, looking at Abby, "and the state doesn't have anything to do with us."

Abby put down the cup she'd been holding. "Isn't Home Away From Home state funded?" she asked.

Marianne frowned, shook her head and resumed brushing. But then, as though coming to a decision, she stopped, and said, "Nick owns Home Away From Home. We're a private institution. The girls all have to be admitted by a parent or guardian, and most of them pay for their board and education. Those who can't afford to pay, Nick funds himself.

"He found the property about five years ago," she continued, scraping melted butter from the sides of the pan. "It'd been vacant a long time, and calling it a shambles would've been kind."

Abby thought of the man she knew, of the generosity she'd already seen him extend. Of course, it was easier to give to a place like Home Away From Home when you had the means, which he obviously did, but still, he was everything her childish heart had ever believed a hero could be.

Except that she'd stopped believing in heroes years ago.

Princes were for fairy tales, St. Nick for the imaginations of little children on Christmas Eve. Love didn't spring eternal in real life.

She took in the shiny wooden floors, the bright, clean walls, the gingham curtains hanging at the picture window that overlooked fenced-in acres of green grass, a pool, padded lawn furniture in the backyard.

"Nick did all this?" she asked.

Sprinkling cinnamon mixed with sugar from a shaker, Marianne nodded. "He had the vision—and the money. Said he wanted the place to be a real home. He let me make a lot of the actual choices."

Abby thought about the rest of the house. The bedrooms that were each a little different in style, the living room that was cozy in spite of its size. The study, with eight pine desks, more suited to teenagers' bedrooms than a schoolroom, arranged along the walls.

"You made great choices," she told the housekeeper.

Marianne shrugged, lifting a heavy sheet of cinnamon rolls into the now preheated oven. Then, returning to the island, she rolled up the dough she'd sprinkled and began to slice it. "I just made the house what I'd want it to be if it were mine." She grinned at Abby. "'Course it's easy to make a place look nice if you have enough money."

But Home Away From Home had a lot more than money could buy. It wasn't just the walls, the carpet, the wooden floors, the furniture. It was the way the house shone with cleanliness, the fresh flowers on the table, the magazines scattered about the living room.

Abby took a sip of her coffee, watching the motherly woman who'd made this house a home. "Do you and Charles have children?" she asked.

The knife Marianne was using slipped out of her hand. "We did."

Past tense. Abby saw the stiffness in the older woman's back. But she wouldn't ask. It wasn't her business.

"Our son died in Vietnam." Marianne's words fell into the early-morning quiet.

"During the war?"

The older woman shook her head. "The war was long over." Wiping her hands on a dish towel, Marianne turned around. "He'd just finished basic training. We don't even know why he was sent there."

"He was in the military?" Abby asked, drawing a picture in her mind of the boy Marianne and Charles had raised.

She nodded. "The army. Just like his dad."

"Charles was in the army?" Abby wouldn't have guessed that. Charles didn't seem gruff enough to be an army man.

"A sergeant," Marianne said. "Fought in the Korean War."

Marianne's husband had made it back from war, but her son had died during peacetime. Somehow that didn't surprise Abby at all. Life had a way of throwing people off balance.

"Was your son married?" Abby couldn't help asking, especially since Marianne didn't seem to mind talking about it.

"He'd met a woman there, fathered a child with her. Died with her." Marianne paused, her eyes swimming with tears. "They stepped on an old land mine."

"I'm so sorry," Abby whispered, hugging her coffee cup with suddenly cold hands.

Marianne wiped her eyes, shrugged again, and gave Abby a tremulous smile. "It all happened more than twenty years ago."

So Marianne had a grandchild almost as old as Abby.

"What happened to the child?" she asked.

Occupying herself at the sink full of sudsy water, Marianne was suddenly busy with the utensils she'd left there to soak. "We never found her," she said. "Charles and I tried for years, but she just seems to have disappeared."

Abby had heard about horrible things that had happened to the illegitimate daughters of American soldiers during the Vietnam era. She hoped to God Marianne hadn't heard the same stories.

"So how'd you meet Nick?" she asked as she helped herself to another cup of coffee.

Even from the side view she had, she could see Marianne's features relax. "My Charlie didn't handle Johnny's death well," the housekeeper explained, reaching for the dough bowl. "He took to the bottle—and to losing jobs, too.

"I knew it was just the grief, that Charlie is and always has been a good man, but after a while, nobody would hire him. Or me, either, after Charlie showed up drunk to every job I had."

The woman shook her head, her short silvery hair bobbing with the movement. "We'd just been kicked out of our fourth apartment for nonpayment of rent when I happened upon Nick one day. He was fresh out of med school then, working in a free clinic downtown."

Marianne poured a cup of coffee, too, and carried it over to the table, her thin little body dropping effortlessly into a chair. Abby followed her, doing a little math as she went.

"Nick must have been still in his twenties," she said.

"Twenty-five." Marianne nodded. "But he was already dedicated to saving the world. Reminded me a bit of my Johnny."

She shook her head, brushing at a piece of lint on the tablecloth. "First thing Nick did was get me a job at the hospital cafeteria. And every week for the next two years, he counseled Charlie and me both. Helped us work through our grief. Taught us how to help each other.

"I'll never be able to repay him for giving Charlie back to me," she said, her eyes tearing again—but she was smiling.

"By the time Nick bought this place," the older woman continued. "Charlie'd been working at the same job for more than three years. Of course, when he offered us the chance to come here, to take care of Home Away From Home, we didn't hesitate...."

"Nick's a good man," Abby said, knowing she could look for ten lifetimes and never find a man she admired more than Nick McIntyre.

"To a fault sometimes."

Abby glanced up, surprised. "Why do you say that?"

"He never asks for anything for himself," Marianne told her. "Somehow that doesn't seem fair."

Maybe not, but it was a quality Abby held in awe. How did he get so involved in people's lives without taking control? Without needing a say in their choices and decisions? Without reassurances that the people he cared for weren't going to desert him?

Bones tumbled into the kitchen through the carpeted doggie door. Nose in the air, he sniffed out the cinnamon rolls in the oven. Even Bones, Abby thought. Nick would give up a dog he'd grown fond of just to allow the animal a happier life.

Except that Bones didn't seem the least bit unhappy right where he was. Abby watched as Marianne got the dog a biscuit from his box in the pantry before she lifted the tray of cinnamon rolls from the oven. Bones chomped his treat with obvious enjoyment, then moved over to nudge Abby's hand for some loving.

Abby complied, scratching the back of the dog's ears, running her fingers through his fur.

The dog had a good life here. So why was Nick insisting on sending him away? And Beanie, too, eventually? Something didn't seem quite right about that, but Abby wasn't sure she knew exactly what.

"Doesn't Nick ever take time for himself?" she asked Marianne. Another couple of minutes and the cinnamon rolls were going to be frosted and ready to eat.

"He dates occasionally."

Abby wasn't particularly glad to hear that. "Anyone special?"

Marianne's arm moved rhythmically as she stirred together confectioners' sugar and milk to make frosting. "No, they vary," she said, her lips pursed with effort. "He says he doesn't have time to find someone special—or time to pursue her if he did." She whipped that frosting so fast it was a wonder some of it didn't fly right out of the bowl. "There is one woman he visits occasionally...." Marianne stopped, looked down at her bowl of icing. "Anyway," she said a minute or two later, "when he's going to be out for the night, he always lets us know in case of an emergency. And he carries his pager."

Abby grew hot with embarrassment when she realized what Marianne was telling her. Nick had sex.

In spite of his schedule, he was a man with a man's needs. And he catered to them now and then.

Just not with her.

Nick could have been perfect for her. By necessity,

his relationships remained casual. He wouldn't miss what she wouldn't give.

Unfortunately he didn't seem to want what she *did* have to offer.

Abby would've laughed if she hadn't been afraid Marianne would question her sanity. And if she hadn't been so damn humiliated.

The one thing she'd never considered when she'd thought about making love with a man someday was that when the moment finally arrived, he wouldn't want her.

SITTING BACKWARD on Brit's desk chair, Nick smiled when Kaylee came into the room. She didn't notice. Her chin was buried so deeply in her chest he knew there'd be a mark to show where it had been. As inconspicuously as possible, she slid into her own chair. Abby pulled Diane's chair over in the otherwise deserted schoolroom and sat next to Kaylee, close enough to share body warmth, though they weren't actually touching. Her gaze locked with Nick's, pleading, yet filled with empathy for him, too, it seemed.

His stomach tightened until it felt like a single huge knot.

And as Kaylee began to speak, in faltering, broken, half-audible sentences, as he witnessed the amount of support the girl needed from the woman at her side in order to speak to him at all, his entire body tightened. With helplessness. With rage.

The despicable act he was witnessing, secondhand, through the defeated and frightened eyes of a devastated young woman was almost more than he could handle, so filled was he with the need to kill the bastard who had done this to her. He'd made it through med school. He'd seen women who'd been battered, sometimes to the brink of death, by the men who'd professed to love them. He'd seen abused children. He'd even counseled rape victims. But he never quite got used to the rage.

He'd also never felt so noticeably, so fiercely, this helpless despair. He dealt with facts, with actions, with taking the necessary steps to cope, to go on, to fix whatever was wrong in whatever way possible. To make things better. He focused on the knowledge he'd gained of human emotions, and the proven ways to deal with them.

But this time was different. He sat with a very special woman and a virtuous, fragile young girl, both of whom had touched a chord he'd never played before, and felt tears burning the backs of his eyes.

Disturbed by his lack of control, he admonished himself. Kaylee needed him to do his job. Her very life, her future happiness, might depend on how well he handled the next few moments.

Pushing back his inappropriate emotions, Nick clasped his hands tightly in front of him and listened to Kaylee tell him how her life had fallen apart. And then he attempted to put the pieces back together.

He'd never faced a harder challenge.

# CHAPTER ELEVEN

BRIT WATCHED. And waited. She couldn't deny that Abby was the best housemother they'd had in the six months Brit had been at Home Away From Home. Couldn't find anything about the woman she didn't like. Or maybe there *was* something, but she just couldn't figure it out. Identify it. Maybe that was the whole problem. There was stuff about Abby that separated her from the rest of them. Stuff they didn't know. Stuff maybe the doc didn't even know.

Mostly what bothered Brit over the first week was that there was no way to get close to their new housemother. Brit sat with the others in the living room early Sunday evening, pretending to pay attention to the comedy they'd voted unanimously to watch. Her legs were tucked underneath her, her long-sleeved maternity dress covered the rest of her body, but she was chilled to the bone. They were in the middle of a balmy California winter and she just couldn't seem to get warm.

Chevy Chase tripped over himself, landing ignominiously, and the rest of the girls laughed. Even Kaylee. Abby laughed, too, although Brit wasn't sure their housemother was really paying a whole lot of attention to the movie. She seemed kind of distracted, watching Kaylee, keeping an eye on Diane, petting

Beanie—and drawing on the sketchpad that was sharing her lap with Beanie.

The little dog had become almost a permanent fixture in Abby's lap. She was always picking him up.
Putting down her sketchpad, Abby shifted, pulling her
knee up to her chest, and Beanie shifted with her.
Standing on his hind legs, he put his front paws on
her shoulder and dive-bombed her face with his
tongue. Dodging the little guy's tongue, Abby
laughed for real and hugged Beanie, planting a noisy
kiss behind Beanie's ear.

Brit wrapped her arms around her belly. She wondered what it would take to get Abby to hug someone
besides the dog. To become their friend.

Brit needed a friend. She needed a woman's opin-
ion. Soon. Before it was too late to change her mind.

Driven from the living room, the gaiety, Brit
slipped outside, hoping a little fresh air, a walk by
the pool, would get rid of the trapped feeling that was
closing in on her more and more with each passing
day. But she was very much afraid nothing was going
to help.

Except a miracle. Like Jimmy finding out where
she was. And coming to get her. She couldn't think
of anything she'd like more than his strong arms
around her, making her feel the way he always made
her feel—the way she'd never felt before in her whole
life. Loved. Wanted. Special.

Jimmy loved her. She knew he did. What she didn't
know was if she was worthy of him. If there was
something wrong with her. If she was as tainted as
her stepfather always made her feel with his pious
righteousness.

And she didn't know where to turn for answers.

Their new housemother? She probably hadn't even noticed Brit leave the room.

According to Kaylee, Abby was wonderful. Saturday night, when Brit and Kaylee were waiting outside for the pizza delivery, Kaylee had finally told Brit her story. And it had been worse than Brit had feared.

But Abby had helped Kaylee see that the rape wasn't her fault. Most important, Abby had helped Kaylee talk to the doc—and to her mother. The change in the girl, in just a couple of days, was amazing. Oh, Kaylee wasn't happy or anything. How could she be, carrying a baby who was a constant reminder of her worst nightmare? But Kaylee did smile some now. She talked a lot more, to everyone. And she was making plans for her future. For afterward.

Tired and achy, Brit slumped in the lounge chair farthest from the pool, from the pool's lights. She needed some time to herself. Time to figure out what she was going to do. She'd tried to talk to Abby a couple of times that day, but the doc was around so much more lately, and when Brit had finally found Abby alone, she'd chickened out.

For all she knew, the woman would agree with Brit's stepfather, anyway. Brit was a slut. Plain and simple. Cut and dried. Case closed. Lord knows Brit's mother hadn't done anything to show Brit any different. Hadn't tried to intervene when Brit's stepfather had made the arrangements to send her away. She wouldn't even agree to forward Jimmy's letters....

Not that Brit would have answered them. She'd given her stepfather her word. She was allowed to live at Home Away From Home because of that. Besides, Jimmy finally had a chance to make something of himself. To get out from under greasy cars, get an education. She couldn't risk the chance that he'd give up his scholarship, that he'd take back his old job at the garage, his apartment out by the railroad tracks. And all because of a girl like her. She wanted so much more for him.

And if she decided not to keep this baby, if she found the courage to do what everyone thought was right, she couldn't bear for Jimmy to know. Couldn't bear to look into the eyes of the man she loved with all her heart and tell him she'd given away their child.

"Something bothering you?"

Brit jumped, her stomach roiling like it had almost constantly those first weeks after she'd found out she was pregnant. Rubbing her hand slowly over her extended belly, she silently apologized to her baby for the sudden upset. She didn't answer the woman standing beside her chair.

Abby sat down in the lounge chair beside Brit's, leaning back to stare at the sky. "It's a lovely night," she said.

Brit nodded. She didn't much care about the weather. And didn't think Abby did, either. Abby smelled so nice. Sweet and feminine. Like flowers. Like the beautiful woman she was.

She intimidated the hell out of Brit. Abby was a good woman. The kind of woman Brit had always aspired to be. Someone who watched out for others. Intelligent. How could Brit hope a woman like that would understand?

She was glad she'd kept her business to herself. She'd rather die than have Abby look down on her.

"Tell me about Jimmy." Abby's voice sounded really loud in the silence of the night.

Brit glanced at the other woman, suddenly suspicious. "Why?"

Abby's gaze, as it met hers, was so warm it almost made Brit feel warm, too. "Because I've never loved a man the way you love your Jimmy," she said, surprising the hell out of Brit. "I envy you that."

Brit had no idea what she'd been expecting, but never in her wildest dreams had she thought there was anything about her that Abby Hayden could admire.

"Jimmy's wonderful," Brit said. "He's so easy to love."

She felt good when she talked about Jimmy. And so she told Abby about Jimmy's mom dying when he was just a kid. About his dad's drinking. About the times Jimmy's father had hit him—and the time he learned never to hit Jimmy again. But she spent longer telling Abby about Jimmy's life after she'd met him. The two jobs he'd worked, the way he took care of his dad when the old man's liver gave out. The fact that he'd been valedictorian of his senior class. The scholarship he'd won to Dennison University.

She looked over at Abby, proud that a man like Jimmy had loved her, Brit Miller.

Abby was frowning.

She hadn't found Jimmy incredible? Did that mean she didn't admire Brit anymore?

"How come a man like that left you to handle this on your own?" Abby's words were so soft, so gentle, they brought tears to Brit's eyes.

"He didn't."

"The baby's not his?"

"Of course it's his!" Brit didn't mean the words to sound so sharp. But did Abby really think that little of her? Brit might have been sexually active, but only with one man.

Abby was quiet, and Brit got nervous again. She chanced a quick look at her, but couldn't make out much in the dark.

"I guess that means you didn't tell him," Abby finally said.

Brit released the breath she'd been holding. "Right."

"Because of the scholarship?"

"Partly."

"Do you think he'd want to know?"

Brit had asked herself those questions a million times. Had agonized over the answers. "Part of him would."

"And the other part?"

"Maybe it would, too." But it didn't really matter, because it was too late to change things now.

"Does he plan to come back for you?"

"I don't know." Brit swallowed hard. "I haven't written to him lately." Not since she'd been kicked out of her stepfather's house.

"And what does he have to say about that?"

Brit did start to cry then, silent tears dripping slowly down her face. "I don't know," she whispered. "My mother wouldn't forward his letters."

"Do you want to go to him?"

"Oh, yes." That was one answer Brit had.

"And will you tell him about the baby if you do?"

Growing unbearably uncomfortable, unbearably hot, Brit shifted in her chair. "Did the doc tell you I'm keeping this baby?" she asked.

"No." Abby paused. "He only said that one of you was."

"It is." Brit shifted some more. And received a hearty kick beneath her ribs for her effort. "When I first found out I was pregnant, I wanted this baby so badly, coming from Jimmy and me, and I knew I could do right by it if I could just finish school. But when my stepfather found out I was pregnant, he wouldn't let me live at home anymore."

Brit burned with humiliation.

"What did your mother have to say about that?"

"Same as she has to say about everything." Brit tried really hard to keep the bitterness out of her voice.

"Which is?"

"Nothing." Brit loved her mom. She didn't always like her, though, which was probably another bad trait. Her no-good father's genes coming through again. "My stepfather said I'd be a bad example to the little kids." Brit shrugged. "I guess he's right."

"How many kids are there?"

"Six, not including me." And Brit missed every one of them desperately. "There's Jenny—she's fourteen—the twins are ten and then three boys. They're seven, four and two."

Abby nodded. Brit couldn't tell what she was thinking.

"So your mother called Dr. McIntyre?"

Brit shook her head. "My counselor at school knew I was having troubles and she talked to the doc for me. He met me and then talked to my stepfather, to get him to let me come here. My stepfather agreed, but only on the condition that I have no further contact with Jimmy."

There, now Abby could blame her for something

else, too. For accepting her stepfather's stipulation in exchange for an easy ride.

"I'm sorry."

Brit looked at Abby, defensive, ready to throw her pity right back at her. She didn't deserve it. Didn't need it. But she wasn't getting it, either. Abby really *was* sorry.

So was Brit. Sorrier than anyone would ever believe. But sorry didn't make things better.

"I think," Abby said softly, "that you're a remarkable young woman, Brittany."

Yeah. Right.

"You could have been weak, could have run to your Jimmy." Abby paused, and Brit stared at her in the dim light. "From the sound of things, he'd have taken care of you and the baby as best he could. Quit school. Got his old job back."

Brit nodded. Of course he would have. She hadn't given him the choice—and in doing that she'd robbed him of the chance to see his baby born.

"But instead of listening to your own need to be loved, you put your baby—and Jimmy—first, giving all three of you a chance at a future."

"You don't think I chose the easy way out?"

"You think being here alone is easier than being with Jimmy?"

"No." Brit could hardly even whisper the word.

"You're giving your baby the best shot at a healthy start in life, Brit. And Jimmy, with his scholarship, has an opportunity to gain the means to support a family."

Brit wished her decision felt as good as Abby made it sound.

"You're one very intelligent young lady, Miss Brit," Abby said.

Gazing into the moonlight shadows, Brit whispered, "Sometimes I'm so stupid I scare myself." Her hands were shaking and she rested them against the mound of her stomach, taking comfort from her baby—Jimmy's baby.

"There's nothing stupid about you, Brittany." Abby's voice was strong, sure, like when she'd been telling Jessie not to cry. "Being scared is normal."

Brit took a deep breath. If she didn't do this now, she never would. And she had to know. For her baby. For Jimmy. She had to know.

"Do you think I'm wrong to keep this baby?"

Abby was quiet again. Brit started to sweat. And to fear Abby's eventual answer. She wished she'd never asked the question.

"I think," Abby started slowly. Then stopped.

"What?" Brit couldn't take it any more.

"That I'm not trained to give you these answers." The words were a huge disappointment. "Have you talked to Dr. McIntyre about it?"

"Of course."

"And?"

"He says the decision is mine to make."

"Then I guess I'm more qualified than I thought," Abby surprised Brit by saying. "Because I was going to tell you to trust your heart."

Abby's words opened a floodgate within Brit, and all her uncertainties seemed to weigh her down, immobilizing her.

"I don't know how to do that," she confessed. "I don't know if my heart's trustworthy."

"Why do you doubt yourself?" Brit could feel

Abby staring at her. "You aren't sure what you feel for Jimmy is love?"

Loving Jimmy wasn't the problem.

"Because I don't think I'll be good for the baby, you know, being what I am." Brit was so afraid of saying the words they hurt her throat.

"What are you?"

"An unwed pregnant teenager. Immoral." The words had been burned into Brit's subconscious for so long she couldn't believe how much they still hurt.

"You're pregnant," Abby said. "I agree with you there. And being seventeen certainly makes you a teenager. The unwed part is negligible, seeing that you probably *wouldn't* be if Jimmy knew you were pregnant...."

Brit wasn't sure what Abby was getting at. She knew what she was.

"But immoral?" Abby glanced over at her.

And because it was dark, because she'd already laid it right out there, because she *had* to know, Brit confessed her greatest sin.

"My body wants...bad things."

"What kind of bad things?"

Brit was shaking so hard on the inside she could hardly stand it. "When Jimmy and I—" She stopped, her whole body hot with embarrassment.

Abby just waited.

"When he touched me..."

She swallowed. Tried to breathe. And when all else failed, caressed her baby through the huge mound of her stomach.

"I liked it... A lot."

IF ABBY HADN'T BEEN conscious of her position, her responsibilities, she'd have cried when she heard the shame in Brit's voice. And the self-hatred. Brit was far too young, far too kind and sweet, to be carrying around such a heavy, needless burden.

She hoped Nick wasn't going to be angry with her for sticking her nose in where it didn't belong. But whether she burned in hell or not, she couldn't walk away and leave that child sitting there, hating herself.

"I'm glad you liked it," she said.

Brit's head shot around, her eyes searching in the darkness. "You are?"

Abby nodded, smiling, her lips quivering, though she hoped Brit couldn't tell that. "It means your Jimmy's a good man, just like you said he was."

Brit was silent and Abby thought maybe the young woman was digesting what she'd said, but as the silence grew she began to wonder, to think about the things Brit had told her about her home life. Her silent, often pregnant mother. Her heavy-handed, unforgiving stepfather.

"Has anyone ever talked to you about making love?" she finally asked.

Brit laughed, but the sound was embarrassment rather than humor. "Of course." Her chin was back down to her chest. "In school they—

"I'm not talking about sex," Abby interrupted. "I'm talking about making love."

Brittany's head turned slowly. Abby could feel her gaze in the darkness.

"Sweetie," she said, wishing she could allow herself to reach over and take the girl's hand. "A woman's body is made to enjoy intercourse just as much as a man's. Our pleasures—our desires—can be just as fierce, just as intense."

Brit still didn't say a word, but Abby could feel the girl's attention.

"The difference between men and women is that more often men can enjoy sex just for the physical release it gives them. Women generally need more than the right body parts in the right places."

Brit nodded—sort of. She was barely moving; Abby suspected barely breathing.

"But when you love a man, when he loves you enough to make certain of your pleasure while he's taking his own, lovemaking can be the most powerful, most spellbinding, most religious experience you'll ever have."

Abby was absolutely certain of what she was saying, remembering the reverence with which Anna had spoken of her first time with Jason. The absolute and utter peace she'd sensed in her sister afterward.

"But…" Brit's voice cracked and the girl fell silent.

"What?"

"I wanted, you know, it, *before* Jimmy even touched me."

"That's natural, honey. God's way of drawing men and women together."

"God's way?"

"Who do you think gave you those feelings, Brit?"

"I don't know." The girl's voice faded. "I guess I never thought about it." Brittany rubbed her belly, back and forth, back and forth.

"Desire is nature's way of ensuring that our species reproduces."

"So you really don't think there's anything wrong with me?" Brit asked a moment or two later.

"Because you felt desire for Jimmy?"

"I did more than that." Abby could barely hear the girl's words. "I, uh, you know…"

And suddenly Abby did know. "You had an orgasm."

Brit nodded. And she didn't turn away from Abby as she admitted the truth. Abby was filled with such a strong need to hug the girl she almost forgot herself.

She blinked back a rush of tears. "I'd say that makes you a very lucky girl." She clasped her hands in front of her. "You experienced one of the ultimate gifts of love."

And for the briefest of seconds, with her own virginity mocking her, Abby was envious of a teenage girl.

"But I'm only seventeen."

"You're young in years, Brit, but not in experience," Abby said slowly, "and I'm not referring just to sexual experience." She knew she was walking a tenuous tightrope between right and wrong. "I'm not saying it wouldn't have been better for you and Jimmy to wait before you made love."

Brit hung her head.

"But what I am saying is that the temptation facing the two of you was perfectly natural, as was your need to give in to it. In your case, you might very well have been fighting a losing battle from the outset. It sounds to me like you and Jimmy were made for each other. Both of you are obviously much more mature than other people your age—and you have an adult relationship. Even the fact that you're honoring the promise you made to your stepfather is very adult, Brit. Jimmy might not like that, but he'll respect it."

"You really think so?" Brit was looking her way again.

"I do."

"But…" Brit hesitated again. "What about the baby?" She moved her hand protectively across her belly. "If I keep it, isn't it going to be hurt by being illegitimate?"

Abby's heart lurched when she heard the fear in the young girl's voice. Did Anna have these same worries?

"I think you've been far more hurt than the baby ever will be," Abby said. "Especially in today's world, where single women are going to fertility clinics and having babies without even knowing the identity of their babies' fathers."

"I never thought of that."

"What I don't see is how any of this matters," Abby told the girl. "The main thing a baby needs to grow and thrive is love, honey, and it seems to me you're overflowing with that."

Brit started to cry then. Big rasping sobs. She cried tears of anguish, but tears of relief, as well. Cleansing tears. And Abby gently dried every one of them, managing—but only just—to keep her aching arms to herself. The effort nearly killed her.

FRUSTRATION WAS killing him. In spite of the fact that his paradigms were clearly delineated, his internal maps engraved, Nick couldn't seem to keep Abby off his mind for more than a few minutes. At nine o'clock on Sunday night, he should've been heading home to his condominium for another couple of hours' work.

He shouldn't have been standing in the living room at Home Away From Home listening to Abby saying good-night to the girls. He shouldn't have been imagining himself the man of the house, eavesdropping as his wife tucked in their children. And he certainly shouldn't have been feeling any sense of loss. Values, not emotions, ruled his life. Love was a verb, he reminded himself. It was something he did, everything he did. It wasn't a *feeling*.

Slipping his hands into the pockets of his slacks, he studied the darkness of the front yard, the shapes of trees that had been around far longer than he had—and wondered why a car would be slowing out by the gate. But before he could do more than notice it, the car was gone. Must've been looking for an address.

Nick glanced over to the Bronco he'd left parked in the drive. He should take a lesson from that car out there—and drive off. One thing was for certain: it was time to act. He'd made a mistake hiring Abby. Not for her. And definitely not for the girls. But for himself.

And—as he wrote in his books—the first step he took after making a mistake was to acknowledge it. To take responsibility for it.

Done. He alone was responsible for the blood burning through his veins as Abby's soft voice floated down the stairs from Brit's room.

"I'm glad we talked," his temporary housemother said.

"Me, too." Brit's voice was muffled but still discernible. Almost peaceful. She'd been more like the old Brit ever since she'd come inside with Abby shortly after he'd arrived.

He thought about the Christmas tree he'd promised the girls tonight. About popcorn strings and cider, Christmas carols and laughter. About having a real family Christmas. With *Abby*. Would she spend Christmas here in the house?

Abby's footsteps fell lightly on the stairs. His nerves tightened with anticipation. In another few seconds he'd be alone with her. If he stayed. The choice was his.

He needed to go.

He'd had another session with Kaylee that evening. A good session. Thanks to Abby, Kaylee was really talking to him, listening to him, allowing him to help her. Kaylee's mother wanted her home for Christmas—and Kaylee wanted to go. Mother and daughter were pulling together in ways Nick had hardly dared hope for, determined to get Kaylee through this nightmare time of her life. They'd decided not to press charges, to spare her the courtroom ordeal. Generally Nick was in favor of pursuing a legal course of action, but under these circumstances, he agreed with the decision.

"You're still here."

He turned from the window at the sound of Abby's voice.

"I wanted to thank you."

"For what?" She walked slowly toward him, then stopped just before she reached the window he'd been staring through. He couldn't decide which was more tempting, the way her jeans molded her thighs or the way her sweater was hugging her breasts.

*Values, dammit. Not feelings. Not reactions. Ethical values.*

"Kaylee." He couldn't look away from Abby's compelling brown eyes—no matter how harshly he told himself to do so. "I think she's going to be just fine."

"I'm glad." Her smile was tentative.

Nick's heart thundered in his chest. *Values. Love as a verb. Giving. Protecting. Doing, not feeling.*

Her eyes implored him. Whatever was going on wasn't happening just to him. It was between them. And she was expecting him to make it better. Or make the next move.

But he couldn't. Or rather, based on the consequences that would follow, he chose not to.

Brushing his hand down her cheek, he brought his fingers slowly around to clasp her neck, urging her forward. Never taking her gaze from his, she came to him, her lips parted. Inviting.

He had choices. He always had choices. And for every choice  a consequence. Which was why hc'd made the choice not to touch Abby. To ignore the temptation to take her into his arms. Values, not feelings, led to effectiveness.

His lips touched hers. Briefly. And then again. Just briefly.

He'd never wanted a woman so much. Nor been more certain he shouldn't have her.

Her lips clung to his, drawing far more than a kiss from him. But whatever she took, he wanted to give her ten times over. He wanted to fill her, with his body, but with so much more. He wanted to make his strength her own, his belief in goodness, his faith in love, wanted to make them an integral part of her. *Love as a verb.* He wanted to give her peace.

Wrapping her arms around him, Abby allowed him to deepen the kiss, all woman to his man. Her body was nearly innocent in its eagerness, unschooled in its heady desire. Nick almost exploded right then and there. How could a man possibly resist such temptation?

With a body hard to the point of pain, Nick tasted her again, one hand on her neck, the other at her back, holding her against him. His tongue explored her sweetness; his body absorbed her heat. He needed more. And he needed it now.

"Nick…"

The hunger in her voice matched that raging through his veins.

The vulnerability did not. Abby was one of the strongest women he'd ever met. And one of the most fragile.

"Wait." He held her away from him as she would have melted back into another heated kiss.

She glanced up at him, her eyes smoky brown. "What?"

Values. Where the hell were his values when he needed them? A paradigm to guide him through the hell of walking away from something he wanted more than he'd ever wanted anything before. Where was it?

"We need to talk."

Abby's arms fell away instantly, leaving him cold, as she sank onto the couch closest to the window. She didn't argue, didn't ask why he'd started something he had no intention of finishing. Didn't look at him right away, either.

Just then Beanie darted into the room, carrying a little blue dog in his mouth. Tossing the toy dog in front of him, he stared up at Nick.

Nick just stood there, unable to move.

Growing impatient, Beanie picked up the dog and shook his whole body, flinging the toy across the room in the process. His back feet raced his front to attack the little blue dog before it could get away.

Abby burst into laughter when he landed in a somersault over the blue dog's back.

Nick gazed at Abby. Her spontaneous laughter excited him all over again.

Taking a long breath, he reached deep within himself, searching for the inner voice, the discipline, that had shown him a world worth living for. Changed him from a juvenile delinquent into a man he could live with. A man he liked.

*Values. Honesty. Integrity. Selflessness.*

Settling a seemingly exhausted Beanie on her lap, Abby looked up at Nick. He'd said he needed to talk. She was obviously waiting.

"I work all the time," he blurted, never leaving his vantage point at the window. He didn't trust himself to move any closer to her.

"I know."

She was so beautiful, so stirringly beautiful as she sat there, her blond hair falling around her shoulders, one knee pulled up to her chest, the other a bed for a four-pound beast.

Nick thrust his hands back into the pockets of his slacks, ordering himself to keep them there.

"I spend my life picking up the pieces of broken relationships."

She nodded. Waiting.

"I know what it takes to maintain a healthy relationship."

"It's okay, Nick," Abby said, surprising him. "I thought you understood. I'm not in the market for a relationship."

He needed honesty. Not denial. "Those weren't casual kisses, Abby."

Her cheeks flared with color, but she didn't turn away. "I didn't mean to imply that they were."

He felt good getting this out. Dealing with it. "I want you more than I've ever wanted another woman in my life."

"I'm glad to know I'm not the only one of us feeling like this," she said, the words catching in her throat. Her eyes burned with such heat he was tempted to forget everything he'd worked so long to learn, forget the man he was.

*Think. Values, man.* Emotions were unreliable. They'd led to every bit of trouble he'd ever been in. Only when he'd learned to depend on something more substantial than emotions—actions based on principle—had he found a way to live with himself.

So why the hell couldn't he get her out of his head? Out of his heart?

"I don't have the freedom to offer you what you deserve," he told her.

"What is it you think I deserve?"

"Love. A commitment. Children of your own. Family."

She shook her head. "Not for me."

"Abby, you're a natural."

"No." She raised her other knee and wrapped her arms around her legs, Beanie cradled across the vee of her body. "I meant it when I told you I'm done with all that, Nick. I won't take the risk."

He couldn't accept that. Abby had too much love to give. The progress she'd already made with the girls only proved what he'd already known. Abby was a born caregiver. Somehow he had to help her see that. And using her as a fling wasn't going to do it.

"Don't you get it?" she continued as he stood silently watching her. "We're perfect for each other."

"How so?"

"I'm...not good at love. I know I won't ever love again and I've been thinking that meant I had to be alone. But since I met you, I can see another way. We can have a relationship, but with you, I wouldn't have to worry about love. Because you don't have time for it."

The twisted logic might have worked if he didn't believe, with everything inside him, that no one was more capable of loving than Abby. Real loving, expressed in action, not just feelings.

"You might not worry about love, but what if I want it anyway?" He regretted the words as soon as they were wrung from him. But they did what nothing else had been able to do. They scared her away.

For the first time in many, many years, when Nick went home that night his values didn't fill up the empty place in his bed.

## CHAPTER TWELVE

THERE WAS a message from Jason on her answering machine. The minute she heard his voice, Abby went for her purse and keys. She was using the phone in the living room at Home Away From Home to get her messages. But she needed privacy to speak with Jason, privacy to deal with whatever news he might have.

On her way out the door, she stopped only long enough to poke her head into the study. "I'm going to run by and pick up my mail," she told the room at large.

Tammy Brown, the girls' tutor, was leaning over Diane's desk. She looked up to nod at Abby. "Take your time," she said. "I'll be here until at least noon."

"Thanks." Abby hadn't known the tiny, bespectacled woman long, but she liked her. Enough to feel comfortable leaving her alone with the girls.

Mere luck kept her from getting a ticket as she sped to the cottage. She didn't adhere to the speed limit at all, driving as fast as the traffic around her allowed and cursing when it didn't.

She thought about the possible reason for Jason's call the entire trip. He called often. Always to tell her more of the same. But every time she heard his voice her breath caught in her throat. Did he have news?

Had Anna remembered something? Or left them completely?

Turning onto her street, Abby cursed again as a blue sedan in front of her drove slowly past her neighbor's drive. And then past her own, the driver craning his neck, peering toward their homes. If he was looking for public access to the beach, he was out of luck. Abby nearly rear-ended him as she pulled in, forgoing the mailbox at the end of the drive until later. She had to get Jason before he left for the station. It might still be morning in California, but it was after noon in New York.

The cottage smelled musty. Leaving the front door ajar to give the place some air, Abby hurried to the kitchen phone. Her fingers shaking, she dialed Jason's number.

Her "should have been" brother-in-law was home alone. But he hadn't been for long. A cab had just taken Anna back to her own apartment. She'd spent the night with Jason.

Deciphering what Jason was really telling her, that he and Anna were finally lovers again, Abby waited for the familiar pangs of jealousy, ready to combat them. But she felt only surprise—and immeasurable relief.

"She's fallen in love with you a second time," she said, grinning out at the panoramic view of the ocean through her kitchen window.

*Thank God.*

"There's more, Ab," Jason said.

Abby clutched the back of a chair. "She remembered."

"Not everything."

"What?" *Tell me, dammit. Tell me before I lose my mind completely.*

"Audrey. You. The day of the murder."

He took a heavy breath and Abby waited, remembering that afternoon herself, the pain that wouldn't ever go away. Her arms ached to hold Anna, to share the burden of grief with her as she had that day. To connect.

Jason started to speak again, and Abby simply turned cold, sinking slowly to the kitchen floor. She didn't want to hear what he was saying, the horror he was describing, the things her sister had seen—and never spoken about.

Audrey had been facedown in the sand when Abby, hearing Anna's cries, had run outside that day. Everyone had assumed that was how Anna had found her. But it hadn't been. Anna had seen their baby sister's face. What was left of it.

"She's better, calmer, this morning," Jason said a while later, having finally told Abby everything, finishing with the fact that Anna still didn't remember him—or why she'd left Abby. She'd remembered their past, but not their present.

"Oh, God, Jason, why did this happen?"

Abby didn't expect an answer to the question. And didn't get one.

"Who would do something so horrible to Audrey?" Abby stared out at the ocean, sick to her stomach. "Why?"

"We may never know," Jason said, but she could hear the frustration in his voice. "I hate that you're there all alone."

Teetering between hysteria and numbness, Abby briefly considered telling Jason about Nick. But she didn't. Nick couldn't matter enough to merit mention to her family. And the fact that he *might* matter that much kept her throat tightly closed. Especially after last night.

A casual affair, she'd been prepared to handle. Had even anticipated. Just the thought of sharing a bed with Nick had given her more moments of pleasure than she'd had in forever.

But she wasn't going to love again.

And then something else hit her. "She remembered me and still didn't call."

"She wanted to, Ab."

Jason knew how much this was hurting her. She could tell by the compassion in his voice.

"You don't know how badly she wanted to."

"Then why didn't she?" Abby looked straight ahead. Seeing nothing.

"She's changed, Abby." He paused. "She's her own woman now."

If he'd ever wanted to repay her for ruining his life, he'd just done so. Abby couldn't have said anything at that moment if she'd had to.

"She needs you desperately, but she's not going to call until she remembers why she left," he continued. "She knows she had a reason and is trusting herself that it was a good one."

Abby sat huddled on the floor, hugging her knees to her chest, as the tears she'd been fighting dripped down, making wet spots on her jeans.

"I'm glad she's *able* to trust herself, Ab," Jason said. "Means a little good has come of all this."

"Yeah." She knew he was right. But the only thing *right* seemed to do these days was hurt her more than she could stand.

Something whispered behind Abby and she jumped, banging her shoulder against the edge of a kitchen chair. Had that been a footstep brushing across the carpet in the living room? Instantly terrified, she lifted her head—and then remembered she'd left the front door open. And realized that the sound she'd heard was a familiar one. Nothing more than the ocean breeze rustling through the front door screen.

Relief left Abby feeling weaker than ever—physically, but emotionally, too. Her feelings were being tossed in so many directions she couldn't keep up with them.

"Anna has got to be able to make her own choices if she's ever going to be happy." Jason's voice was faint. Abby's hand holding the phone had drifted away from her ear.

She quickly returned it. "I know."

"She misses you."

Abby wanted to believe him. But she said nothing.

"She's wearing her necklace again," he offered. "She told me about your parents making you wear them to tell you apart, but also that they'd had the necklaces specially crafted, that each is really one-third of a whole and pieced together they form a heart."

Abby started to shake, trying to hold back the sobs that were robbing her of breath. "Audrey was buried with hers."

"I know. Anna told me."

"I'm not wearing mine anymore."

Jason's silence hung over the line, and she knew he was hurting for her—for all three of them.

But she had to let go. Or risk controlling Anna all over again.

She wanted so badly to call her sister. Just to speak with her after all these months. To hear recognition in her voice. They wouldn't have to talk about anything that mattered. About anything at all. Abby just needed to hear Anna say hello.

To wipe away Thanksgiving.

Surely, since Anna had remembered so much, a phone call wouldn't hurt at this point.

"Take care of her for me?" She could barely speak, the words painfully abrasive against the dryness of her throat.

"You know I will."

"You still love her, don't you, Jason?"

"More than ever."

She wasn't going to call Anna. She couldn't. Because if she did, Anna would know how badly Abby needed her to come home. And she'd rather die than interfere in Anna's life again.

Abby's tears fell harder. "I still can't believe it about Audrey," she whispered. "God, to think of Anna seeing that…"

Abby couldn't remember what Jason said then. She had to get off the phone. She just made it to the bathroom before she was violently sick to her stomach.

HOME AWAY FROM HOME was a welcome respite after that. An escape. A place for Abby to hide from the life she'd handled so abominably. A place where no one could find her.

Over the next few days, she got to know the girls. Gradually figured out how to relate to each one of them. To guide them as she knew Nick was counting on her to do.

And she got to know Nick better, too. As Christmas drew closer, he continued to stop by the home almost every evening, and whether the girls were around or were already upstairs in their rooms, Abby enjoyed having him there. She didn't confide in him anymore, not like she had that weekend they'd spent together at the cottage, but they talked about the world, about rock concerts they'd both attended, about the girls. And one night, less than a week after their talk about relationships, when she walked Nick to the door to say goodbye, he kissed her good-night. The kiss was so brief Abby almost thought she'd imagined it. But the aftermath of desire he left behind assured her she hadn't.

So she began to hope that maybe Nick was going to see things her way after all. Maybe he'd realized that a casual affair was perfect for them. She began to look forward to Christmas. To the magic. To the anticipation of receiving something she really wanted.

As long as she hoped small. Wanted only temporarily.

Her parents were gone until the new year. She'd been banned from Anna. She was surrounded by good people who were including her in their immediate plans. It had been made surprisingly easy for her to ward off her life until January.

Of course, she'd never escape completely. There were more and more times when she felt Anna calling out to her—and every time, the feeling drove her to the phone, to call the cottage and retrieve any messages from her answering machine. None was from Anna. But she and her sisters had never needed a phone to communicate. So every time Abby "heard" Anna calling, she "answered." She had no other choice.

And she still checked the shop for messages, too. But unless they were urgent, she didn't return them. Someone named Maggie Simmons had called a couple of times, but Abby wasn't up to returning business calls to strangers. She'd handle all the Maggie Simmonses after the holidays.

The Friday following Abby's talk with Brit, Tammy phoned to say she wasn't feeling well, a flu bug, she thought, and was worried about infecting the girls. Agreeing with the tutor that she should stay home to recover, Abby gave her the day off. And then, faced with the unexpected holiday, she piled all the girls into the seven-passenger van and headed into the city for some Christmas shopping. Even Deb was in good spirits.

She took them to the Beverly Center, treated them to lunch at the Hard Rock Café, a far cry from the healthy, nourishing meals Marianne made sure they consumed three times a day, and then ushered them into the mall. The colorful lights, the fancy gold trimmings, the decorated trees, were a bit much for her taste, but the girls were excited about them—oohing and aahing over every last merry detail—and their holiday moods were contagious. Abby was happy to follow them up and down the mall, listening to their stories, their laughter.

Because Deb had run away a couple of times before she'd come to Home Away From Home, Abby couldn't leave the girls alone, but when they complained that they couldn't shop for one another if they had to stay in the group, she quickly worked out a system.

She paired the girls off, with Brit and Deb together, and sent them into three separate stores, all within her view. Watching the three shop entrances, she sat and waited for them—then repeated the process again and again. No one was going to have a penny left of the money Nick had given them for Christmas shopping.

She was actually having fun until she noticed the looks the girls were getting. Abby was used to the girls, saw them as the individuals, the people, they were. But suddenly she was seeing them through the eyes of the strangers around them. The shocked, condemning eyes. All of them but Kaylee were so obviously pregnant. All of them so obviously young.

Abby's heart ached for them. She knew they were paying dearly for their mistakes.

Just as she was paying for her own.

Oddly enough, the girls didn't let the stares ruin the fun they were determined to have. Rhonda sampled the most expensive perfumes, dragging Kaylee into all the ritziest shops. Abby was astounded by the number of times the girl pulled out her father's credit card.

Becca came out of an accessories shop sporting purple nail polish on her thumbs—and green and orange on her fingernails. Diane tested some brown lipstick. And all the girls took turns trying on watch rings. Abby made a mental note to pick up one for each of their stockings.

"Ugh, my feet hurt," Deb complained about halfway through the afternoon.

"*Your* feet," Diane snorted. "I'm further along than you."

"Just wait, guys, the back goes next," Brit said, laughing at them.

Concerned, Abby stopped in the middle of the mall. "You girls had enough?" she asked. "We can come back another day."

"No way!" The chorus of six hearty voices drew attention to their little circle.

"You're sure?"

"What's a couple of sore feet?" Deb shrugged, her stomach protruding from her overalls. "Let's check out that bath shop."

So Abby followed them into an entire shop full of lotions and body oils. They tested every skin lotion they could find—and ended up purchasing six different scents.

"Come on, Abby, you pick one," Kaylee cajoled.

Wanting to be part of their fun, part of their family, Abby picked up a plastic bottle from a basket of creams. She sniffed the jasmine-scented lotion. Liked it.

And put it back. She'd been hired to watch out for the girls. Not to share with them. Because when Abby started sharing, she didn't stop. And pretty soon, she was controlling the whole damn show.

She tried not to notice the disappointed looks the girls exchanged as she walked away.

She did, however, notice that they averted their faces when they passed the shop window next to the lotion store. She noticed their sudden silence even more. None of them wanted to acknowledge the precious little pair of newborn shoes in the window.

Except for Brit. The older girl didn't even pause, out of deference to the other girls, Abby was sure, but Abby saw the longing on Brit's face again later, as they passed a specialty children's wear shop. A shop that carried some of Abby's stuff. Or what used to be her stuff.

Right then, Abby knew what she could do with the extra stock and samples she had left at the shop. Assuming Brit had a little girl, Abby had the child's wardrobe covered, at least until she started school. And if it was a boy, well, there were plenty of newborn and toddler outfits that would work. She'd call Maria in the morning and let her know what to set aside.

"I came up with a couple of ideas for a line of denim maternity wear," she said casually as they walked.

"How soon can you have something done?" Deb spoke first.

"No kidding? Maternity wear?" Brit sounded pleased.

"Cool!" Becca and Diane said together.

"Jinx!" Diane called. "I jinxed you."

"That's so lame," Deb told her.

Abby smiled. Her idea had passed muster. She'd get some designs to Doug as soon as she could.

Abby was sitting outside a record-and-video shop later that afternoon, waiting while all six girls browsed what seemed to be every single title and debating whether to call Marianne and tell her not to bother with dinner. She'd actually considered calling Nick's office to see if he'd be free to meet them all for dinner but had pretty much decided not to. She was afraid of the intimacy, the almost wifely feel, of doing such a thing.

Glancing around as she waited, Abby noticed a person leaning against a shop window across the crowded mall. From that distance it was hard to be sure, but the guy seemed to be watching her.

Or maybe she was just being paranoid again. Maybe the stares the girls had been receiving were getting to her.

She looked back at the record shop and counted all six bodies in her charge. And then, unable to help herself, ran her gaze briefly toward the other side of the mall.

The guy was still there. Still appeared to be staring at her. Not that she could be sure with the baseball cap covering half his face. He was wearing jeans, expensive-looking ones judging by the fancy stitching, and a jacket to match.

Immediately nervous, Abby got up and hurried into the store to join the girls. She was overreacting. She knew she was. In a city the size of L.A., there were millions of people who wore baseball caps and expensive jeans. And even if he had been watching her, that didn't mean anything. She and her sisters, with their California-blond looks, had always attracted their share of attention.

"See what we found for the doc?" Diane called out as soon as she saw Abby enter the store.

Glad of the diversion, Abby moved toward the girls, who were all clustered at the register.

"Air Supply's Christmas album," Diane said before Abby had a chance to get close enough to see what the girl was waving.

"He'll like it, don't you think?" Kaylee asked as Abby approached.

Becca stepped in front of Kaylee. "Remember, you guys both went to that same Air Supply concert? You

were talking about it the other night.'' The girl's ponytail bobbed. ''He said the concert was great.''

''You don't think he'll like it, do you?'' Rhonda
asked. Anything less than a fourteen-carat diamond-
studded tie tack would have a hard time meeting with
Rhonda's approval.

Looking over the worried faces, Abby smiled, feeling better.

''I think he'll love it, girls.'' She was surprised at
how thoughtful their choice had been, how important
to them that Nick like their gift. And just a bit pleased
that they thought *she'd* know his tastes.

As they all left the shop moments later, she
couldn't help one more glance toward that spot across
the mall. Nor the relief she felt when it was empty.


''HEY, BONES, where is everyone?''

Firmly ensconced on the hallway rug between the
living room and the kitchen, the dog cocked an ear
but gave no other response.

Slipping his hands into the pockets of his jeans,
Nick glanced through the door into the kitchen, and
on to the backyard through the huge windows. Not a
soul to be seen. Midafternoon on a Saturday, he
wouldn't have expected Marianne to be there, but
what about the six active teenagers in residence or
their housemother? What about little Beanie? The
weather was so nice Nick found that even a T-shirt
was a little too warm. So why weren't they all outside
basking in the good weather?

''Oh, hi, Doc.''

Nick turned at the sound of Brit's voice. The denim
maternity dress she was wearing was filled to capacity—and Brit still had another six weeks to go.

"Where is everyone?"

"In the study with Tammy." Brit grabbed a tray from one of the kitchen cupboards.

"On a Saturday?"

"Yeah." She poured six glasses of milk. "Tammy had food poisoning yesterday so we took the day off. She was better today."

Nick nodded, feeling a little lost. He'd been up a good part of the night finishing his book and hadn't checked in with the girls at all yesterday, having simply assumed that everything was running, as it always did, according to the routine he'd established.

"So, what'd you do with the time off?" he asked, lifting the tray of glasses for Brittany.

"Abby took us into the city to shop."

Which was exactly what he'd hired her for—to take care of the girls, to make decisions for them, to handle the daily crises so he didn't have to. Because he didn't have *time* to handle them.

It still felt odd not to have known.

Stepping over Bones, Nick followed Brit down the hall. "Where's Abby?"

"In her room drawing, I guess." Brit opened the study door for him. "That's where she usually goes when Tammy's here. She's working on a line of maternity wear." Brit sounded like a proud parent as she imparted this last bit of news.

"Hey, Doc!" Diane bellowed, looking up from her desk as he entered the room.

Tammy shook her head at the girl. "Diane, shh."

"Don't forget, you promised to take us to get the tree tomorrow," Becca whispered as he set her glass beside her.

"I won't," Nick whispered back.

Deb's desk was next, and when he approached the sullen teen, another mystery was solved. Beanie was curled up, sound asleep, on Deb's lap. Nick left her milk without a word and moved on.

When his tray was finally empty, Nick walked quietly out of the room and closed the door behind him. He'd see them all the next day.

Nick could have left then. He could have gone out to the guest house to check in with Charles and Marianne. Or puttered in the yard.

But he didn't. He climbed the stairs, instead, in search of Abby. She was working on a line of maternity wear, Brit had said. Nick smiled. He liked the idea. And even more than that, he liked the fact that he and his girls were becoming such an integral part of her life.

Calling himself all kinds of a fool, he knocked lightly on her door. He'd had no business climbing those stairs.

He heard something move in Abby's room, or what he thought was something moving. There was definitely sound coming from behind her door, but she didn't answer his knock. A little concerned when his second knock went unanswered, Nick slowly opened the door.

And wished he hadn't. Dressed in jeans and a short-sleeved pullover, Abby was sitting on the floor, leaning back against her bed. She was holding some kind of necklace in one hand, and what looked like a Christmas ornament in the other. And she was crying.

Not gut-wrenching, heart-breaking tears. She was crying silently, tears rolling slowly down her cheeks, as if she just didn't have it in her to fight anymore.

Or even to sob. She was crying as though she was simply too tired to stop.

Never had Nick felt such a powerful need to make things better. Nor this inexplicable fear that he might not have the ability to do so.

"Abby?"

She jerked when he said her name, turning away quickly, as though by hiding her face, she could hide what he'd seen.

"What are you doing up here?" Her voice was muffled. And angry.

"The girls are all in the study with Tammy." Which was no explanation. "I knocked," he added, as if that would somehow clear him of his crime.

Abby said nothing, her shoulders ramrod straight as she continued to hold her back to him.

"I didn't want to leave without saying hi, seeing if you need anything."

"I don't." She didn't turn around.

And though he knew he should, Nick could not just walk away and leave her like that, sitting there all alone. Hurting.

He wanted to take her in his arms, to hold her. He sat on the end of her double bed, his elbows on his knees.

"You want to talk about it?" he asked softly.

She shook her head.

"I thought we'd at least reached the point where we could confide in each other."

"It's nothing."

Her voice was so thick he knew she'd been crying for a while. And that she was still crying.

"Just PMS," she added.

"You don't really expect me to believe that."

"Go away, Doc."

The girls called him "Doc." Abby didn't. He hoped that meant she didn't really want him to go. Because he knew he couldn't.

And regardless of what she called him, it was the man who sat beside her, not the doctor. Nick's fingers weren't itching to pick up pad and pen, to make notes. They were itching to grab hold of Abby's shoulders, to pull her against him, to wrap his arms around her until nothing could ever hurt her again.

He waited a long time. He didn't move, didn't touch her, didn't speak. Just waited. Not because his training told him to do that, but because he simply didn't know what else to do.

His stomach was one huge knot by the time she finally moved, reaching into a drawer of her nightstand. He waited, unsure what she needed from him. Unsure how to help her. Abby wasn't his patient, he reminded himself. He was there as a friend. And yet...

She turned, handing him the picture she'd removed from her drawer.

Nick leaned forward, taking the picture, careful not to touch the fingers that were reaching out toward him.

He looked at the glossy color photo, then looked again. And just kept looking. What he saw made his blood run cold, his heart fill with dread. He suddenly understood so much. More than he'd ever wanted to understand. He knew what had stolen away Abby's belief in magic—in herself. And he wasn't sure there was any way for her to get it back.

Because Abby hadn't just been the caretaker of younger sisters, as he'd believed. She wasn't just suffering from empty-nest syndrome or misplaced guilt. She was trying to get by without two parts of herself.

Not even asking, he knew why she hadn't told him she was a triplet. She'd been floundering helplessly since Anna left. He could see that now, recognized the signs in the way she'd clung to their cottage, to anything that made the bond she'd had with her sisters more tangible.

But she'd reached an impasse in her life. Either let go. Or die—at least figuratively. And the only way to let go was to see herself, to be seen, as an entity unto herself.

He'd counseled a female twin once—the sole survivor of a car accident that had taken the lives of her twin sister and also her parents. It had been many, many months before the woman was able to see herself as a fully alive, capable human being, existing in her own right.

He looked again at the picture, the three breathtakingly beautiful women smiling up at him. And understood the trust Abby was placing in him, sharing this part of herself.

Three images of the woman he'd grown to care about more than any other person in his adult life smiled up at him from that photo. And yet not one of them was familiar to him. He'd never seen Abby smile that way, never seen her eyes glow with happiness. With love.

Even so, he knew instantly which of the three was Abby. She was the one in the middle, her arms linked with a sister on either side. She was the one wearing plain old jeans and a sweater.

"Which one is Anna?" he asked.

"In the dress." She spoke softly, lifelessly. "She always wore those crazy earth-mother dresses."

Nick continued to study the picture. He could hardly believe that it was Abby's image staring back at him. Abby and her sisters, her *identical* sisters.

"Audrey's the one who looks like she stepped out of a fashion magazine," she said.

He'd already figured that out for himself.

Abby fell silent again, moving only to grab a tissue when she needed one. And the longer he sat there, looking at that picture, the more anxious Nick became.

An expert on family relationships, he was well aware of the intense bond shared by identical siblings. A bond that went beyond science, beyond explanation. A bond that, in cases of identical siblings, was often as necessary to living as life itself. A bond that, for Abby, had been shattered.

Abby handed him the ornament she held, lifting it over her shoulder. "Anna made this," she said.

Nick took the patchwork angel from her, noticing the intricate detail of the stitching.

"I can feel her calling out to me, Nick."

He believed her.

"She needs me."

"Have you talked to Jason?"

"Monday." Abby nodded. "Anna remembered some things."

"You?" he asked.

"Partially." Abby sighed, her breath shuddering through her body. "But she doesn't remember why she left." She wrapped her arms around her knees. "And she doesn't want to talk to me until she remembers why she cut herself off in the first place."

"That's fair." And healthy. From the sound of things, Anna's sojourn had been a successful one. At least for Anna.

He wasn't so sure about Abby. Her tears were still falling slowly down her cheeks.

Remaining on the edge of the bed took self-control; keeping his hands to himself, even more. "Just as you feel incomplete without Anna, she'll feel incomplete without you, Abby. As soon as she's well."

Abby silently shook her head.

"She left you to become her own person, but she's going to discover that you are a vital part of who that person is."

"She left because I made her choose between me and the man she loved," Abby whispered. "I did this."

# CHAPTER THIRTEEN

NICK FROWNED. "You made her choose? How?"

Abby finally faced him, her eyes red with tears, her beautiful mouth twisted with scorn. "When Jason was offered the lead anchor job in New York, he asked Anna to marry him. I panicked, okay? After losing Audrey the year before, I couldn't face losing Anna, too. I knew the control I had over her. And I, with my superior knowledge, thought I knew what was best for her, also. I figured if I couldn't survive without her, she wouldn't be able to survive without me, either."

"Don't you think you're being a little hard on yourself?"

Abby shook her head. "Just ask Jason. My focus was so narrow I didn't see anything beyond what *I* knew, what *I* felt. It wasn't until Jason came to me just before he left town that I saw what I'd done. I hadn't just broken Anna's heart—I'd broken his. And it just continues." She rocked slowly, side to side, her arms still wrapped around her legs. "That baby Anna's carrying should be Jason's. *Would* be Jason's if I hadn't interfered." Abby looked up at Nick, and the despair in her eyes cut him to the quick. "She's fallen in love with him all over again, Nick. So, how do you think she's going to feel about me when she remembers that it's my fault she's pregnant with another man's child?''

"Surely she was the one who made the choice to sleep with someone else.''

"Because her heart was breaking. Because she was trying desperately to find out who she was, to make a life for herself apart from the one I'd stolen from her.''

"She still made the choice.''

"And it's still one she wouldn't have made if I'd given her my blessing to move to New York.''

He was getting nowhere. Wasn't even sure at this moment if there was anywhere to go.

"You did what you thought best at the time, Abby. And you did it out of love. If Anna's half the woman you are, she'll see that.''

"Love isn't this magical thing you think it is, Nick.'' Abby met his gaze head-on, conviction in every taut muscle of her body. "It's evil. It makes people vulnerable, it controls, it disappoints. It hurts like hell. And sometimes, it even destroys.''

Nick stood up, turning away from her, then swung back around. "That isn't love, Abby. Everything you're describing is the downside of human nature. It's why we *need* love in our lives. Love heals.''

"Right.'' She stood, too. "Look at all the healing we have downstairs,'' she said, flinging her arm toward the door. "Six unwanted babies, six lives destroyed in the name of love.''

"Five.'' The more she spoke, the angrier Nick got.

"Five?''

"Five unwanted babies. And you're confusing the word with the deed.'' He forced himself to speak calmly, knowing that everything rested on these next moments. "It doesn't take love to say love, Abby. Nor does a feeling constitute a deed."

Her hands clutched behind her back, Abby faced him down. "Tell me something, Nick."

He nodded acquiescence, the cords in his neck stiff.

"Why, if you're so gung ho about this love business, about your so-called magic, do you keep yourself so…free? So outside the fray?"

Had the woman lost her mind? "I don't."

"No?" She stepped closer. "What do you risk, Nick? Where do *you* put your heart on the line? Hell." She laughed, but there wasn't a hint of humor in the sound. "You don't even give your heart to the dogs, let alone the people around you."

He couldn't believe what she was saying. Couldn't believe she was saying it. "I love people each and every day of my life, Abby. At the clinic, the books I write, the homes I visit, here." And he couldn't believe he was defending himself to her. That he'd given her words enough credence to warrant an explanation.

"Those are all things you *do,* Nick," she said, visibly crumbling before him. Her shoulders slumped, her expression fell. "I'm talking about *feeling.*" She held her clasped hands just beneath her breast. "Deep inside here."

And then she touched him. One slim hand reached out to his chest, just above his ribs. He felt that soft contact through every nerve in his body. "Right here," she said, as though he didn't even know where his heart was. When he moved to cover her fingers with his own, she dropped her hand and turned away.

Nick had answers for her. Full explanations about the validity of action-based loving—the fickleness of emotion. He just couldn't come up with any words at that moment.

He'd dismissed emotion from his life long ago. So why was he suddenly *feeling* so damn much?

He'd been up all night. Just needed some rest.

Without another word—he left.

THE HOUSE WAS QUIET. Resting peacefully. Or most of it was. Abby hoped so, anyway. She lay in bed because it was expected of her. She even closed her eyes, doing everything possible to fall asleep. But she didn't.

She'd hurt Nick. And for what? What had she gained by belittling everything he held dear? What harm could have come from leaving him with his illusions?

She'd never felt so alone in her life. Not even when she'd lived by herself in the cottage on the beach. Because that was before she'd known Nick. Before she'd known how much pleasure it brought a woman to have a special man in her life. Before she'd lost what she'd never really had.

Lying there, contemplating shadows on the ceiling, she wasn't prepared for the tiny pitter-patter of feet across her carpeted floor.

Completely unaffected by the fact that the rest of the household was sleeping, Beanie sat ramrod straight beside her bed, his big brown wide-awake eyes staring up at her expectantly. He gave a little growl-like cry.

"It's the middle of the night," Abby whispered sternly. "You should be asleep."

Beanie's whole body wriggled with his wagging tail, but he still managed to stay seated. He held his mouth slightly opened and Abby swore he was grinning.

"It's not time to play."

His sounds got a bit louder, a bit more insistent.

"Oh, all right," she said softly, reaching down to him. Beanie hopped back.

"Fine, then." Abby pulled her arm beneath the covers and waited. If this was the ritual he expected, she didn't want to disappoint him. But she kept a close watch on him just the same. She wasn't going to take a chance on his running out on her.

Skittering forward, Beanie jumped up against the side of her bed, crying again.

Abby tried to snag him again. And again he jumped back, just out of reach.

Settling back on her pillow, she was determined to ignore him. Until he started nipping at her mattress and making so much noise she feared he'd wake the girls. She expected him to run off as she climbed out of bed. Instead, he rolled over on his back, lying at her feet, all four paws hanging out at his sides. Abby picked him up. Looking at her, he licked her chin once, then tucked his head against her and sighed.

In the interests of keeping him quiet, she got back into bed. And that was how she fell asleep, half sitting, a four-pound ball of fur sleeping on her breast.

"COME ON, Abby, you need to have a say in this...."

"It's the Christmas tree, Abby."

"Come with us...."

"Listen, you guys, it's just a stupid tree!"

"I can't believe you don't want to help us get the tree...."

Nick didn't know how Abby managed to resist the

girls' appeals, but despite their cajoling, she continued to shake her head.

"I'll stay here and make sure Beanie doesn't eat the decorations while you're gone," she said, avoiding Nick's eyes as she balanced the little dog with one arm against her body.

"More like make sure he doesn't pee on them," Deb muttered.

Brit, who'd been standing silently by the door as the other girls begged, stepped directly in front of Abby. "You're sure you don't want to come?"

Gazing into Brit's pleading eyes, Abby hesitated and Nick dared to hope she'd change her mind.

"I'm sure," she finally said.

He wasn't surprised. Cutting down a Christmas tree was too much of a family thing. Abby might actually start to feel like she belonged. Might have to love them a little.

Besides, he hadn't asked her to come. A part of Nick knew that was one of the reasons for Abby's refusal to join them. After he'd walked out on her yesterday, the next move was up to him.

"Come on, gang. If we don't get going we won't make it home before dark."

Nick didn't like himself much as he backed the van down the drive, leaving Abby alone with the dogs. Not even Charles and Marianne were home, having gone to an all-day holiday social at their church.

Ever since he'd left Abby so abruptly the day before, Nick had begun to wonder if he was at all the man he'd thought he was.

"Why wouldn't she come, Doc?" Brit, who was sitting in the passenger seat next to him, asked as he turned onto the highway.

"Probably thinks she's better'n us," Deb groused from the seat directly behind them.

"She does not!"

Nick would have grinned at Kaylee's uncharacteristic vehemence if he hadn't been so busy chastising himself for not trying to get Abby to join them.

"She might." Diane's voice carried from the far back seat. "You guys ever notice she doesn't hug any of us?"

The van was suddenly, accusingly, silent.

"She hugs Beanie all the time." Brit turned toward Nick, and he heard the question she wasn't asking. "So why not us?"

"Yeah, and that time my baby kicked, she only touched me 'cause Brit made her. Then she jerked her hand away."

"She helped me," Kaylee said, quieter now but still defensive.

"Me, too," Brit added.

"I like her," Becca piped up from beside Diane.

"I think we all like her," Rhonda put in. "But she *does* hold herself apart. Maybe she looks down on us."

"No, she doesn't." Nick had to make a quick decision. Abby's problems weren't his to tell, but he couldn't have the girls thinking so poorly of themselves. Not after all the effort they'd put in to creating positive self-images. They all had tough roads ahead of them, even Rhonda. Their best shot at reaching the end of the road intact, of making happy, productive lives for themselves, started with their self-images.

And he couldn't have them thinking less of Abby, either. For one thing, she didn't deserve it. For another, she needed these girls. She needed their affection. She needed their love.

"Abby's going through a pretty rough time right now." Glancing into his rearview mirror, Nick saw six pairs of eyes trained directly on him.

"She talked to you?" Brit asked.

Nick nodded, determining how much he should say.

"She's an identical triplet."

"You mean there're two more just like her?" Diane blurted from the back of the van. Everyone else sat silently, trying, he was sure, to picture three women as beautiful as their housemother.

"There were."

"Ohhhh." The word was drawn out as Diane slumped against the seat.

"One of them was murdered a couple of years ago."

"Murdered?"

"How?"

"What happened?"

"Was Abby there?"

The questions came at him so fast Nick couldn't possibly answer them all. Nor did he want to.

"Abby's other sister, Anna, found her," he said slowly. "Anna had some problems dealing with things after that, and just this past summer, she left Abby, too."

"That was mean," Becca said.

"Where'd she go?" This from Brit.

"She went to New York. She had some things to work out and needed time by herself to get through them."

"Oh."

Nick glanced at Brit, saw the frown on her face as she considered what he'd told them.

"Abby's lost a lot, girls. She's hurting. And she's afraid to care too much ever again."

"She didn't tell me all that," Kaylee said.

Looking in the mirror again, Nick saw tears in several pairs of eyes. Including Kaylee's.

Deb, he noticed, was staring out the side window, her face hidden from the rest of them. He'd have given a lot to know what she was hiding.

"That's why she's all alone this Christmas," Brit said a couple of silent minutes later.

Turning off the expressway to the side road that would take them to the evergreen lot, Nick nodded, telling the girls that Abby's parents were gone, too, in Europe.

"We'll just have to give her a good Christmas ourselves, then," Diane said.

Nick smiled as the van resounded with agreement all around.

*Watch out, Abby. Here they come.*

ABBY WASN'T MUCH of a cook, but she could pop some mean corn.

"It's not for you, little rat," she told Beanie as he sat at her feet in the kitchen, wagging his tail at the big shopping bag she was slowly filling with popped corn. She'd found some colored glitter in the school-supply room and had it sitting on the counter, ready to shake over the popped corn.

She had colored thread, too. Seven long strands of it, already threaded into seven needles, just waiting for the girls to get home.

Beanie jumped up and down against her leg, talking to her. "Okay, but just one piece," she said, throwing him a popped kernel of corn.

Moving fast, as he did only when food was around, Bones suddenly appeared at her side, expecting his share. "Two for you, big guy," she said, dropping them into his mouth.

Beanie looked up at her, his big brown eyes imploring. "It is, too, fair," she told him. "He's bigger than you are." She scooped Beanie up and hugged him, planting a kiss behind his ear.

She was popping corn one-handed when the phone rang.

It was Nick's parents, calling from Florida.

"You're the new housemother he told us about," Mrs. McIntyre said when Abby introduced herself.

"Right." Abby was a tiny bit pleased that Nick had found her important enough to mention to his family.

"We left a message for Nick at his place, but he'd said he was going to be at the home today and I was hoping to catch him."

Abby scratched Beanie's ear absently. "He should be back within the hour."

"We'll be gone by then," Mrs. McIntyre said. "We've got tickets to the symphony this evening and we're meeting friends for dinner first, but I did so want to reach him."

"Is there a problem?" Abby's fingers stilled in Beanie's fur.

"No!" Mrs. McIntyre sounded embarrassed. "I just read about some great airfare rates in the paper, and I'm afraid if we don't book today, they might all be gone. We were thinking about coming to L.A. to spend Christmas with Nick."

"I'm sure he'd love to have you," Abby said. Family was Nick's number-one priority in life. He'd be thrilled to have his parents for the holidays.

"I don't know…" Nick's mother hesitated.

"The boy's awfully busy." Mr. McIntyre spoke for the first time. "He hates to have us come when he can't spend time with us."

"And his work is so important we certainly don't want to be in the way," Mrs. McIntyre added. "We're very proud of him."

"How long has it been since you've been here to see him?" Abby asked.

"Not since we retired five years ago," Nick's mother said. "Nick insists on flying out here for quick visits whenever he can get away. But we miss him so much," she went on, "especially through the holidays."

Abby could understand that. To have a son as dynamic, as special, as Nick and not be able to see him would be torture.

"I really want to book these tickets," Mrs. McIntyre said.

"I can have Nick call the second he comes in."

"I think we'll just book them," Nick's father said. "We can stay in a hotel, and that way, we won't slow the boy down."

"Oh, you don't have to do that," Abby said, without even thinking. "You can stay here with me and the girls. We have plenty of room, and Marianne's happiest when the house is full…."

Long after she'd rung off, Abby was still thinking about the offer she'd made, surprised to find she really liked the idea of having Nick's parents here over the holidays. She'd love to visit with them, get to know the people who'd dared to take a juvenile delinquent into their home, to love him. Who'd helped mold him into the incredible man he'd become.

But one thing must remain clear. She was okay with the visit from Nick's parents as long as her pleasure had nothing to do with getting closer to the man himself.

AFTER THEIR TREE excursion, the girls seemed more than happy to sit on the living-room floor stringing popcorn while Nick got the tree straight in the stand and hung the lights.

All except for Deb.

"This is dumb," she said, her thread fuller than anyone else's. "Beanie and Bones are just going to eat these." She continued to poke her needle through kernels of popped corn. Broken pieces littered her overalls.

"Ow!" Becca cried, stabbing her thumb with the needle. Then, "They will not."

"Sure they will." Deb wasn't daunted. "And they'll probably knock over the tree in the process."

The culprits in question had been relegated to the backyard for the evening.

"What's with you, girl?" Rhonda asked, her thread almost empty. "Don't you ever have anything good to say?"

"What's it to you?" Deb shot back. The other girls sat silently, concentrating on the strings in their laps. Even Diane seemed completely engrossed.

Rhonda glared at Deb. "The rest of us have to live with you—that's what it is to me." She dropped her needle and thread. "And let me tell you, it ain't no joy having you around."

Abby exchanged glances with Nick, as she wondered which of them should jump in to stop the girls before war broke out.

"Who says it's my job to bring anyone joy?" Deb went on stringing popcorn, jabbing one piece after another onto her needle.

Abby glanced at Nick again. Wasn't he going to say something? Do something? Almost imperceptibly, he shrugged. He continued to hang the lights as though he couldn't hear the conversation in the room around him.

The other girls fidgeted, clearly uncomfortable. Deb and Rhonda were breaking the unwritten rule at Home Away From Home. The rule about everyone getting along, no matter what. The rule that said they were all any of them had; they were all in this together.

"Who says you have the right to make the rest of us miserable?"

"Who says I don't?"

"I say you don't." Abby couldn't stand it any longer. Nick had gone to a lot of trouble to give these girls a little of his magic for Christmas. The least they could do was pretend to appreciate it.

They all froze, their eyes on Abby. All but Nick. He continued to hang lights.

"Life might have dealt you some rough cards, Deb, but you aren't the only one who's holding a bad hand."

"Yeah, well, look at us." She pointed to herself, her pregnant housemates. "You gotta admit, we're a pretty revolting bunch, all getting as big as elephants with our illegitimate kids."

Abby could feel the gazes of the other girls, every

one of them, although she never took her eyes from Deb. "I don't think your pregnancies are the least bit revolting."

"Pathetic, then," Deb said, still stringing popcorn.

"No."

"Come on, Miss Goody Two-shoes." Deb set down her needle and thread. "Why don't you just admit you're secretly disgusted by us."

She glanced up then. And Abby's heart started to pound. If she wasn't mistaken, there were tears in Deb's eyes.

"I don't think you're disgusting, Deb. Not pathetic, not revolting, not even shocking," she said, holding the girl's gaze. "I think you're human beings who made a mistake, human beings worthy of a second chance, human beings I admire because you're here, trying to make something good come out of that mistake. You're forfeiting nine months of your lives to give a family to someone else—someone who might never otherwise have the chance.

"And beyond that, I couldn't think poorly of you even if I wanted to. In each and every one of you—" she glanced from one girl to the next "—I see a part of someone I love very much—my sister, Anna."

The girls looked at one another, looked at Nick, and Abby knew he'd said something to them. Even before she saw the silent apology he sent her way, the shrug of his shoulders. She supposed she should be angry with him. But she just couldn't make herself believe that Nick would've told the girls anything more than he found necessary, for whatever reason he found necessary. He hadn't told them anything she wouldn't have told them herself. She knew him that well.

"I haven't seen Anna in a while. I miss her terribly." Abby paused, tried to get through the words without thinking the thoughts that accompanied them. Not then. Not when she had a roomful of needy girls looking to her for strength. "And each of you brings her closer to me.

"You see, Anna's pregnant, too." She addressed the sweet faces staring up at her. "And every time one of you can't reach to tie your shoes or has trouble getting up out of a chair, every time someone's back aches or feet hurt, each time one of you has a doctor's appointment or takes your vitamins, I think of Anna. I wonder if she's feeling the same things, doing the same things."

"She's pregnant?" Diane asked, glancing at Nick as if to ask why he hadn't told them that.

It only confirmed what Abby had already known. Nick hadn't betrayed any confidences that mattered.

"Yes, she's pregnant."

Suddenly the room started to come to life. "How far along?"

"She's married?"

Abby turned to Becca. "No, she's not married." And to Brit. "She's due at the end of January."

And to Deb she said, "Not only is Anna not married, she doesn't even know who the father of her baby is."

Every one of the girls glared at Nick, who was standing still at the top of the stepladder he'd been using. Abby almost felt a little sorry for him. The girls obviously thought they'd been entitled to this information.

"So, you see, girls—" Abby looked straight at Deb

"—I, of all people, would be the last to throw stones at you."

Climbing down from the ladder, Nick plugged in the lights and the room was suddenly lit with a colorful glow. Everyone stared silently, emotions running high.

"Let's get this thing decorated." Deb finally broke the silence, stirred the girls into action. They ripped into the boxes of ornaments Nick had carried down from the attic, oohing and aahing over the bright glass bulbs.

Brit unwrapped the ceramic nativity scene, then set it up beneath the tree. Diane worked on the train set, fitting the pieces of track together to form a circle around the tree.

The popcorn strings were the last to go on, and they were about done when Nick called to Abby from across the room.

"What?" she asked, tying off one more string of popcorn before deeming it ready to be hung.

"Why don't you go get that ornament you had yesterday. The one Anna made."

Abby's heart dropped. Her throat closed around the air she was trying to pull into her lungs. He'd done that on purpose. Mentioned the ornament—and Anna—in front of the girls. He'd left her no out.

Nodding, needing to escape, she handed the string of popcorn to Brit and ran upstairs to her room.

Anna's ornament had hung on every Christmas tree the sisters had ever had since she'd sewn it in their seventh-grade home economics class. But it wasn't meant to hang this year. Abby was alone now. She had to get used to that fact.

A good twenty minutes passed before she made it

back downstairs, ornament in hand. She tried not to think about what she was doing as she walked up to the tree and hung the ornament on the first branch within reach. She tried not to cry.

"You think she's scared?"

Abby jumped, startled as Deb spoke softly beside her. She hadn't realized the other girl was so close. Everyone had been involved with packing up the decoration wrappings when she'd come back into the room.

"I know she is," she said, just as softly. Deb was the last person she'd expected to understand.

"Yeah," the girl said, looping her arm through Abby's. "Me, too."

Abby squeezed that young arm to her side, holding on for all she was worth, realizing that Deb needed the contact as badly as she did. Just for a moment. Just until each of them was strong enough to stand alone once again.

And suddenly Nick was there, too, just behind her and Deb, one arm around each of their shoulders. "She looks beautiful," he said.

He was looking at Anna's angel, but from the satisfaction in his voice, Abby had a feeling that he'd been referring to far more than a piece of cloth hanging on the tree.

He knew he and his girls were getting to Abby. Damn him.

# CHAPTER FOURTEEN

NICK WASN'T READY to be alone with Abby. He was well aware, in spite of the things she'd said the day before, that the minute he had her alone, he was going to be hauling her into his arms and kissing the mouth that had been tempting him all evening. Every time she spoke to the girls, laughed with them, he'd wanted to feel her lips beneath his own. He'd even been tempted when her lips were trembling with carefully suppressed emotion—especially then.

But he couldn't kiss Abby. Couldn't hold her. Couldn't have the satisfaction of loving her. Their values were too different, their lives too diametrically opposed.

And he didn't have time to love Abby as she needed and deserved to be loved.

So he grabbed his keys just as soon as the girls collected their things to head upstairs for the night.

"Would you mind waiting a minute?" Abby asked from the foot of the stairs. "I need to talk to you for a second."

She'd left him no choice but to wait. And to think some more about the absurd theory she'd thrown at him the day before. He didn't use his schedule as an excuse to stay uninvolved as she'd implied. He was simply a man with a calling. Something she obviously didn't understand.

Of course, the little voice that had been nagging him over the past weeks piped up louder than ever. Reminding him he knew many people who had callings—and still had families of their own, who still had healthy personal relationships.

"Sorry to keep you. I know after being here all day you must have a thousand things to do."

Though he listened carefully, though he didn't detect a note of sarcasm in her voice, he assumed it must be there. Someplace.

Nick shrugged, watching her. Abby was walking down the stairs, her long hair falling like a halo around her shoulders and over the violet sweater she wore. She was an angel. A beautiful angel. Sent to him from his Maker.

Or not.

He had to get out of there. Spend some time alone. Think about his goals, his values. Remember his mission in life. He'd set that mission for himself before he'd even left college and he'd never strayed from it, never questioned it. Until now.

"What's up?"

"Your parents called today," she said, reaching the bottom of the stairs. She smelled good. "They want to come out for Christmas."

He backed up a step or two. "I'd love to have them," he said. And he would. If he had the time. "But I've got meetings right up until Christmas Eve and a speech to make the day after Christmas."

Abby swallowed, looking uncomfortable. "I said they could stay here."

He didn't say a word. Just stared at her.

"I'm sorry, Nick." Her brow puckered with worry. "I really thought you'd want them here. I thought it might be good for the girls, too.'' She rushed on. "And if they're at the house with us, you wouldn't have to worry about entertaining guests. You could just come see them when you had time.''

She was right. The plan was a good one. So why was he more bothered than thrilled? He loved his parents. Very much. Owed them his life. He always enjoyed the time he spent with them in Florida and hated being apart from them at Christmas. Didn't he?

"They got some special airfare but had to book today,'' Abby said, still looking worried.

He'd never had his parents come to visit him because he hadn't wanted to leave them at the condo by themselves. But if they were at Home Away From Home with Abby and the girls, with Marianne and Charles, he wouldn't have to worry about entertaining them. About feeding them. And the girls would have more of a family Christmas than any of them had expected.

"Thanks,'' he finally said, smiling at Abby. "It'll be great to spend Christmas with them again.'' There was no logical reason it shouldn't.

"You're not mad at me?'' Abby asked, her sweet face full of concern.

"Of course not.'' He didn't think he had it in him to be angry with her. "Your idea was inspired.''

And it was. Then why was he suddenly feeling so…so…trapped?

A COUPLE OF DAYS later, Abby left to do some Christmas shopping of her own. She wanted the girls to have presents under that tree they'd been so excited about. To have the stockings they'd all hung on the wall filled to the brim. She wanted them to believe in Christmas—even if just for one more year.

The girls were on Christmas break from their studies, and Marianne had them busy in the kitchen, making cookies. Dozens of cookies. Chocolate pixies, golden tassies, snickerdoodles, accordion treats, cutouts. And based on the finger licking Abby had already seen, they wouldn't need to eat again for at least a week. Neither would Beanie or Bones. Abby figured she was doing herself a favor, getting out of temptation's way.

The first purchase she made was six of the watch rings the girls had tried on the day they'd gone to the mall. Other packages quickly followed. A battery-operated hedge trimmer for Charles. Aprons for Marianne. A leather-bound gold-embossed diary for Brit. A collection of wildly colored nail polish for Diane. A new pair of boots for Deb. It wasn't hard to find special things for each of the girls.

She didn't intend to get anything for Nick. Wasn't looking for anything, didn't have him on her list. But when she saw the carved wooden St. Nick, grinning, surrounded by miniature wooden children clamoring for hugs, she knew she had to have it. This was Nick. He never ran out of giving.

She'd been so wrong to criticize him, so damned nervy to think she had any answers. So what if Nick kept himself out of the fray? Anyone with as much love to give as he had, and as many places to give it, didn't have a chance to develop anything close and personal. She'd just been too selfish, as usual, to accept that. She'd wanted more from Nick for herself. And that would have meant taking from someone else.

Just like with Anna. She'd tried to rob Jason to keep her sister for herself.

And then there was the thing with Nick's parents. She should never have invited them without asking him first, airfare or no. She'd thought it would be what Nick wanted, thought it would be fun to have them, would be good for the girls. But that was the problem. *She'd thought.* And the lives involved had not been hers. Would she never learn?

Paying for the colorful carving, watching while the clerk wrapped the package, Abby knew she had to apologize to Nick. And soon. Maybe now Nick could see why she was all wrong for Home Away From Home. Maybe her inability to love in a balanced way went back to her childhood, to growing up with absentee parents. Maybe her capacity to love had been warped during those years.

And maybe love was a highly overrated emotion, saved only for special people like Nick.

And Brittany.

And Anna and Jason.

And Marianne and Charles.

Abby left the shop and went to buy a double-dipped chocolate ice-cream cone. Something guaranteed to make her feel good. At least for a moment.

SHE WAS ABOUT three-quarters of the way home when she noticed the car behind her. A blue sedan. Like the one that had been behind her a couple of weeks earlier. At least she thought it was the same kind of car.

Suddenly frightened, Abby sped toward home. The country road she was traveling was relatively populated with homes, a small farm or two, and had quite a few people going into the city. There were many places she could stop for help if the need arose. Careful not to move her head, to be obvious, she glanced in her rearview mirror. Her heart started to pound so heavily she could feel it. The car was still there. Still the same distance behind her.

She tried to get a better look at the driver, to find something by which to identify him, but could only make out a shape. A shape—but no baseball cap. Thank God.

A baseball cap certainly wasn't a permanent fixture, but Abby took comfort from the fact that the mysterious driver wasn't wearing one. She debated stopping, calling Nick, calling the police. But what would she tell them? That a blue car was driving down the road behind her? That a blue car had driven behind her before? That someone at the mall had looked at her? That she'd become irrationally frightened of baseball caps?

That she was going slowly out of her mind?

No, she wouldn't need to tell them that last part. They'd figure that out on their own.

She wondered if she should even go home. If she'd be endangering the girls by bringing whatever was lurking behind her into their midst. Living near L.A., she'd heard some horrible stories about ungodly things happening to innocent people who'd just been in the wrong place at the wrong time. She couldn't do that to the girls, to Charles and Marianne.

And then she thought about explaining her absence. She hadn't come home because there was a blue car driving behind her on the road. And because she'd seen a blue car outside her shop once, and later there'd been one on the road behind her. Of course nothing had come of it the last time she'd been "followed." The car had turned off, gone harmlessly on its way.

Abby cringed just thinking about Nick getting wind of this. Oh, he'd have some nice words to put her at ease. He'd talk about natural reactions and reassure her that time would take care of these insane fears. But counseling wasn't what she wanted from Nick McIntyre.

She had to quit allowing her paranoid thoughts to overtake her—starting immediately. She refused to live the rest of her life in fear. She refused to give someone else that much control. The damn blue cars of the world could follow her all the way to hell— their drivers wearing baseball caps, every one of them.

With that thought, Abby turned boldly into the drive of Home Away From Home, angry with herself for going weak with relief as soon as the blue car went speeding past. It was time to remember who she was. What she was about. Audrey had been the needy one. Anna, the silent one. And she, Abby, was the strong one. Whether she had her sisters with her or not. She would be strong.

THE KITCHEN WAS STILL buzzing with activity when Abby came through the door. Beanie hopped up and down in his Beanie-style greeting. Cookie-filled lengths of foil covered every available bit of counter space. The girls were all sitting with Marianne around the massive oak table, each with different bowls of colored icing, and dozens and dozens of sugar cookies piled in front of them. Bones was asleep in the corner.

"Just in time!" Marianne greeted her, holding up a knife.

"Yeah!" The girls all grinned up at her.

For a moment, before she had time to remember herself, Abby felt warm and good inside. Welcome. Wanted. Part of this odd little family.

"We've got sprinkles," Becca said.

"Nonpareils," Deb corrected.

"And silver balls. They're cool!" Diane held up the decorator bottle filled with what looked like little silver BBs.

Deb smirked. "They'll break your teeth."

"Did you get your shopping done?" Brit asked. She was already spreading a Christmas-tree-shaped cookie with green frosting.

"Most of it." Abby finally got a word in edgewise. After washing her hands at the kitchen sink, she slid into a seat between Kaylee and Rhonda.

"Where's your bowl of frosting, Rhonda?" she asked.

The girl flicked a lock of silky blond hair over her shoulder. "I'm in charge of carrying the cookies over to dry as soon as you guys finish decorating them."

Deb shook her head. "She doesn't want frosting under her nails."

They worked steadily for half an hour, barely making a dent in the cookies. Sitting there with the girls, with Marianne, looking at the unending pile of cookies that awaited them, Abby smiled at the good-natured groans, secretly glad they were a long way from done. The cookies were a job, but she was enjoying this togetherness.

Beanie jumped down from Deb's lap and wandered over to the doggie door. Stopping in front of the flap

Bones had just disappeared through, he scratched once, then turned, gazing up at the table full of people, waiting.

"It's your turn," Deb told Becca.

"Uh-uh. I just did him when you were taking that batch of snickerdoodles out of the oven."

"Then it's Diane's turn."

Beanie scratched again, looking up expectantly. There was obviously no doubt in his mind that one of them was going to do his bidding.

"Rhonda, you go open it for him. You're not doing anything." Diane slopped some blue frosting on a Santa Claus.

"I am so." Rhonda started gathering finished cookies onto her empty tray. "And Santa's red."

Finishing her fifteenth bell, Abby pushed away from the table. "Someone's got to teach this little guy to get through the door himself."

Marianne agreed. She decorated two more cookies in the time Abby stood by the doggie door, waiting for Beanie to do his business and come back to be let in.

THEY WERE ABOUT halfway through the stack of cookies when Kaylee dropped her knife.

"Omigosh!"

"What?" Abby's heart leaped at the fear in the girl's voice. Had she cut herself?

Kaylee looked at Abby, her eyes filled with terror. "I'm all wet!"

That was when Abby noticed the red stain spreading across Kaylee's chair.

"Call an ambulance." Abby stood, rubbing Kaylee's shoulder as she tried to figure out what to do.

Tried not to let any of them see that she didn't *know* what to do. "And Nick," she added, glancing at Brittany.

Brittany rushed for the phone just as Marianne cried, "Oh, my God! Something's wrong!"

The other girls started to talk at once, all with varying degrees of worry, some craning their necks to see what Marianne was looking at. Others trying not to see. And then, as if on cue, they turned to Abby.

Those frightened eyes trained on her were all the incentive Abby needed.

"Marianne, take the girls down to the guest house with you," she said, her hand never leaving Kaylee's shoulder. "Take the dogs, too."

Marianne nodded, dropping a cookie on the floor in her agitation. "Maybe I should stay with you."

"Take the girls and go." Abby didn't have time to be gentle.

The kitchen emptied in seconds and Abby immediately turned back to Kaylee. "I want to try to get you to the bathroom, honey," she said, holding Kaylee's gaze with her own. She didn't want Kaylee to look down at herself again. Didn't want her to see how the dangerous stain had grown.

*God, please, if You're really out there someplace, if You know who I am, please help me just this once.*

"Do you think you can walk?"

Kaylee stared at her silently, her face as white as the icing she'd been using on the snowman cookie she still held.

"It's okay, honey," Abby murmured, trying to loosen Kaylee's fingers from the cookie. "Come on, let me help you stand."

The cookie crumbled, but Kaylee didn't move.

"They're on their way," Brit said, rushing back into the kitchen. Her face was pinched with worry when she saw the spreading stain.

"Help me get her to the bathroom," Abby said. "The ambulance is coming?"

Supporting Kaylee on one side, Brit nodded. "And Nick."

Gently, slowly, Abby and Brit raised Kaylee from her chair. "I'm scared," the girl whispered.

So was Abby. Especially after she saw the chair where Kaylee had been sitting. Her heart filled with the same terror she'd heard in the young girl's voice. And she prayed a second time. She honestly didn't know if she had faith anymore or not; she simply knew that Kaylee's life wasn't going to end this way.

She couldn't even think about the life of the baby Kaylee had been carrying.

NICK MADE IT to the hospital just after Abby had arrived in the ambulance with Kaylee. They'd given the girl something for her pain and Kaylee had been dozing on and off.

"How is she?" he asked quietly. His hair, always a little long, was mussed, as though he'd been running his fingers through it on the way to the hospital.

Abby leaned into him, welcoming the arm he slid around her. "I don't know. They're with her now." She turned her face into his suit jacket, wishing she could wipe away the last hour, the fear that still left an acrid taste on her tongue. "She lost a lot of blood."

Nick nodded. Had she not known him so well, Abby would have been amazed at his calm. But she saw the flare of his nostrils, the intent look in his eyes. Nick was worried.

He led her to a couple of chairs in the emergency waiting room. "I called her mother, and she's on her way."

Abby nodded, her heart aching for the woman, knowing how frantic she must feel, how frustrated to be more than an hour away.

"How are the rest of the girls?"

"Scared." Abby fiddled with the cuff of Nick's jacket. She needed the contact. Needed him. "I sent them to the guest house with Marianne."

"What about Brit?"

"When I came out of the bathroom after the paramedics arrived, she was cleaning the chair in the kitchen," Abby's eyes teared as she remembered the sorrow on the girl's distraught face, the tears that had mingled with the soapy water.

"I sent her down to Marianne before we left."

And now all any of them could do was wait. And those who were capable, who knew how, could hope.

TAKING ABBY'S HAND, Nick settled back in the hard plastic chair, med school statistics running through his mind. He'd done a research project on problem pregnancies—on miscarriages and dangerous levels of lost blood. Of course, at the time, he'd been studying grown women. Chances of recovery weren't nearly as high for a child.

"You think she's going to be okay?" Abby's voice was soft beside him. Searching.

"I do." Because he refused to consider anything else.

Abby nodded, squeezing his fingers. And squeezing

his heart, as well. Abby took so much on herself. Suffered for those around her.

Kaylee's mother was ushered straight in to see the doctor the moment she arrived.

"What do you think that means?" Abby asked. Her face was white, pinched, as if she was going to be sick.

"Could just be they didn't want to leave her sitting out here worrying," he said, although he didn't really think so. "Or Kaylee could've been asking for her." Which was what he hoped.

It could also mean they'd lost her.

But he wasn't going to consider that possibility. Not yet. Not ever, if he had any say in the matter. If personal will, faith, had half the power he'd always believed.

Abby leaned her head against his arm. "I'm glad you're here."

He was glad, too. Glad that, for once, Abby wasn't handling things all alone.

THE DOCTOR FINALLY appeared what seemed like hours later but had probably only been minutes. He was accompanied by Kaylee's mother. Mrs. Mc-Donald was crying.

"We lost the baby," the doctor said.

Nick had never doubted that. Abby stood up beside him, clutching his arm stiffly to her side.

"And Kaylee?" she asked, her voice strong. But Nick could feel her trembling.

"She's going to be fine," Mrs. McDonald said. And started to sob.

Abby released Nick's arm instantly. With one arm around the distressed woman she guided her gently to a quiet corner in the nearly vacant waiting room. As he listened to the doctor report on Kaylee's loss of blood, their fear of hemorrhage—unwarranted as it turned out—Nick watched Abby console Kaylee's mother. He was struck by the obvious empathy Abby had with the older woman, the tender way she wiped the woman's tears.

One thing was for certain. Whether she believed in herself or not, Abby Hayden had stores of love to give. She was just too busy caring for other people to notice. Nick wished he'd been too busy to notice, too.

# CHAPTER FIFTEEN

NICK DROVE Abby home, not only because she didn't have another way back, but because he wanted to be with her to break the news to the other girls.

The girls were subdued. Still a little frightened, knowing the same thing that had happened to Kaylee could easily have happened to them. But they were more relieved to hear that Kaylee was going to be fine. That she'd be released from the hospital in a day or so and that she'd be moving back home with her mother and brother.

"Freaky, isn't it? That just so fast it can all be over," Diane said. They were sitting together in the living room, the light from the Christmas tree their only illumination.

Everyone contemplated Diane's comment silently, each of the girls lost in thoughts of her own. Abby sat by herself at the far end of Nick's sofa, Beanie in her lap.

"That was one baby who wasn't meant to be," Brit said, sharing a look with Abby.

And Nick supposed Brit, who was way too wise for her years, was right.

HE WAS ALONE in the living room a while later, listening once again as Abby wished each of the girls good-night at their bedroom doors. He'd shed his jacket earlier, and now reached up to loosen his tie, staring at the tree they'd all decorated together. He thought of Kaylee, her life before the pregnancy— and the life ahead of her now.

And he thought of how Abby had helped make Kaylee's coming life one the girl could face with optimism.

Now Abby was saying good-night to Brit. Nick could hear the soft, personal exchange between the two, the warmth in their simple communication. Since Abby had talked to her, Brit seemed to be facing the birth of her baby, the hard months afterward, with equanimity. With peace.

Abby moved across to Deb's room, and surprisingly enough, there were more soft words. More than just a brief good-night. Looking back at the tree, Nick stared at the angel right in the middle. He remembered the way Deb had gone to Abby the night she'd hung that angel, remembered the thin thread by which Abby had clung to her composure, and the way Deb had strengthened that thread.

As Abby moved from room to room upstairs, Nick's eyes strayed around the living room, taking in the homemade Christmas stockings hanging haphazardly along one wall. He thought about the anticipation, the hope they represented, there in a home where one might be forgiven for thinking that hope had long since taken a hike. His glance skimmed over the few surprises already under the tree. He knew there were more still in the planning stages.

And suddenly, in the midst of this refuge he'd created, Nick had to face a truth he'd somehow missed along the way. The presents, the stockings, were all there because these girls truly cared about one another. And that caring included the giving of gifts. But just as important was the taking, the acceptance of what was being given. Accepting not only the gifts, but the caring. Nick had long ago mastered the giving part. It was the taking he'd failed to do. The personal *caring* he hadn't allowed.

And by refusing to take, he was robbing those who cared about him of the joy of giving. His parents, who'd been asking to come out for Christmas every year since he'd bought them their retirement home in Florida. A home, now that he thought about it, they'd never actually said they wanted.

And...

Nick stopped, thought for a moment of the other people in his life. Charles and Marianne were part of it. So were Sally and the girls, and all his patients, and the people he worked with at the clinics, his racquetball partner and his editor, his agent. But did any of them feel more for him than admiration? Had he ever allowed them to?

As if sensing Nick's disturbance, Beanie trotted up to him and began scratching him on the leg. Looking down at the little beast, then over to where Bones lay sleeping beside the lit tree, Nick didn't like himself much at all. He was so far gone he'd even refused to take affection from a couple of loyal, loving dogs.

Love was action—doing—just as he'd always known. But love was taking, needing, *feeling,* too.

"Whatcha thinking about?"

Wrapped in his horrifying self-revelation, Nick hadn't even heard Abby come in. She stood next to him, gazing at the tree.

"You were right." He said the first thing that came to his mind.

"Oh. Good." She frowned. "About what?"

"My steering clear of the fray, as you called it."

"No!"

He could feel her staring at him.

"I should never have said that, Nick. I had no business saying that. I was wrong and I'm so sorry."

The sardonic glance he sent her said more than any words could have.

"I mean it, Nick." Her brown eyes met his squarely. "All you do for people... They need you. The world's a better place because you're in it."

There was nothing she could have said that would have affected him more. Because she'd hit on the core of his mission. To live in such a way that the world was a better place for his having been there.

But was it? If he himself had missed a vital experience, a vital part of what he preached?

Abby grabbed his hand urgently. "Please, don't change who you are, what you do because I stuck my nose where it doesn't belong."

He wasn't even sure he could change. "I may do good things, but it doesn't get *personal,* does it? And isn't that what love and life are all about? *Persons?* I teach about love, but I don't even know what it is."

"Who says you don't? Don't you see, Nick?" She jerked on his hand. "This is exactly what I was talking about. I think I know everything. I get close to someone, and I think it's my job to control how they live." She laughed bitterly. "I must really be good if I can make someone as committed as you doubt himself."

Nick took her other hand in his, turning to face her fully. "Did you ever stop to think that maybe you have a gift, too? That maybe you see things in perspective? See things in ways other people don't always want to see them? Or bother to see them?" Somehow, in spite of his own turmoil, it was important that she recognize she might not be wrong. As much as he wished she were. "Did you ever stop to think that maybe you're right?"

"Nope." She stared down at their clasped hands. "At least, not anymore."

"So how do you explain the fact that I want you more than any other woman I've ever known? That I can't seem to stay away from you? And yet I don't make love to you."

Abby raised her head slowly, her eyes searching his. "I just figure it's me," she said, honesty shining through the pain on her face. "When you get right down to it, there's something about me that turns you off."

And with that look, those words, Nick knew he'd lost. Pulling her into his arms, he buried his face in her hair. "No," he said against her neck. "It's definitely not you.

"Your smile tempts me, your walk." The words were torn from him. "The way you listen when the girls speak. Your enjoyment of Marianne's cooking. How much you care about your sister. It all keeps me up nights. Keeps me coming back for more."

And then he did what he'd been needing to do forever. What he'd sworn he'd never do. He kissed her. Really kissed her. Like the starved man he was. Everything he'd become, everything he'd ever hoped to be—and everything he'd ever been afraid of—went into the kiss. And somewhere, in the process of giving Abby the passion he'd kept pent up for too long, he took from her, too. He took her sweetness, her warmth. He took absolutely everything she had to give him.

And savored it all.

Some part of him remained mindful of the girls upstairs. Nick somehow got Abby and himself to the study, managed to shut and lock the door behind them, before his greedy hands divested Abby of the clothes she'd been wearing. Sweater, jeans, shoes, socks—they all just landed where he dropped them, until she was standing before him in the sexiest underwear he'd ever seen.

Following his hungry gaze, Abby glanced down self-consciously, looking at the French-cut thong panties, the lacy bra that barely concealed what it covered. "Audrey made us all wear nice undies." She shrugged. "She said a woman had to feel good on the inside to look good on the outside."

Nick laughed. "I think the inside that statement usually refers to is a little farther in."

"Yeah, well, that's Audrey for you." Abby smiled up at him.

Warmth flooded through him, a hot, sexy, wanting kind of warmth. But it was more than that. He drank in Abby's smile, her happiness to be in that room with him, doing what they were doing. And the heart he hadn't even known was empty suddenly started to fill.

So unexpected was the feeling that Nick paused. Years of personal discipline, of fighting against emotions that had led him to serious trouble at such an early age, came to the fore, making him doubt the rightness of what he was doing. Doubt followed doubt. Doubt about the way he'd been living his life.

Taking time for relationships was the core of a good life. He'd said so in all his books. In every speech he'd ever given. In a million counseling sessions. And it was something he didn't do.

In the split seconds it took for these thoughts to chase across his mind, Abby had his shirt undone. Her fingers along his chest felt not just right but necessary, and his doubts fled, leaving only sensation. Only life. The life that was flowing between him and this woman. His slacks quickly joined his shirt and tie on the floor.

"You are so beautiful." He drew his fingers through her hair, letting the silky lengths cloak his wrists.

His hands fell slowly to her shoulders, caressing the slender bones, and traveled lowered until they brushed over her breasts.

Abby's eyes never left his face. "I've never felt beautiful before."

Moving from her breasts to her face and back again, his gaze drank in all of her. "How could you not?"

She shrugged. "I always knew Audrey and Anna were gorgeous. I just never saw myself that way."

His hands continued downward, caressing her waist as he pulled her to him, their bare thighs meeting for the first time.

"You're beautiful to me far beyond the physical beauty you shared with your sisters." He ground his body lightly against hers, the contact a huge relief in itself—and shockingly painful, as well.

Her hands splayed against his back, her arms clutching him as if she'd never let go.

Gazing into her upturned face, seeing the tears that threatened to spill from her eyes, Nick knew he'd come home. That this moment was as perfect as life could be.

And then he couldn't think anymore. He urged her gently down on the carpet of their clothes, slowly removed her bra and panties, and more quickly his own briefs. He wanted to know every inch of her, with his eyes, his hands, his kisses. He wanted to know how she tasted, to fill his mind with her sweet rose-scented fragrance. To give her pleasure like none she'd ever known before.

Because her pleasure was as important to him as his own, and because he didn't trust himself to hold on for long once he finally entered her, Nick loved her first, with his kisses, his caresses. And when she came that first time, it was like she'd never come before. Her eyes, at first closed, flew open, staring at him with smoky astonishment. He rode the waves with her, encouraging her, turned on by the excitement he'd helped her discover.

And then, as he felt the last waves drifting away, he pulled his hand away and reached for the wallet in the pocket of his slacks.

"Were you so sure of me?" she asked, grinning like a spoiled cat as she figured out what he was after.

"Hardly." Nick grinned right back.

Abby watched while he shielded himself. And even that aroused him.

"Let me guess," she teased. "Being such a responsible man, you always carry one, just in case."

"Always." Nick was no longer smiling, too overcome with the intensity of what he was about to do, what they were about to share, as he settled himself over her.

Abby welcomed him wholeheartedly. Until he started to penetrate. The resistance that met him was too great to be misunderstood. And Nick was too far gone to do one damn thing about it.

His body finished the thrust before his mind could tell him not to, breaking through the tight resistance of her body. Hurting her. But as his gaze flew to hers, Nick saw only satisfaction there—and happiness. And Nick's heart plunged that much deeper into Abby's. For someone who never took anything from anyone, Nick had just taken a very precious gift.

"You should have told me," he said, holding himself within her. He was hesitant to move, to hurt her further.

Abby shrugged. "The choice was mine."

"I've waited so long I'm not sure I can go slowly." The tension in his body was almost killing him. He felt as if he had to move, or die.

Lifting herself, Abby flicked her tongue lightly against his mouth. "Love me, Nick," she whispered. "Please love me."

So he did. And the experience was like none he'd ever had before. It was one he knew he was going to have again. And again.

His life was suddenly flying out of control. The entire center of his being had shifted. His paradigms were no longer in focus.

And that scared Nick to death.

THEY DRESSED QUIETLY, quickly, going about their own business as clothing was collected, buttons were buttoned. Completely unschooled in mating protocol, Abby had no idea what happened next. She just wished Nick would say something. She needed to know what he was thinking. What she should be thinking.

She needed to know she hadn't disappointed him.

"I guess taking care of your sisters all those years, and the shop, didn't leave much time for pursuing romantic relationships of your own."

Whatever she'd been expecting, it wasn't that. "That was certainly part of the reason." She pulled up the zipper on her jeans. "Also the fact that I didn't know the rules, was embarrassed by my inexperience. It just seemed easier to be alone."

He nodded, tucking in his shirt. "I'm glad." His fly lay open, and as much as she told herself to, Abby couldn't pull her gaze away.

"Me, too."

Nick reached out, tilting her chin until she was staring straight into his eyes. "You're very certain?" He wanted the truth. "You're not sorry?"

Abby shook her head. Gave him the truth.

"I'm not ready to change my life," he said, fastening the waistband of his slacks.

"That's good." He was just what she wanted—right? A man who didn't have time to get too involved.

Nick looked as though he'd expected her answer, but he didn't seem to feel any happier about it than she did. He nodded. "As long as we understand each other...."

"We do." But without warning, Abby was fighting back tears.

And a few minutes later, after Nick gave her a lingering, hungry kiss goodbye, Abby locked the door behind him, ran up to her room—and wept. She wanted more. *Oh, God. I want it all.* But finally making the admission didn't change a thing. Because *all* was something she would never have again.

THERE WAS ANOTHER message from Maggie Simmons when Abby called the shop the next day. And this time Abby asked Marianne to keep the girls company for her. She had to get to the cottage. Had a phone call to make. In private.

Because this time Maggie had said why she was calling. *For Anna.*

All the way to the cottage she kept telling herself that Anna was okay. Jason would've called if something was wrong.

Unless something had happened to Jason, too.

The other thing that didn't add up was the number this Maggie had left. It wasn't a New York number. Maggie Simmons was here in California.

Did that mean Anna was, too?

She had to dial three times before her fingers got the numbers right. Then she waited through four long rings before the phone was picked up.

"Yeah?"

Abby wasn't sure she liked the woman's style. "Maggie Simmons?"

"Yeah, that's me."

The New York accent threw Abby. "This is Abby Hayden."

"It's about time. I was beginning to think I had the plague or something," the woman said. "You been out of town?"

"You could say that," Abby said slowly. Who was this woman?

"Yeah, well, I'm calling only because I can't say no to Anna. She's just too damn sweet."

"You know Anna?" Abby felt a little breathless.

"Lived right down the hall from her."

"Oh, my God." A real connection to Anna's new life. A connection other than Jason, who was also a part of Anna's previous life. "How is she?"

"Good as can be expected for someone who's big as a whale."

Abby grinned, and teared up, too. "I wondered if she'd gained a lot of weight." She thought about Brit, how the girl could barely get around anymore without her back hurting.

"Only her belly," Maggie said. "Last I saw her, she looked like she was hiding a basketball under those pathetic dresses she wears."

Abby's smile grew bigger. "So, she found a used clothing store there, too, huh?"

"Three of 'em. And then dragged me with her so she could buy exactly what I told her not to buy."

Leaning forward on the kitchen counter, Abby searched for ways to keep the other woman on the phone. She needed the connection so desperately. "You said last time you saw her—how long ago was that?"

"Couple months. Moved out here to make a pilot."

"You're an actress?"

"So they tell me."

"How'd it go?"

"Depends on what NBC says when they call my agent later this week."

"Listen." Abby was scrambling. "Would you like to get together for coffee or something?"

"Can't stand the stuff. But…"

Maggie paused and Abby had a feeling that this brash New Yorker wasn't usually at a loss for words.

"God, your sister's a pain, you know that?"

Anna, a pain? Not the Anna she knew. If anything, Anna had always been too accommodating, blended in *too* well—until she became like the paint on the wall. Noticeable only if you cared to see that it was there.

"What's up?" Abby asked.

"I'm supposed to move in with you."

"*What?*"

"I told her it was a crazy idea."

"What idea?"

"You got a cottage on the beach, right?"

"Right."

"And Anna's half owner."

"Yes."

"She called me a little over a week ago, asked if I'd move into her room."

"You need a place to stay?"

"Not really."

Abby frowned. "Then why…"

"She remembered some stuff, you know?" Maggie's voice was softer. "And there's stuff she still doesn't remember, or at least she hadn't last I talked to her."

"I know." Abby turned, leaning her back against the counter. "Jason called." But Abby hadn't heard from him since.

"Well, I don't know what she remembered, but she's worried about you."

"About me?" Abby was fighting tears again.

"That's what she said."

"Why?"

"How the hell do I know? Guess she loves you." Maggie was clearly wishing she could get out of this conversation. "Said she didn't want you to be alone."

"I'm not."

"Oh. Well, good, then. Nice talking to you—"

"Wait!" She didn't want Maggie to go.

"Yeah?"

"I could sure use someone here," she said, liking

the idea immediately. "I took a job—at a home for unwed pregnant teens. I'm their housemother."

"Anna told me you two look alike. You wear flower-child dresses and help old ladies across the street, too?"

Abby liked Maggie Simmons. The woman made her smile. "No. And neither did Audrey."

"Who's Audrey?"

"Anna didn't tell you we're triplets?"

"No way! There're *three* of her?"

"There were." Abby paused. She had no idea why she was talking so freely with a woman she'd never met. "Audrey was murdered a couple of years ago."

"Oh, no… I'm sorry."

"Anna found her." Abby looked out at the waves, the ocean she loved. "That's part of the reason she had to get away."

"My God!"

"Yeah."

The line was silent for a moment.

"So, this cottage. It's just sitting there empty?"

"Yeah." Abby glanced around. The place seemed so empty. Too empty. "I'd feel a lot better if someone was here, looking out for things."

"How close is it to the beach?"

Abby mentally measured the back porch. "About three feet."

"You got yourself a house sitter."

Abby suspected she'd just gained far more than that. She could use a friend like Maggie. Someone who saw the world exactly as it was—and liked it anyway. Besides, any friend of Anna's…

## CHAPTER SIXTEEN

IT WAS LATER than she'd planned when Abby finally made it back to Home Away From Home. She and Maggie had arranged for Maggie to move into the cottage Christmas Day, as that was the first day Maggie didn't have an audition. Then Abby had stayed home long enough to spruce the place up, vacuum the floors, clean the bathrooms. Anna would have killed her if she'd let a friend come to the house looking the way it had.

Her sister would also have been sure to note that one thing about the job at Home Away From Home that suited Abby was the housekeeper.

She could hear voices coming from the living room when she finally let herself into the house. And something didn't sound quite right. Frowning, Abby hurried into the room.

Brit was standing in front of a woman Abby didn't recognize. The obviously affluent woman's hair was short but still tied back in a ponytail. There was a baseball cap sticking out of the pocket of her denim jacket. Brit's normally sweet face was puckered with concern. And she seemed far too relieved when she saw Abby.

"What's up?" Abby asked.

The woman turned, her eyes taking on the strangest light when she saw Abby. Brit grimaced at Abby over the woman's head, shrugging. "I thought she was a potential client, here to check out the place for her daughter or niece or something."

The woman neither verified nor denied Brit's claim. She just continued to stare at Abby, breathing like she'd been running for miles.

"Did Dr. McIntyre call to say someone was coming?" Abby asked. Her heart was beating frantically.

"No."

Something was wrong. Very wrong.

"Can I help you?" Abby asked the woman.

The woman spit at Abby's feet. "That's what your help is worth," she said. "But don't worry. I'm going to make sure you don't ever help anyone again."

As she drew closer, Abby could see that the other woman's eyes were dark, her pupils dilated. She had to be on some kind of drugs. And she was older than Abby had originally assumed. Closer to forty than twenty.

Scrambling for her next move, Abby motioned Brit to leave the room. "Do I know you?" she asked.

"You should." The woman practically bit out the words. "All those times you slept with my husband you did it in *my* bed." The woman reached out to touch Abby's face. "I'll bet you even felt the wedding ring I put on his finger sliding over that pearly white skin of yours."

Abby moved instinctively, but not before the woman reeled and landed a resounding crack across Abby's cheek.

Her head was flung back from the force of the blow, hitting the wall. Eyes watering, she said, "I have no idea what you're talking about."

"At least have the courage to admit what you did,"

the woman screamed, leaning closer to Abby's face. "Don't let me know that he killed himself over a coward!" Her voice was getting shriller by the second.

Abby was worried about the girls. She had to get rid of this woman. Quickly. "Why are you here?"

That stopped the woman for a second. She blinked, looked at Abby as if she'd expected Abby to know.

"To kill you, of course."

Her heart stopped beating; her breath froze in her throat. And that was when Abby understood. The jeans the woman was wearing. The boots. She'd seen them before. The day she'd met Nick.

This woman was really going to kill her.

She looked up to see the woman pull a knife from the inside of the denim jacket she was wearing.

*Oh, God. Not like this.*

*Not again.*

*Not here.*

"I told you that day on the beach, before I cut your pretty little face to shreds. I won't die until I see you dead first."

"You killed Audrey." Suddenly Abby's heart was pounding too fast. She felt light-headed. She was going to throw up. "You killed my sister."

The deranged woman didn't even hear her. She approached Abby slowly, as if savoring every step, her expression gleeful. "You young things, you think you can just steal away any man you want. You don't care about the lives you ruin. You don't even care about the men. You leave them like that—" she snapped the fingers of her other hand, the hand without the knife "—as soon as someone richer comes along."

"No." Abby backed toward the door, though

whether to shut the woman in, away from the girls, or try to get outside she wasn't sure. "I'd never do that," she said.

The knife floated within a foot of her face. "My Bob wasn't good enough for you, was he? He was so depressed after you left him he finally told me about you. Told me he'd been sleeping with you right under my nose."

Was the woman stark raving mad?

Or had Audrey really had an affair with a married man?

Something the woman had said clicked in Abby's fear-crazed brain.

*Bob?*

"Was his name Robert Winters?"

"So you *do* remember." If anything the woman became more enraged. She made one quick sweep of the knife, cutting Abby's sweater.

Abby remembered Audrey falling head over heels in love with a man she'd met only twice. Bob Winters had come into the shop asking for directions. And asked Audrey out for a drink. A month later it had ended abruptly, and Audrey had moved on to someone else. Audrey had never said why things had fallen apart with Bob, but Abby could guess.

"You have the wrong woman."

The man had never told Audrey he was married. Contrary to what his deranged wife thought, he hadn't worn a wedding ring the couple of times Abby had seen him with Audrey. And though she was weak and sometimes irresponsible, Audrey would never have slept with a married man.

"I'm warning you, don't do this," the woman hissed, lashing out a second time with the knife. But her aim was wild and she missed Abby altogether. "You already admitted everything to me, the first time I found you."

Abby choked on her fear, her grief. This woman had heard Audrey's last words. God, how frightened Audrey must have been. As frightened as Abby was now?

"You'll never get away with this."

"What're they going to do to me? Put me back in that asylum? Give me drugs until I can't remember what day it is?" The woman shrugged. "Doesn't much matter anyway. Bob's gone, put a gun to his head the day after he told me about you. What else have I got to live for? I'm ready to die." The woman came slowly closer, steadier now with her purpose firmly in mind. "Just as soon as I take care of you."

Abby had backed up as far as she could go. She'd missed the door and retreated straight into a wall. Where were Charles and Marianne? Had anyone called the police? Did they even know Abby was in danger? Abby couldn't remember how much Brit had heard before she'd sent the girl away.

The woman lowered her knife, peering at Abby's face. "They really did an amazing job," she said.

Abby could barely speak. "I'm a different woman. You killed my identical sister two years ago."

Either the woman didn't believe her or just plain hadn't heard. And Abby could tell by the anticipatory gleam in the woman's eyes that it probably didn't make any difference. The woman was looking forward to disfiguring Audrey a second time. Abby fought for a clear thought, for something to stall the inevitable.

"It was you on the street that day, wasn't it?" she

asked. She hoped to God that what she'd found in every mystery novel she'd ever read was true. Criminals liked to talk about their crimes, their cleverness.

"I would've had you that day—if that stupid man hadn't come along."

"And at the mall?"

The woman smiled and nodded. "I made it all the way into your cute little cottage on the beach, too. Just walked in one day when you were on the phone. I'd have had you then, right by the beach where we were together the last time, but you had to go and throw up and that spoiled things." The woman's eyes were alight with a satanic glow. "But I knew, just like before, that if I waited long enough, the right time would come."

"How'd you find me here?" Abby asked. But she already knew. She'd led the woman to her front door. The woman and her blue sedan.

"Followed you home one day," the woman said. "Couldn't believe you'd be living with all these pregnant girls." The woman paused, scowling as if she'd just thought of something. "How'd you know about this place, anyway?" she asked, glancing around at the obvious signs of dormitory living, the many couches, the lack of family knickknacks and photos.

"I met—"

"You had his baby, didn't you?" The woman came closer still, the knife almost at Abby's chin. "That's how you knew about this place. You lived here. You were pregnant, too, weren't you?" the woman screamed.

"No!"

"Where is it? Where's my dead Bobbie's baby?"

That was when Abby knew how she was going to

buy herself some time. She'd stumbled upon something the woman wanted.

"Tell me." The knife grazed Abby's chin.

But before she could make anything up, before she could promise to take the woman to this imaginary child, there was a sound from the doorway and a rolling furniture dolly came speeding toward them, knocking the woman off her feet. Then, with one quick chop from Deb against the fallen woman's wrist, the deadly knife flew across the room. Coming out of nowhere, Rhonda picked up the knife and ran out.

Deb sat on the woman's back, twisting her arms up behind her, while Diane threw a blanket over her feet, sat on them and proceeded to tie them. Becca stood in the doorway crying. Brit was holding Abby up.

"Let me go!" The woman started to scream hysterically and then, suddenly, wilted, going limp beneath the girls as she continued to cry quietly and moan about her Bobbie.

"Charles took Marianne to the store," Deb said as though that explained everything.

And in a way it did. With no other immediate option, the girls had just risked their lives to save hers.

"Did anyone call the police?" Abby finally thought to ask, her head clearing a bit as she started to breathe more normally.

"I did. And in case you're wondering, I called Nick, too." Brit still hadn't let her go. "Bones is down at the guest house. Charles thinks he has a piece of glass in his foot. And Beanie's locked in the pantry."

Abby didn't know what to say, what to think. She just stood there, still shaky, with her arms around the girl. Unexpectedly, Brit's baby walloped Abby a good one, right in the ribs.

"Ow!" she said, jumping back.

Brit laughed, somewhat wildly, but it was enough to lighten the tension around them just a bit. "No kidding," Brit said, rubbing her belly. "This kid's trying to do me in before she even hits puberty." She gave Abby a sharp look. "Your chin's bleeding!"

Until that moment, Abby hadn't even been aware of the sting. Lifting her hand to the bottom of her chin, she wiped away a small dab of blood. "It's just a scratch."

Just then, a siren came wailing up the drive.

"Thank God," Abby heard Brit whisper.

*Thank You, God,* Abby reiterated, shaking so hard she could barely stand. She saw a policeman flatten himself against the side of the house, peer in the window and raise his hand in a signal. The front door crashed open, and two more uniformed men burst inside.

They were already taking the woman into custody when Nick came running in.

He went straight to Abby, hauling her into his arms, crushing her to him. And suddenly, knowing that it was over, that they were all safe, Abby lost what little control she had left. It had been only a matter of hours since he'd held her. It felt like forever.

Nick got the police to agree to give Abby a few minutes before they took her statement. He just kept hugging her while she trembled, didn't even seem to mind the embarrassing weakness, the blubbering. And the girls gathered around, too. Becca, talkative now, was telling Nick everything that had happened. A couple of the girls rubbed Abby's back.

Slowly returning to her senses, Abby thought of what the girls had done. The danger they'd put themselves in.

"Y-you g-girls are pregnant!" she said, admonishing them, frightened all over again when she thought of what might have happened, how differently things could have turned out.

"She's just now noticing." Deb's drawl made everyone laugh, Abby included.

Until she looked around at them, still so innocent in so many ways, with full lives to lead ahead of them. "You girls should never have—"

"If the situation had been reversed," Brit interrupted, "isn't it what you would have done?"

Nick didn't say a word. Just stood there. Watching. Abby realized something then. Strength, real strength, came from caring. And doing whatever it took, right or wrong, for those you cared about.

Still, she would never have forgiven herself if something had happened to the girls. As always, loving came with a price.

"ABBY!"

Dropping the dispenser of tape, Abby left the pile of half-wrapped Christmas presents on her bed and ran for the hall. Something was wrong with Brit. Only three days had passed since the incident with the Winters woman, so Abby—and the girls—were still a bit shaky.

"I'm coming," she called out, trying to figure out where the girl was. She'd be glad when they'd all made their appearances in court and could put the whole Winters episode behind them. Unfortunately, because of psychological examinations and previous history, the police didn't expect the trial to take place until sometime in the spring.

"Hurry!" Brit cried again. This time the girl's voice just sounded weak, as opposed to far away as she'd originally suspected. She headed toward Brit's room.

"What's up?" she asked, poking her head in the door. No Brit. Not on the bed, not at the bureau or in the chair by the window...

"Oh, Abby, it hurts. Bad."

That was when Abby saw her, lying on the bathroom floor, her lower body wrapped in a towel.

Rushing forward, lifting the girl's head onto her lap, Abby helped Brittany breathe through the pain. The girl was a sweaty mess and Abby wondered how long she'd been having contractions. Why hadn't Brit called her sooner?

"Mmmmm," Brit said as the contraction relaxed. "It's not supposed to be like this."

Abby gently pushed the hair back from Brit's face, waiting for the girl to recover some of her strength. "What, you thought you were going to get to do this without the contractions?"

"No, you don't understand." Brit struggled for breath. "It's way too sudden, too fast—"

Almost before Abby knew what was happening, Brit's body contorted with another pain. And Abby felt the first stirrings of panic.

"Nick! Girls! Anybody!" she hollered. Thank God it was Saturday and Nick was there helping Charles string lights on the outside of the house. Thank God Nick was there, period. She hadn't seen him in three days. Not since the police had finally left late on Wednesday afternoon.

"Mmmm." Brit's moans frightened Abby.

It sounded like the girl was ready to give birth any second. But she couldn't be. She was supposed to be in labor for hours.

"Hold on, honey, just ride the pain," she said. "Help!" She threw the word over her shoulder. Surely not everyone was out back.

Nick had told her when she'd first started at the home that often with girls so young, the birthing process followed no set patterns.

Brit's eyes, opening as the pain subsided, were filled with terror. "I just came in to go to the bathroom and my water broke," she gasped between breaths.

That explained the towel. "How long have you been having pains?"

"They started just after my water broke."

Beanie came barreling into the room, attacking Brit's sweaty face with his tongue. Abby shooed him away. "Okay, we've probably only got another minute before the next one. Let's get you to the bed."

Beanie gave a second shot at joining the fun.

"Beanie, go!" She forced herself to remain calm as she half lifted Brit from the floor, helped her around Beanie's wiggling little body, and into bed, then pulled the girl's soaked dress over her head as she lay back against the pillows.

Brit tried to grin, so involved in what she was experiencing that her nakedness didn't seem to faze her. "That feels so much bet—ohhh, here it comes again."

Abby pulled the covers up to Brit's chin and took the girl's hand, rubbing it gently as she coached her through another contraction. She was going to have to get to a phone. Immediately. But she was afraid to leave Brit alone.

Abby had just opened her mouth to holler for help one more time when she heard footsteps thundering up the stairs.

"The girls said you called," Nick said, striding into the room. He was wearing jeans and a T-shirt. And looked sexier than hell.

"We need a doctor," Abby told him, turning back to Brit. She wanted to cry as she saw the pain contorting the girl's face. "Just a little longer, honey," she said. "Breathe."

Brit tried to pant, but Abby could see the effort it cost her. "I have to push."

Reaching for the girl's wrist, Nick felt her pulse. "How long's she been like this?"

"Not long." Abby's panic subsided just a bit as he took over. He'd make everything right. He always did. "Her water broke and the pains were almost immediate—and three or four minutes apart as far as I can tell."

Nick nodded, looking a little pinched around the mouth. "Go call her doctor."

"Mmmm," Brit groaned.

Abby fled.

"And call an ambulance!" Nick's voice followed her down the stairs.

The girls were all outside helping Charles untangle a long string of lights spread across the grass in the backyard. Marianne appeared to be supervising. The housekeeper hurried toward the house when she saw Abby in the kitchen.

"Brit's having her baby," Abby said as soon as the woman was in the door. "Would you please go out front and wait for the ambulance?'' She remembered how flustered the older woman had been during Jessie's birth.

After assuring herself that everything was going as well as possible, Marianne hurried to the front door.

Frustrated with the time it was taking her, frightened, Abby could hardly focus on the list of doctors' numbers Nick had hung by the kitchen phone. She felt only minimally better after getting through to Brit's O.B., who said not to move her. The pains were too close, the baby's arrival imminent.

And then she gave Abby a list of things to do in case she or the paramedics didn't get there in time. Abby's sole thought as she raced back up the stairs, having shoved Beanie outside and told all the girls to stay put in the backyard, was that the doctor hadn't asked her to boil any water.

''She's on her way—'' Abby broke off as she rushed into Brittany's room. Nick was sitting at the end of Brittany's bed, surrounded by a tent of sheets, and it looked like Brittany was ready to give birth any second.

''We're not going to be able to wait,'' he confirmed as Abby came up beside him.

''I have to push,'' Brit told Abby almost apologetically.

Exchanging a glance with Nick, Abby nodded. ''Then push, honey.'' She took hold of Brit's hand. ''The doctor said to—''

''I know what to do, Abby,'' Nick said. ''I *am* a doctor.'' He gave her a quick, reassuring grin before once again focusing on the job at hand.

She'd forgotten that Nick had a medical degree.

She wanted to ask him how many babies he'd delivered, but was afraid of the answer. Afraid to have Brit hear the answer.

"I've—got—one—lucky—baby, huh?" Brit panted, a sheen of sweat on her face. The girl's hair was plastered to her forehead, her eyes wild.

"How so?" Abby asked gently.

"She's got—two of my—favorite people in the world—delivering her."

Abby smiled down at her. "And what if she's a he?"

"She's not." For the moment Brit looked so peaceful. So serene. Abby could only wonder at the strange miracle of birth.

And hope that Nick knew the signs the doctor had told her to be aware of, knew what to do in case the birth didn't go as planned. She kept an eye on Brit's face, her pupils, making sure the girl wasn't going into shock. And prayed that the doctor, or the paramedics, arrived soon.

"Mmmmmm!" Brit practically sat upright as another pain hit.

"Easy, Brit," Nick crooned. "Push easy." He looked at Abby. "Head's crowning. You want to see?"

Fascinated, Abby couldn't not look. She'd never seen a baby born before. She was amazed it was really going to happen. In just a short while, they were going to have a little baby in the room.

Brit relaxed as the contraction passed, her eyes closed. Abby knew the girl had to be exhausted.

"She's been having sharp back pains for two days," Nick told Abby. "But her back's been hurting for so long she didn't think anything of it."

Abby continued to watch what Nick was doing, so

awed by the process that she wasn't the least bit un-comfortable with the intimacy they were sharing. "She's been in labor for two days?"

Nick nodded, moving forward as another pain came. "I'd say so."

Two whole days. Ever since— Abby froze, dread making her entire body go numb. Had she done this? If Nick was right, Brit's premature labor had started just hours after the incident with Robert Winters's deranged wife. Dammit, she'd *known* better than to drive straight here the day she'd discovered the blue sedan behind her. But she'd done it anyway.

Nick talked to Brit, to the baby he was birthing— and occasionally to Abby. And as she watched him, as she realized that if she couldn't have an obstetri-cian, there was no one in the world she'd rather have delivering her own baby, Abby could no longer deny that she'd fallen irrevocably in love. She'd realized it the night she made love with him. She'd probably known weeks before that. Just as she'd known she could never allow herself to give him her love.

She could see the pulse beating at the side of his throat, the cords of his neck tense. Coaching Brit, Abby watched Nick, too, quick to follow his orders.

As the minutes passed, she prayed long and hard for a safe birth, a healthy baby.

Maybe there was more of Audrey in her than she'd thought. Maybe she *was* foolish enough to believe in fairy tales. To fall in love with Prince Charming. That discovery frightened Abby almost as much as the rapid, early birth of Brit's baby.

Brit's daughter was just sliding out when the doctor appeared beside them, pulling on sterile gloves. She took over effortlessly, catching the baby easily. While the doctor tended to the baby, Nick assisted with the afterbirth, and between the two of them, it was only another couple of minutes before an exhausted but happy Brit was holding her new baby daughter.

"Isn't she's gorgeous?" She gazed down at the red, wrinkled little body squirming against her. Judging by the wails she was emitting, the baby's lungs were healthy. Brit looked from Abby to Nick, her eyes full of tears. "Thank you," she said, her voice breaking. "Thank you both so much."

Leaning forward, Abby kissed Brit's face, feeling weak with relief. "You're the one who did all the work, Mom." She didn't even try hiding her tears.

As Abby straightened, her eyes met Nick's and her heart caught in her throat when she saw the raw emotion on his face.

She loved him.

## CHAPTER SEVENTEEN

THE PARAMEDICS ARRIVED shortly after the doctor and Brit's room was suddenly far too crowded. Leaving the girl alone with the experts, Abby and Nick went downstairs to wait.

"They're going to take her to the hospital, aren't they? Just to make sure everything's okay?"

"I'm sure." Nick nodded. "If nothing else, they'll want to monitor the baby for several hours."

"You don't think anything's wrong, do you?"

"I'm sure there isn't." He took her hand as they reached the bottom of the stairs. And because she needed the surge of warmth his touch sent through her, Abby let him. Just for a moment.

"How is she?" Marianne was pacing the foyer outside the living room.

"Just fine." Abby smiled. "We have a healthy baby girl."

Joy burst over Marianne's features. "A girl!"

"And a bed that's going to need changing," Nick added. Abby grinned again at the stereotypical male response. "Just throw the sheets away—"

"I'm sorry, ma'am, but I demand to know what's going on...."

Abby and Nick turned simultaneously toward the unknown male voice coming from the doorway of their living room. The owner of the voice, a tall muscular dark-haired man in his late teens or early twenties, stopped in his tracks when he saw Nick.

"This young man is asking about Brit," Marianne said, wringing her hands. "Says his name is Jimmy something or other."

"Jimmy Henderson." The young man stepped forward.

"And what did you tell him?" Nick asked his housekeeper, but his eyes were sizing up their surprise visitor.

Marianne shook her head. "I haven't told him anything."

"Is something wrong with Brit?" There was fear in the young man's voice.

"Let's go sit down, shall we?" Nick's request brooked no refusal.

Jimmy followed them back to the living room, but he wouldn't be put off. "What's wrong with Brit?" He shook his head. "You have to tell me!"

Letting go of Nick's hand, Abby stayed in the doorway, afraid to know what would happen when Jimmy heard Nick's news. Would the young man come through for Brit? Or would he abdicate his responsibility, proving, once again, that so much of the world's pain came in the name of love?

It was a lesson Abby didn't want sweet Brit to learn. Not ever. But especially not that day.

LEANING AGAINST the end of a couch, Nick studied the young man for several seconds and then, satisfied, made a decision.

"Nothing's wrong, exactly."

The veins in Jimmy's neck were taut, his lips tight

as he waited. He was braced for bad news. Nick hoped to God he didn't get any.

He saw Abby standing in the door, hadn't missed the significance of her drawing back. And suddenly he was doubting, too. Doubting that a young love could possibly be strong enough to welcome the challenges ahead.

"How did you find her?" he asked. He was a doctor. A psychiatrist. It was his job to be impartial, not defensive.

"I had to," the young man said simply, pacing in front of Nick. "She didn't return a single one of my letters all semester. I love her. I want to marry her, bring her back to school with me. I have an apartment, a full-time job—" He stopped. Composed himself. "I have to know what's going on."

"You really think you can work full-time and go to school full-time, too?"

"Why not? I worked two jobs all through high school." He sounded impatient, as if ready to get on to what mattered. "Besides, I've been doing it all semester."

Nick was starting to admire this young man. "How were your grades?"

"This term 4.0, but that was probably because Brit wasn't there." Jimmy gave a cocky little grin. "I've already accepted the fact that my GPA's probably going to drop to 3.6 or so."

"You still haven't told me how you came to be here." Did the kid know what they did at Home Away From Home?

"I went to her house." He shuffled his feet, his shoulders slumped. "They shut the door in my face."

He looked up at Nick, perhaps still a little shocked by the unexpected reception. "What'd I do?"

Nick wasn't ready to tell him that. "If they didn't see you, how'd you end up here?"

"Her sister called my aunt's house, left this address. No phone number. No explanation. Just the address." He swallowed thickly. "I got here as fast as I could."

So Brit had an ally within the family after all. She'd be very happy to know that.

Standing, his hands in the pockets of his jeans, Nick faced the young man. "This is a home for pregnant teens."

Jimmy's face was blank. "For...but—why is Brit here?"

Nick watched as truth dawned. The young man turned white, then a mottled shade of yellow, as myriad emotions chased across his face. Shock. Pain. Regret.

But no repulsion. No denial.

"I want to see her." He stepped closer to Nick. "I don't care what you say—I have a right to see her. This is my problem, too."

Nick breathed his first easy breath since he'd entered the room. And chanced his first glance at Abby. She was smiling. And trying not to cry.

"I'm not sure Brit sees her daughter as a problem," he said, looking back at Jimmy.

Jimmy turned white again. And then lit with such joy Nick knew for sure love had won another round.

"I have a daughter?" His voice was incredulous. And thrilled. "A real daughter?"

Nick nodded. "As of twenty minutes ago."

"She just had it?" Jimmy ran for the door, stopping when Abby didn't move to let him out. "Which hospital?"

Just then, steps could be heard coming down the stairs.

"Is she okay?" Abby asked whoever was approaching.

"Just fine." Nick heard the doctor's voice moments before the woman appeared behind Abby. "They're just getting her moved to the gurney to take them in."

"Who?" Jimmy demanded. "Take who in?"

Nick exchanged one quick glance with Abby, heard her silent plea and gestured Jimmy toward the stairs. "Second door on your left."

They were all the words Jimmy needed.

NICK INVITED Abby out to dinner that night. Takeout at his place. He was getting nervous about the mixed signals she was sending, and needed to get her alone.

"You think they'll make it?" she asked on the way to his condo. She'd been talking about Brit and Jimmy since she'd climbed in the Bronco.

"I do."

"It's going to be hard."

"They're tough enough to deal with it."

"Brit said something about doing day care out of her home."

"She's resourceful. She'll find a way to make things work. To help Jimmy get through school."

She laid her head back against the seat, smiling. "I'm glad."

Abby was feeling the magic. He hoped to God it would last.

SHE WAS DISAPPOINTED with Nick's home. The condo was nothing like the man at all. Stark. Cold. Unadorned. There wasn't a single Christmas decoration.

The leather furniture grouping in the living room was nice. The accent tables, the lamps, the carpet— all of good quality, but the room looked like a model home. Minus the prerequisite generic knickknacks. This room had no knickknacks at all.

"I'll get some paper plates," Nick said, carrying the bags of Chinese takeout into the kitchen with him.

"Would you like some wine?" he called.

"Sure." Abby followed him into the kitchen. Which was more of the same. Expensive-looking countertops and appliances, but there were no canisters on the counters, no towels hanging from the oven bar, no curtains to cover the window above the sink. Everything was so...detached.

Something like the man himself after all.

"Zinfandel okay?" He'd pulled a couple of matching wineglasses down from the cupboard.

"Fine." But as she watched him uncork the wine, as she noticed the muscles in his forearms strain with tension, and almost felt those fingers working their magic on her, Abby had to wonder if wine was really such a good idea.

If dinner had been.

"Thanks." She took the goblet he offered.

He lifted his glass. "To Christmas," he said. "And the miracle of babies." Abby allowed her glass to clink against Nick's. Took a sip, her gaze still locked with his.

And then she looked away.

She'd come here to talk to him. To set things

straight. Not to make love with her eyes. Or any other part of her, either.

"Hungry?" Nick asked.

"Famished." At least, she'd pretend to be if that would forestall having to say what she'd come to say. She helped him set the table with their cartons of Chinese takeout, paper plates and napkins. Then she sat down to eat with him, savoring, despite herself, the intimacy of being alone with Nick, in his home, sharing a meal at his table. They talked about Brit some more, about the other girls' varied reactions when they'd briefly seen Brit's daughter. Some gushing, some pretending disinterest. One not pretending.

They talked like the friends they'd become, two people who knew each other well. Who cared for each other.

And then the meal was over and Abby felt as if she'd just finished the last supper.

She'd be seeing Nick again, she reminded herself. She'd be seeing him a lot over the next week as they followed through with all their holiday plans.

She just wasn't going to be intimate with him. She'd searched her heart for a way to be Nick's lover and still keep things casual, but she couldn't do it. Abby wasn't a casual person. And that was probably a big part of her problem. She got too involved in everything she did. She drew a couple of children's wear designs in class and ended up with a shop. She worked as a housemother and became an unofficial midwife. When she cared for people, she had to control them, too.

"COME HERE." Nick settled on the couch in his living room, opening his arms to Abby. He might be unsure about a lot of things in his life, but holding her was inevitable.

Poised between him and the door, she looked from one to the other, but Nick knew she'd already lost the battle. She felt it, too, this insatiable, inexplicable need to connect.

But she wasn't any happier about it than he was. He felt her resistance even as she sank down beside him, melting naturally into his embrace. She wouldn't look at him, didn't offer her mouth for the kiss he had to take.

He understood. He didn't want what was happening between them any more than she did. He just didn't know what to do about it.

Except to kiss her. Being with Abby was the only thing that felt right in a life that was careering out of control.

With one finger, he tilted her chin toward him, no longer expecting any resistance. And getting none. His eyes focused on her lips, on the way her tongue moved slowly across them, inviting him. Tempting him. And then he lowered his head, covering those delectable lips with his own. He took from her greedily, insistently. Reveling in her eager response.

He avoided her eyes.

She was wearing another sweater, and his hands couldn't get beneath it fast enough. Dealing with the sexy little bra with one pinch of his fingers, he availed himself of her sweet, heavy breasts.

"I love your nipples," he whispered against her mouth.

She stifled his words with her lips, kissing him hungrily, her tongue exploring as his had done seconds before.

Nick was so on fire for her he felt rational thought slipping away. Years of self-control, of discipline, lost their strength. Abby was his.

"No."

He barely heard the word, but her withdrawal left him with a pain he wasn't sure would ever go away.

"Stop." Her voice grew stronger. "We have to stop."

The most excruciating thing of all was to know she was right.

He let her go, his body hard and throbbing as he slumped into the corner of the couch, one of his arms flung along the back, one resting on the arm.

Abby got as far away from him as the room allowed. "I just can't do this."

"Maybe we don't have a choice."

Her head jerked up, her eyes penetrating points of determination. "We always have a choice, Doctor. Isn't that what you tell your patients?"

With supreme effort he kept himself seated where he was. "Can you tell me you don't feel something here? Something stronger than your will, or mine?"

She shook her head. "I can't tell you that."

Because she wasn't sure? Or because she couldn't tell him? Nick had a feeling it was the latter, though that didn't make him any happier.

"So you think that if we pretend it doesn't exist, this need is just going to go away?"

Abby turned her back on him. "The only thing I know is that I can't do this."

He should be glad she was strong enough for both of them. Relieved that she was letting him off the hook, freeing him to resume the life she'd interrupted. "How can you dismiss us so easily?" he asked, honestly wishing he knew. "After seeing Brit and Jimmy today, how can you not believe in the ultimate power of love, the magic?"

"I do believe." She should have sounded joyful admitting such a thing.

"How can you not want a piece of what they had? How do you reject it so easily?"

"Easily?" She whirled around, her face twisted with anguish. "You think this is easy for me?" Her laugh was choked, bitter.

Nick didn't know what he thought. Why wasn't he just letting her go? It was what he wanted, too, to be free from the force that was turning his life inside out, making him question the very center of his existence.

"I finally know what it feels like to be in love." She stopped. Swallowed. Looked up at the wall above his head. "For the first time in my life, I know what Audrey felt for Robert, and probably for Jeffrey and Dan, too. I understand why Anna's separation from Jason devastated her."

It was the most tortured confession of love Nick had ever heard.

"And it's the cruelest joke of all," she said, looking at him again. "Don't you see?" Her beautiful eyes were shadowed with dark emotion. "Before, knowing I wouldn't ever love again was sad, but now I know what I'm missing. Now it's like death in life."

Was he right back where he'd started, then? Had these past weeks proven nothing to her?

"Not if you embrace it."

She turned away again. "You know I can't do that."

"How can you see Jimmy with Brit and not believe

that love is a good thing? Not see the strength Jimmy's love gave Brit? Enough to carry her through the worst time of her life."

"I believe love can bring goodness. I didn't believe it before but I do now." Several weeks ago, that confession was all he'd been after.

"So why not embrace it?"

She whirled suddenly, coming closer. "Why all the interrogation, anyway?" She was angry. "You don't want me expecting anything from you except an occasional romp, maybe dinner now and then when you have time."

Nick inclined his head, acknowledging what she'd said.

"So what right do you have to demand so much more from me? What's the point of loving you? What would I do with it?"

"I don't know." The admission was hard. Because the sad fact was that his not knowing was more than simply an answer to her question. Not having that answer meant he no longer had some of his other answers, either. Maybe he didn't have any at all. He, whose entire life revolved around giving people answers.

"What you do, the people you help, the happiness you make possible in so many lost lives—that's important, Nick. I believe in you. In the vital good that you do."

He didn't understand why her words didn't make him feel better. Why they didn't validate his need to remain uninvolved.

"I believe in the love you talk about." She sat down, close but not touching him. "I just can't embrace it for myself."

"You're not making any sense." *But she was.* And he didn't want to hear it. He wondered if he'd ever smell roses again and not think of her.

"I love you, Nick."

His breath caught. But only for a second, until reality intruded.

"But I can't trust myself to...*manage* my love for you," she continued. "When I care, I suffocate.

"And if I suffocated you, Nick, I'd be suffocating all the good works you do. I can't take that chance. My love for you won't let me take that chance."

It was by far the most selfless act Nick had ever witnessed. And that was when he knew he'd won, but by winning he'd lost. He'd shown her the very real power of love, and that power was giving her the strength to walk away.

She waited for him to speak.

He couldn't think of a single thing to say.

Finally, her eyes averted, she gathered her purse, called a cab and, with one last glance at him, quietly left.

Hours later, Nick was still sitting on the couch, in exactly the same position, more frightened then he'd ever been. His entire adult life, his work, his service, was a front. A very effective barricade behind which he could hide. A barricade so clever, so convincing, it not only kept other people at arm's length but even had him fooled.

Looking deep into himself, searching for the man he knew himself to be, Nick found...nothing. Except pain. And fear. And doubts. The deeper he traveled, the worse it got. Until finally, he came face-to-face with a little boy who'd been hurt far more than he could bear, who wanted to die more than he wanted to live. A boy who never wanted to be vulnerable again. Who never wanted to have to depend on anyone, ask for anything. A boy who'd grown into the man he was.

And suddenly Nick was face-to-face with that man. He had good principles, lived by them, but he was only half-alive. Abby had been right that day in her room. Even then, she'd loved him enough to see—and more, to tell him what she'd seen.

Was it too late to resurrect the parts of him he'd lost?

Or would he lose so much more in the process he'd be better off half a man?

# CHAPTER EIGHTEEN

WEARING HER BLACK velour Christmas Eve jumpsuit, Abby poked her head into the kitchen, Beanie in her arms, "You need any help?" The place smelled divine. Christmas dinner wasn't for another twenty-four hours, but Marianne already had preparations well under way.

"Nick's parents settled in their room?" The housekeeper glanced over her shoulder, still peeling a carrot.

"Yes, and Becca's giving them a tour."

Turning fully around, carrot suspended in midair, Marianne frowned. "Becca? She'll drive them crazy. Do you think—"

"Don't worry," Abby laughed. "They asked her."

"Where's Diane?"

"Pestering Rhonda."

"She's going through the table linens for me?"

"Yes."

Marianne nodded, picking up a knife to slice the carrot. "Send Diane in here. She can help with the vegetable tray."

Abby, still holding Beanie, was back in a flash, Diane in tow. Bones had left for his new home that morning.

Marianne put Diane to work, breaking apart florets

of broccoli. "This stuff is gross," Diane said. "Look, there're little green dots all over my hand."

"At least green's a Christmas color." Abby leaned over to make sure the girl was following Marianne's instructions. "I've got the rest of the presents wrapped," she told Marianne when she saw how easily Diane was accomplishing her task. "I can do something."

"Not in here you can't." Marianne grinned at her.

"What about dinner for tonight?" Abby leaned against the counter, watching Marianne. "You need me to run and get anything?" Nick's parents, Nick, Marianne and Charles and the four girls still with them meant there'd be a lot of mouths to feed. Brit and the baby were at Jimmy's aunt's.

"We're having chili—and it's already done." With the last of the carrots cut, Marianne moved on to a stalk of celery.

"There're a couple of lights out on the tree."

Deb clomped into the kitchen. The girl insisted on wearing heavy work boots even now that she was so weighted down with her pregnancy, hanging on to her identity for all she was worth.

"I'll get them." Abby jumped on the job. If she wasn't careful, the excitement in the air was going to infect her, too.

THE LIVING ROOM WAS full later that afternoon as they all shared some cheese and crackers before dinner. Abby sat on a couch with Nick's parents, Marianne and Charles shared another couch, while the four girls sprawled on the floor. Christmas-tree lights gave the room a warm glow, and the piles of presents falling out from beneath the tree filled everyone with anticipation.

"So Nick tells me you're designing maternity wear now, too," Nick's mother said to Abby.

Abby nodded and smiled. "Doug Blair agreed to carry the line for a year to see how it does. There's no reason women can't be pregnant and fashionable, too."

Deb picked at the new maternity top she'd only just conceded to wear. "Too bad nothing'll be done in time for me."

"I'll see what I can do," Abby told her. "One of the ladies who used to sew for me is a friend of mine. I bet she'd sew up some of the designs for us."

"For me, too?" That was from Diane, who was swinging a Christmas ball back and forth from one of the bottom branches of the tree.

"Of course."

"Wow. Cool clothes." As usual, Rhonda knew just what mattered.

As she sat there with her new extended, albeit temporary, family, Abby couldn't help but feel the magic of Christmas. The sense that anything could happen. That miracles were possible. And even though they couldn't change what she was, she was glad to believe in miracles again.

Nick was due in another hour or so. Brit and Jimmy were going to be joining them for Christmas dinner the next day. For now, for this one moment, Abby's life was full.

A lot fuller than she'd ever thought it would be again. And maybe, if she could keep her love for Nick under wraps, if she could be certain he'd accepted her no as final, just maybe she could stay on at Home Away From Home. For a while, anyway.

There was a loud rap on the front door.

"Who's that?" Becca asked as everyone looked at Abby.

Rhonda lazily said, "Nick doesn't knock."

Abby was only about halfway across the room when the knock sounded again. "Whoever it is is mighty impatient." Nick's father chuckled.

Muffled voices, resumed conversations, followed Abby as she went to the door.

"My God! You do look just like her!" The curly-headed vibrant woman on the doorstep could be only one person.

Grinning, Abby held out her hand. "You must be Maggie."

Bypassing Abby's extended hand, Maggie pulled her forward into an awkward hug. "What the hell," she said, stepping back to stare at Abby. "With both of us being Anna's suckers, we're almost related or something." She took stock of Abby's black velour jumpsuit. "I gotta say, though, you have better taste in clothes than she does."

Abby laughed, ushered her new friend into the living room and made introductions all around.

"I got the job!" Maggie shared her early Christmas present as soon as the introductions were over. "Can you believe it—the station loved the pilot!"

Abby quickly explained about the audition that had brought Maggie from New York to California and soon everyone was congratulating her, as though she'd been a part of their odd family for years.

With no need to go on the audition she'd set up for that day, Maggie was at loose ends. She was promptly invited to use one of the vacant rooms in the house for the night, and to join them for Christmas dinner the next day.

Suddenly Abby was looking forward to Christmas. She had a piece of her own family there now. A piece of Anna. Slipping upstairs for a moment while Marianne and Nick's mother refilled drinks and the cheese tray, Abby grabbed the necklace she'd taken off so many weeks before and put it back on.

There might always be holes in her life. She might be lonely as hell sometimes. But she was going to be okay. Somehow, as she felt that familiar necklace against her skin, she knew she was going to make it.

NICK WAS LATE. Dinner had come and gone. The girls were all in the living room with Nick's parents watching *Miracle on 34th Street*. Maggie was upstairs taking a shower, and Charles and Marianne had retired to the guest house.

Abby had been watching the movie, too, an hour before. In fact, she'd suggested it. And the popcorn they'd all consumed, also.

But as the movie progressed, as Santa Claus's identity, his very existence, was being denied, she couldn't sit still. Determining that it had been a while since Beanie had been out to do his business, she excused herself to pace the backyard. Beanie pranced along behind her, lifting his leg on every upright surface along the way.

"You're supposed to smell things first," she muttered, watching him leave a few drops on the water spigot attached to the house.

Beanie grinned at her, proudly following at her heels as she walked across the lawn. The movie would be over soon. She couldn't stay out too long. Just long enough for Nick to arrive.

She hoped.

Stopping beside a lawn chair, Beanie watered one of the legs. "Yep, we'll all be wanting to sit there, bud. Thanks a lot," she said. He wagged his tail. She supposed that was as close to "you're welcome" as she was going to get.

Halfway around the big yard, Beanie grew tired of keeping up the pace and hopped against Abby's leg.

"No," she told him, continuing to walk. Surely Nick was there by now. Skirting around to the side of the house, she peeked toward the spot where she knew his Bronco would be.

It wasn't there.

Beanie resumed his hopping and added a pathetic yowl to his plea. Abby bent down, intending to have a heart-to-heart with the mutt about independence and self-sufficiency. She picked him up, instead. His warm little body was oddly reassuring.

She was being ridiculous. Nick was always late. Always.

But this was Christmas Eve. He hadn't even seen his parents yet, since he was at the clinic when their plane landed earlier that day. He'd finished with his last appointment at four o'clock. And he'd called at six to say he was on his way out.

So where in hell was he?

Butterflies took up residence in Abby's stomach, fluttering so fiercely she felt she had to sit down. But she couldn't. Something had happened. Something Nick hadn't foreseen. Something so horrible he couldn't even get to a phone. Abby felt sick to her stomach.

Fear rendered her weak, robbing her of rational thought, replacing logic with horrible visions of Nick beside the road, on a stretcher, his blood flowing out of him while the Bronco lay smashed beside him. Some drunk, someone who'd celebrated a little too much, was standing beside the Bronco, too engrossed in his alcoholic stupor to understand that he was the one who should have been hurt.

Just like Robert Winters should have paid for his affair with Audrey. Instead, it had been her baby sister, whose only crime was her appreciation for the opposite sex—and a too-trusting nature.

As she allowed her mind free rein, as she loosened the death grip she'd had on her thoughts for so long, Abby sank down to the wall beside the pool. And faced the truth. She was paralyzed with fear.

Stunned, she sat there, staring at the water.

She wasn't just scared because Nick was late. She was numb with a bone-deep fear that had been her constant companion for more than two years.

*She was afraid to care too much. Afraid to hurt anymore. Afraid to love Nick.*

She wasn't just afraid she'd smother him. It had started out that way. She'd hurt the people she'd loved most with her possessive, controlling ways. But the mistakes she'd made had been made in ignorance. She wasn't ignorant anymore. And with her new awareness came the faith that she could control her tendency to take over. She could stop to think before she interfered.

Remembering the past weeks, remembering Kaylee, Brit, she saw signs of her new awareness, her ability to love. She'd interfered with both of the girls' lives—guided them. She'd known what to say. She'd known what they needed. Because she'd put herself in someone else's shoes. Not to live their lives, but to feel *what* they were feeling. Her biggest flaw, her need to jump right into other people's lives, had, in actuality, been her greatest strength. She'd helped two young girls find happiness.

That same strength had seen her and her sisters into adulthood.

Her problem was no longer that she loved the wrong way. Her problem was that she'd become afraid to love at all. She'd tried to fool herself into believing she *didn't* care. That she *couldn't*. Yet what she'd really been doing was trying to lessen her chances of losing another loved one. She'd been protecting herself from any more pain.

But the thing was, denying herself the relationship she craved wasn't taking away the fear. She could taste its rusty flavor on her tongue, smell the acrid stench in the air, feel it beating through every shaky nerve in her body. Something had happened to Nick.

"Abby!" She stopped when she heard his voice. She'd lost her mind. Just like that, she'd finally gone over the edge. "Abby, you out here?"

Abby froze, afraid to turn around, to have proof that he wasn't really there, proof that she was imagining him.

"Didn't you hear me, honey?" He was standing beside the wall. She could see his feet. Beanie was struggling to get away from her, to greet his master.

"There's someone here to see you."

Abby barely heard the words. She glanced up at Nick—and knew that she would love him until the day she died. She wanted a chance to share that love with him....

"Nick?" She stood, sliding her arms around him, holding him tightly, never wanting to let him go.

"I'm happy to see you, too, honey," he said, but he was pushing her away from him. And grinning. "But there's someone else to see you."

Not anyone Abby needed to see. Not anyone who mattered. She'd had enough visitors for one day. What she needed was to be alone with Nick. To convince him that he could love her, no strings attached.

But instead of taking her back into his arms as she wanted, Nick turned her around.

And held her up when she would have fallen. Her knees gave out on her. Her strength gave out on her.

"Anna?" The word was barely a whisper. The tears were so thick Abby couldn't be sure she wasn't imagining her identical sister standing there. Wasn't imagining Jason just behind her. Wasn't imagining the tiny baby in his arms.

But she knew she wasn't when she felt Anna's tender arms slide around her. Or felt her sister's huge burst of joy, deep inside her soul, where she'd always felt Anna.

"Anna?" Abby leaned back, running her fingers over her sister's face, through her hair. "It's really you," she said. Then she started to sob.

Anna held her, rocked her, crooning to Abby as Abby had always crooned to Anna when they were children. She held her until Abby's tears ran dry. And then she just held her.

"I missed you," she said, her own voice thick with tears.

Abby nodded. Beyond words. Almost beyond coherent thought.

"I have someone for you to meet," Anna finally

said, turning from Abby only long enough to take the newborn baby from Jason.

"She missed you, too," she said, placing the baby in Abby's arms.

Peace settled on Abby as she looked down into that precious little face. "When?" she asked, hardly able to believe that this beautiful sleeping child was related to her, had some of her genes, her blood.

"Two weeks ago today."

Right about the time Abby had begun to fit in here.

The baby stirred, blinked, opened her eyes. "Hello, little Audrey, welcome home," Abby said, and promptly dropped a tear on the tiny baby's cheek.

A life given for a life lost.

Jason coughed. "Hey!" He came forward, holding out his arms. "Don't brothers-in-law get welcomed home, too?" he asked.

Abby stared from him to her sister, still holding fast to the child in her arms. "You two got married?" she asked.

Anna slipped her arm around Jason, staring adoringly up at him. "Yep."

Holding his wife to his side, Jason said, "Audrey insisted that her mother and father be married if we were going to live together."

Abby's stomach tensed. *"Father?"* Did this mean they knew who the other man had been in Anna's life? That he'd relinquished his rights?

"That would be me," Jason said proudly. "There was no one else. Anna was underweight, which made the baby measure small on the ultrasound—or so they figure."

"Thank God." Abby's relief was far sweeter than

any she'd ever imagined. There'd been a miracle for her this year after all.

Nick stepped up, putting an arm around Abby before gently lifting the baby from her arms. "Why don't us guys—" he looked at Audrey "—and girl leave you two ladies alone for a bit."

After a quick kiss for Jason, Anna turned and took Abby's hand, leading her toward the lawn furniture. "There's so much I have to tell you...."

"Don't take all night!" Jason called as the men disappeared into the house.

"Maggie's here," Abby said, sitting beside her sister. She could hardly believe Anna was really there, touching her.

"I know, I saw her." Anna smiled. A sweet, peaceful Anna smile that spread clear through Abby.

"Oh, Anna, I'm so sorry," she said, rubbing her sister's hand where it lay on her lap.

"Don't be." Anna's eyes teared up as she locked gazes with Abby. "Don't ever be sorry for loving me."

"But I—"

"Ssshhh." Anna placed one finger against Abby's lips. "I was wrong, too, you know. All those years, all that responsibility—I just let you do it all. Never gave you back the nurturing you gave us so freely."

"I smothered you."

"But you wouldn't have if we'd given a little in return. When you're taking, there's no room for giving. And that's the thing." Anna's eyes were compelling, earnest. "Love is doing both."

"'Course, you'd probably have given if I'd stopped to let you." Abby couldn't relinquish her burden so easily. She'd been carrying it far too long. Was afraid to let go, lest she fall back into her old ways.

Anna shook her head and smiled. "Or did you smother us because we let you? Because we never gave?"

"You were always the smartest one of us," Abby said, smiling back at her sister. "You tell me."

"Uh-uh." Anna shook her head. "You're the smart one."

"Well, one thing's for sure, Audrey wasn't," Abby said. And with a shared, sad smile, both girls said goodbye to the triplet they'd lost.

Abby would tell Anna about the circumstances of Audrey's death soon. But not now. Not this night. For now, it was enough to be together. And to know that wherever either of them might travel in the course of their lives, they'd never be apart again.

ABBY WAS ALONE in the living room just before midnight, having told the others that she'd unplug the lights. Nick had gone upstairs with his parents; he was staying in the room across the hall from them for the night. Jason, Anna and the baby were in a spare room on the third floor. Everyone else had just turned in, too. Including Beanie. He'd gone up with Becca. They'd all be up early to unwrap gifts the next morning.

Looking at the loot, not only under the tree but now in every conceivable space around it—once Jason and Anna had added what they'd brought—Abby's heart was full. She could wait for Nick to give their love a chance. Wait for years if she had to. She knew what was important now.

"I have something for you."

She turned at the sound of his voice. He was standing in the middle of the living room, holding a small package in the palm of his hand.

"Shouldn't I wait until morning?" She stood where she was.

"I don't think so."

He didn't come any closer. The box lay there in his hand.

Never taking her eyes from that small present, from the possibilities it might hold, Abby reached out, her fingers barely grazing his palm as she grabbed it.

"You were right." Nick's voice was soft, not quite even. "I was hiding behind my job."

And with her newfound confidence, her new understanding, Abby almost believed him. She continued to stare at the little package he'd brought her.

Nick cleared his throat. "I'm not hiding anymore."

With trembling fingers Abby untied the ribbon, ripped through the paper. The jeweler's box glowed under the Christmas lights. Abby hesitated. Afraid to open it. Afraid to find the earrings that were certainly waiting inside.

And then she couldn't wait anymore. As eager, as undisciplined, as a child, she popped the lid open—and stared.

A star-shaped solitaire shone up at her. Like the star on top of their Christmas tree, this one was many faceted, glittering with promise. With hope.

"Will you marry me?" Nick asked, still standing where she'd left him.

She'd never seen him so hesitant, so exposed. He wasn't sure of her answer. But he was taking the risk anyway. He was putting himself on the line. Making himself vulnerable. He was jumping into the fray. For her.

"You're sure?" Abby still couldn't quite abdicate control. Still had to look out for one she loved.

"More sure than I've ever been about anything in my life."

"You'll still be able to do your work."

"Together, we'll be able to do more."

"I was afraid to love again."

"I know."

She nodded, still holding that box, looking at him across the carpeted floor. The intensity vibrated between them.

"Yes, I'd be honored to marry you." Abby's words were strong, sure.

And then she was in her lover's arms.

"Yes!" She barely heard the whispered cheer behind them.

"All right!" She heard that one more clearly. If she wasn't mistaken, Diane had just broken curfew.

"Thank God." Yes, that would be Anna.

"What's with you two, hogging all the great ones?" Maggie was there, also.

"Put the ring on her finger already." And Deb.

"It's about time...." Nick's mother.

A little growl with human inflections joined the chorus. Beanie wanted down from whoever was holding him.

"Give the guy a little privacy, girls." Jason had obviously joined them, as well. If he hadn't been there all along. Abby could already tell that she and Anna were going to have their work cut out for them when Jason and Nick got together.

Breaking off their kiss before they embarrassed

themselves or their gate-crashing audience, Abby still clung to Nick, sharing with him a secret smile, a promise of what was to come. Later. When they were alone.

Just before she turned to receive the congratulations of their loved ones, she caught a glimpse of the Christmas tree behind Nick. Anna's patchwork angel stared back at her. Nick had been right all along. Christmas was about love. And love was magic.

She couldn't help wondering if maybe her soon-to-be husband had some insider knowledge here. After all, no one knew for sure that St. Nick didn't really exist....

## HARLEQUIN SUPERROMANCE®

### MEN OF GLORY

*They're ranchers, cowboys, men of the West!*

# O LITTLE TOWN OF GLORY

## by Judith Bowen

**Visit the town of Glory in December 1998!
A good place to go for Christmas...**

Calgary lawyer Honor Templeman makes a shocking discovery after her husband's death. Parker Templeman had another wife—and two children—in the small town of Glory. Two children left to the care of their uncle, Joe Gallant, who has no intention of giving them up—to Honor *or* her powerful father-in-law.

Available wherever Harlequin books are sold.

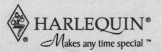

## HARLEQUIN®
*Makes any time special* ™

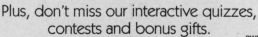

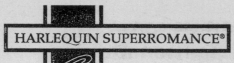

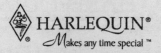

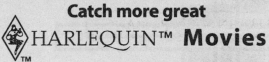